WITCH GIRL STUDY GROUP

An Isekai Fantasy Harem

MILO STORM

Cover art by AbbeysHollow

Even if you don't want to leave a review, feel free to contact me at MiloStormBooks@gmail.com with feedback on your favorite characters, scenes, anything!

You can also find me on Facebook to hear about cover reveals, and future release dates!

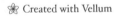 Created with Vellum

ABOUT THE BOOK

Dark Gods and Witch Girls, name a more iconic duo.

Jake works at the newest, and technically oldest, excavation site in America.

As a janitor. Not quite an archeology major's wet dream.

But then an ancient Pillar awakens, and Jake switches lives with a doppelganger in another world. This world's Jake happens to be a top prospect at the magical Aether Academy... and a servant of a dark God who expects repayment for his boon.

If he's going to live long enough to find a way home, Jake will need a little help. Luckily, beautiful witch girls are lining up to form a study group with the man they think is a genius. He's not. But who is Jake to turn away busty witch girls in need?

When they learn about a bond that will help them all cheat on their deadly exams...well they've worked their whole lives to get into that school, and they'll do whatever it takes to pass!

But exams are just the beginning.

Witch Girl Study Group is an 18+ isekai fantasy harem story with adult situations

1

FOR THE THIRD NIGHT IN A ROW, I DREAMED OF ANOTHER world. Another life.

Between a full load of classes and a night job, I took the opportunity to sleep whenever it presented itself. Blackout curtains meant I could take advantage of a few free hours, whether the sun was up or not.

In the first dream, I found myself the subject of some kind of dark ritual. Shrouded figures surrounded me on all sides, and it was dark. Too dark to see anything but the candles lit on the stone wall behind the mysterious group. They chanted something that seemed to make sense at the time, in my dreamlike mind, but I'd never been able to remember since.

Then they stabbed me in the heart. And I *felt it*. Not like a normal dream at all, where I just *thought* I felt it. When I woke up, my hands flung to my chest to check for leaks. It seemed so real. A bit hazy, maybe, as I looked back, but even though I watched the scene from above, I felt everything.

That was a week ago.

Tonight, I seemed nervous. Well, the dream-version of

me, did. He speed-walked through a crowded hallway that must have been a university. Several beautiful girls walked by, carrying books, or chatting with friends, and they never failed to look at me. Ah, *him,* not me. But he ignored them completely. I had been hoping the dream was about to take a much more fun direction, but he just walked right by.

And that's how I knew he was not me. Not quite, anyway. A pretty girl's smile was an opportunity I just couldn't pass up. Especially some of the girls at that college, or whatever it was. Their outfits were extravagant, and tight in all the right places. Many of them even wore tall, pointed hats and carried weapons, staffs usually, like witches or wizards.

But this alternate-Jake didn't so much as glance. He stomped through the hallways, shoulders tight, and grimacing at the floor until he left the building and entered a dorm. Then, what must have been his own room.

It was small and sparsely furnished, the size of some of my friends' dorm rooms, but it seemed like he lived there alone. Just another clue that it wasn't real; any real university would have packed at least two more students into a room that size. A wardrobe stood a foot or two away from the end of a bed on one side of the room, while a large desk filled the other. Books were splayed out over it, as well as a few beakers, a couple empty, but a few of which contained odd-looking mixtures of shifting colors.

He fell into the bed, then sat straight up. Clenching and unclenching his fists, glancing around the room. He looked like a madman, to be honest. A bead of sweat gathered on his forehead and he took a deep, shuddering breath. Then another, and they started to come faster. Soon he was hyper-ventilating, hunched over and cradling his head in his hands.

"You alright, man?" I said. Tried to, anyway, he didn't hear me.

But then his head snapped up and his eyes shot wide for a

brief moment. For how broken he seemed a minute ago, he was able to adopt a calm appearance with shocking ease. One particularly deep breath and he was back to normal. On the outside, anyway.

I turned to see what he was looking at and, if I were actually there, I'd have been the one hyperventilating.

A shadowy gateway had appeared in the wall above the desk that just a few seconds before was solid white brick. After a few seconds, a figure stepped out of it with an ornate purple gown, like she just came from a ball.

She stepped across the desk with no respect for the items on it. She kicked a beaker over, pushed a book the floor, and then cleared off a space for her to sit. On the desk. With her feet resting on the chair. Her head was shrouded behind a black mist, but I could see a long braid of brown hair falling out from the behind the cloud.

Fake Jake immediately launched himself to the floor, kneeling at her feet, so she must have been important.

She definitely made that dress look good. It clung to her slender body like it was painted on, and yet she moved without restriction. One sleeve covered her left arm, while the other was bare, and they were crossed under her chest. The dress's deep neckline gave a generous view of cleavage that threatened to spill out.

Dream-me had his eyes on the floor. Mine, however, were glued to that woman.

"Good. They train you kids well these days. Already know to kneel to your betters. Worry not, one day, you might be in my place. If you do as I ask," I could hear a smirk in her voice, even if I couldn't see it. She hopped down and took a few slow, relaxed steps toward the bed and sat down next to my prostrate doppelganger. Then she glanced around the room, checking out a few books lying around. "They really have you reading Strativade's? His take on physical magic is just so... boring. You can find far more fun things to do in Occulin's textbook. She at least had the will to include weaponization methods."

She almost seemed normal for a minute, there. Like an older sister visiting her brother at college. She reached down and pressed a hand into the bed. "These are way better than they used to be. Mine was made out of fucking straw. My days here were some of the most demeaning of my life," her nostalgic voice darkened, and she changed the subject. "Now. Are you ready to get your hands dirty, new boy?" He nodded but didn't move anything else. "Good. You know the plan, so don't mess it up. You will be rewarded for your success. Think of those fools out there scraping together every bit of Pholl's power that they can manage."

The woman scoffed and held up her hand. A black fire gathered around it. As she spoke, she bent down closer, lowering her voice as well. "You and I have another option, don't we? You may only be able to access a small portion of the dark energy available to us but serve well... and the things you are capable of one day will scare the shit out of you."

The woman sounded so proud. Like she was offering him the chance of a lifetime. I had no idea how far those powers could go, but I'd be lying if I didn't say I was intrigued. Dream or not, magic was probably the coolest thing that didn't actually exist, much to my disappointment as a child.

When the woman walked back through her portal, it slowly dissolved until no sign of it was left. It wasn't until minutes later that the Jake on the floor rose. He was breathing heavily and had a sheen of sweat on his forehead, but a determined look in his eyes. They focused on his outstretched left hand as it rose, palm up.

He stared hard, focusing on his palm, until a small, black flame appeared.

The smile on his face then, was pure evil.

A KNOCK AT MY DOOR WOKE ME UP. NOT IN SOME BLEAK, magical dorm room, but in my own bleak, lame bedroom.

It was not all that different, really. My bed seemed more comfortable, I had a closet instead of a wardrobe, a bookcase that held more video games than books, and my desk was home to a computer. There were a few books lying around, mostly fantasy but some sci-fi.

I usually left textbooks in my backpack because just looking at them could be depressing. Those thick volumes filled with hundreds of the most boring pages imaginable were enough to turn my hobby of reading into a chore.

Archeology was supposed to be interesting. But it didn't take long to realize that Indiana Jones lied to me. Then at the end of my freshman year, a cave-in about an hour away, in a rural part of Rhode Island of all places, revealed an enormous, ancient chamber with a singular Pillar in the center.

Being an archeology major at the University of Rhode Island, or URI, which managed the excavation, I was able to land a job at the site.

As a janitor.

I never said I was *a good* student.

"They're still making you work nights?" My mom's shrill, worried voice calls through the door to me as I hopped out of bed to get dressed for work. "I thought that was supposed to be temporary."

Pushing my foot into a boot, I called over my shoulder to her. "Mom, it could be one of the biggest discoveries in history. No one wants to stop working. They've got people excavating the area around the clock!"

Not that I was one of those people, but she didn't need to know that. She was just so proud to hear that I landed a job at the excavation, I didn't have the heart to tell her what I actually did there.

I scrambled around my bedroom, stuffing supplies into my backpack. Headphones, a few packaged honey buns for break time, and A Storm of Swords. I was still trying to get the bad taste out of my mouth since the damn show ended.

"I just wish they'd let you take the day shift once in a while. You need time for your classes too, dear. You're falling behind as it is." I couldn't help cringing at that.

At least she didn't know I was barely scraping by. At this point, I would just be happy to leave with an Archeology degree and my sanity intact. Hell, one or the other would be good enough.

Slinging the backpack over my shoulder, I opened the door, gave my Mom a kiss on the cheek and bounded down the stairs. She followed me into the kitchen where I grabbed a bottle of water from the fridge.

"I just don't want you to run yourself ragged. It's good to work hard, but you'll burn yourself out at this rate and I can't stand to lose you like your father." She crossed her arms and stood in the middle of the kitchen with a worried look on her face.

I took a break from rushing around to give my mom a

hug. Lame, I know, but I was her only son. If it weren't for me, she would've devolved into crazy cat lady territory years ago. Especially after my Dad walked out on the two of us when I was five. The asshole couldn't at least leave a few years earlier? He had to wait until I was able to form just a few memories of him before he left? Sometimes, I thought it would have been easier if I never even knew him at all.

"Don't worry, mom. I'm not going anywhere, not for a long time. So, get used to having your deadbeat son living upstairs!"

"Oh, don't talk about yourself like that! You need to put a good attitude out into the world if you expect it to give you anything back," she snapped at me.

It was a nice idea, but a little too vague for my taste. Bad things happened to good people too often, and my mother was a prime example of that. She was the sweetest person in the world but look where it landed her. She managed a used bookstore and we lived in a small upstairs apartment in Westerly, Rhode Island. It was a nice beach town that we could barely afford to live in, but she always refused to leave, and I stopped trying to convince her a long time ago.

"You're right, Mom. I'll try to be more positive," I replied with my best smile.

"There's my good boy. Have a nice night! Oh, and pick up some creamer on your way home, we just ran out!" She stood in the entrance to our apartment, calling after me. She added, "I love you!" then, like she couldn't believe she almost forgot it.

"Sure thing, Mom! And I love you too."

WESTERLY WAS A NICE PLACE. PLENTY OF RESTAURANTS, right on the beach, got a nice big park.

The only downside? I worked in the middle of fucking

nowhere. Rhode Island wasn't a big place, but I managed to fit an hour-long drive into the smallest state in the country.

It was a small price to pay, though, to be a part of history. I was enthralled with the Indiana Jones movies as a kid. Always wanted to be an archeologist. But the reality of the job was about as far from what I'd imagined as it could possibly be. There were no adventures into lost tombs, no golden idols to switch out, or rolling boulders to run away from, just a lot of dust to carefully brush away.

So, in a way, my janitor gig was just training. My brush was a lot bigger than the real archeologists', but we basically spent our days doing the same thing.

It was a drive I'd made dozens of times, so I just listened to some music and let the world pass by. The dark sky was clear, and more stars came out the closer I got to the excavation site. It was a few turns off the highway, and about a mile down a dirt road.

Somehow, a few hunters stumbled across a new cavern on their land that went far deeper than they could have imagined. They kept expecting to get rich, but there wasn't all that much down there. Nothing like treasure or artifacts, anyway. Plenty worth writing about, but nothing worth selling.

The cave led to an enormous chamber with carvings covering every inch from floor to ceiling. Words, pictures, everything. For a historian, or an archeologist, it was the find of the century. For a treasure hunter, though? It was a bust.

Still better than working at Dunkin Donuts.

A couple of my professors passed by as I walked in, leaving for the night while I was coming in to clean up after them. They gave me a polite nod, the ones that noticed anyway, and headed home. I was the only person there overnight. The location was kept secret, so there was no real need for security. But wherever trash built up, they needed someone to clear it away. *That's right kids; you want job security? The world will always need janitors.*

The last person left just as I reached the chamber. Just like every time before, I got goosebumps stepping into that place. It was carbon-dated to be billions of years old; it changed everything! And I got to clean the floors. *How glorious.*

It had to be a hundred feet around, and just as many high. The light from the standing lamps spread throughout the chamber barely even reached the ceiling. It was actually pretty creepy at night, when everyone else went home.

Especially after I turned all those lights off. Then, all they gave me was a battery-powered headlamp so they could save money on electricity. It was dark, cold, and ominous down there. The echo that reverberated at the smallest of sounds was terrible. My own feet scraping against the ground always managed to sound like there was someone else walking around, just out of sight.

And on top of all that, today, there was a hum that just would not go away. I assumed it was a machine running overnight, maybe a computer finishing up a simulation or something. But when I saw someone return to grab a jacket they had apparently forgotten, I called out to them. "Hey, do you hear that?"

"Hear what?"

"Sounds like a computer fan running, or a fridge maybe."

He lazily glanced around, then gave me a flat look. Graduate students were so condescending. "Maybe get yourself checked out for tinnitus," the guy scoffed and walked out.

"Well, I don't even know what that is, so jokes on you!" I called after him, but all he did was wave.

Whatever. Something was making that sound and I could just bust through my work, then spend some time looking around for it. Which was basically my plan every day, except I usually spent my spare time reading a book since there was no cell reception down here.

Even after throwing headphones on and playing some music, the low hum didn't go away. It wasn't drowned out by the music, muffled by the headphones, nothing. Just a constant level, no matter how hard I tried to ignore it or block my ears.

It grated against the inside of my head the entire night. As I swept the floor, I kept my eyes peeled for anything suspicious. Movement, out-of-place computers, anything. And since the hum pierced any noise I tried to distract myself with, I didn't bother with music. Couldn't focus on it anyway. Yeah, it was a boring, paranoid night and I was not proud of the work I did, but hey. It was a cave. It was gonna be dusty.

After a couple of hours, I couldn't take it anymore and headed to where I ultimately knew the sound had to be coming from. The Pillar. The only thing that changed the sound was my relative location to that hundred-foot-tall cylinder of stone. As I got closer, it got louder. Not by much, but after a while I could tell the difference.

I leaned my broom against the outer wall and clipped an extra light to my jeans' pocket. It was just enough to light about a ten-foot radius around me. Pausing to make sure that I was alone, despite hearing nothing but the hum for the past few hours, I ducked under the caution tape that usually kept grunts like me away from the more important stuff, and made my way to the Pillar, slowly. I edged forward, glancing in every direction constantly.

A part of me expected some alarm to ring out and my professors to pop out of nowhere to tell me I'd failed all my courses by crossing that line.

But when nothing happened, I just shrugged and started to walk normally.

That's when the voices started.

The Pillar was just getting close enough to catch some of my light and I could hear people whispering all around it. More than one voice, but I couldn't tell how many.

"Hello? The excavation's closed for the night, you know." I called out, but the whispers didn't skip a beat. The only response was my own echo.

In front of me, the Pillar rose high into the darkness. I'd never seen one, but I thought of the Redwood trees that were wide enough for a car to drive through. This thick, silver-blue pillar must have been at least that wide and covered with a mixture of lettering and drawings like nothing I'd ever seen before.

And then there were the whispers. It was nothing I could make out. Like someone talking in another room just loud enough for me to hear, but too muffled to decipher. As I reached a few feet from the Pillar, I circled around the ancient wonder a few times just to make sure no one was hiding on the other side and messing with me.

"The fuck is going on," I finally said on my fourth trip around, and the voices stopped. Just for a few seconds, but they stopped. Started again for a second, then went back to normal.

Can they hear me? Or was it just some kind of fucked up, slow-moving echo?

I decided to test it. "Helloooooo!" I called out, then tried to drown out the echo and focus on the strange voices.

Sure enough, the whispering stopped again. This time, when they started up, they sounded in a rush, all trying to speak over one another. One of them got loud for a moment and then they all went silent.

A pale blue light suddenly rose from the Pillar. There was a strip of carvings separated into eleven equal portions that wrapped around the Pillar. One was lit solid blue and contained a glyph of an open eye.

At the same time that the voices started up again, in unison this time, the light started to pulse. First lightly, but it grew more intense over time until it was almost fading out entirely before rising to a blinding white light. The voices grew louder in the same fashion, eventually blocking out any other noise. I spoke but couldn't hear the words.

I screamed as pain shot through my head, my eyes and ears overwhelmed.

But all I could hear were the voices, and a high-pitched whine getting louder and louder until I lost consciousness.

3

"Hey!"

A girl's voice woke me up with a start. She was shaking me by the shoulder and looking down at me with dark purple eyes, almost black.

Purple eyes.

Alright, either I was dreaming again, or I hit my head when I fell. But I squeezed my eyes shut, and she was still there when they opened.

And still beautiful.

A tall, dark, pointed hat with a wide, floppy brim sat atop her fiery red hair that fell down just past her shoulders, framing a cute face twisted with anger. Which, on her, just made her even hotter. She wore some kind of robes, oddly enough, the likes of which I'd only ever seen on priests. Or... in a dream that was starting to feel oddly relevant. They were dark purple, with orange accents, and seemed like they were made with twice as much fabric as was actually needed.

And from the way she was bending down to check on me, I got a peek down her modest neckline. As slim as the girl was, her boobs looked almost out of proportion.

Just as I was starting to enjoy the view, though, my vision went haywire. It was almost like the zoom function on a camera malfunctioning. As I focused on her body, my vision *passed through* her clothing for a split second. I saw her in nothing but her smooth, pale skin, crouched and pushing her boobs up in an intoxicating view.

But it didn't last. After that, my vision kept zooming through layers of cloth, then skin, and muscle. In the span of a few seconds, I saw through every layer of her being, and finally through her body entirely. My head swam and a pounding headache hit me like a sledgehammer. I threw a hand up to my temple and gritted my teeth against the pain.

"What the fuck are you doing?" I hear a deep voice coming from behind me. Not from the girl.

My vision returned to normal, and I forced my eyes to focus on the world around me. Not on what was underneath that girl's clothing. She was hot as fuck, but I had bigger concerns just then. Like, how I was supposed to get home if I couldn't even stand because my eyesight kept fucking up.

It was like I suddenly had a new muscle in my eyes that I had no control over. A zoom function that also served as x-ray vision, somehow? And I felt like a newborn calf, trying out this new muscle, kicking and flexing to figure out my limits. Except it wasn't like a leg that I could voluntarily stretch. Just checking out that girl's outfit managed to activate the strange ability, and there was nothing I could do to stop it.

I'd have to figure out what the fuck all that meant later.

I turned around to face the unfamiliar voice and found a proud-looking dude maybe a year or two older than myself, but in much better shape. Blonde hair and blue eyes, he looked like a stereotypical rich frat boy that I'd seen walking around my university. Except he was wearing a tunic of dark green and gold, like he'd just been to a renaissance fair.

Who the fuck are these people? At least this one didn't have purple eyes. I addressed him because it was hard to focus on the girl without undressing her with my eyes. *Literally.*

"Nothing," I grunted, my throat feeling so tight that I was forcing the words out. I shifted to my knees and tried to stand, but my legs felt weak. "I work here. I clean the place overnight and wanted to check out the Pillar. What are you two doing here? How did you even get down here?"

The two shared a suspicious look. The guy's eyebrows scrunched down. "We came in with you," he muttered, a hand coming up to rub his chin as he looked down at me in thought. He let out a sigh and crouched down, chuckling to himself, "I told you not to touch the pillar, Jacobus." I reared back as that name hit me. *The guy in my dream was named Jacobus.* There was familiarity in his tone, but I didn't think I'd seen him before, neither in my life or while asleep. "The Lady is not going to be happy when she hears about this, but," he shrugged and made an amused expression, "that's not my problem, is it?"

"I wouldn't be surprised if she killed you," the girl snapped. The guy gave another shrug, like he didn't care either way.

I struggled to finally get my feet under me, taking notice that neither of them made even the slightest move as if to help.

"I don't know about that. They've taken an interest in him, for some reason. And now that he's captured a Pillar? Oh, The Lady will be pissed alright, she wanted to do that herself, but these things have been buried for hundreds of years. Thousands, maybe. Who knows what the side-effects are? They might just appreciate you falling on your sword like this. Especially if it wipes your memory," he added. "You really don't remember coming in with us? You literally led the way." There was a bite in his tone now. He squinted and spoke down to me, like he was talking to an idiot.

I was no genius, but I was not going to just put up with that. "Fuck you, man," I snapped back, but that just made him smile.

"There he is! Maybe you're still in there after all, Jacobus."

Feeling more than a little confusion and frustration, I decided to just go along with is. "Right. But, uh, for the sake of the moment... let's just pretend I did lose my memory. Who are you two?" I let the words out slowly, testing the grounds.

"Brock," the muscular blonde boy says, clearly amused by the situation.

"Filomena. Filo, to you," the girl bit off each word, and I was struck again by her beauty. When she caught me staring, she crossed her arms over her chest and glared back at me with those haunting purple eyes.

"What's the power like, anyway?" Brock asked. It was always an effort to look away from this Filo, and her crossed arms just squished cleavage up past the neckline of her robes.

"Uh, what do you mean?" I say, trying to focus on anything but her chest. It wasn't easy.

"You know," he starts listing off powers that belong in comic books, "Immortality, Truevision, Omnitongue. It's gotta be Truevision, right? The section that lit up was an eye, anyway."

Truevision. Sounded about right. I considered asking more about it but didn't want to let these two know how little I knew.

Especially the girl, Filo. She was damn fine to look at, but not much for conversation if my first impression was at all accurate. Whatever the case, I still had no idea what just happened, and I was not ready to trust them.

Instead, after thinking for a moment, I just shook my head. "No clue. I don't even know what any of those mean, so I guess I did lose my memory." *Might as well go along with that little detail, they might start getting suspicious at my obviously simple questions.*

Filo scoffed and took off toward the entrance. She held her right hand up next to her and a ball of light winked into existence just a few inches above it. Like a perfectly spherical light bulb hanging in the air, lighting up the room to a startling degree considering how little it was.

My eyes nearly popped out of my head before I could school my expression back to something resembling normal.

But, fuck! That was *magic*. It had to be. And she just pulled out that ball of light with the same nonchalance as I would have pulled out my phone and turned on the flashlight.

The thought triggered an instinctive reaction in me, the pocket check. My hands idly tap where my pockets usually were, and my heart dropped. The square bulges of my wallet and phone, the jingling sound of my keys, were all missing.

For the first time, I looked down at myself.

And I nearly shit my pants... er, robes, at the shock.

❧ 4 ❧

THESE AREN'T MY CLOTHES.

I felt past the black robes, pressing into a surprisingly taut stomach. Without really meaning to, my vision phased through my clothing and I suddenly looked down on myself, naked. Instinctively, my hands jolted toward my waistline, covering myself up before I realized no one else would be able to see it. Filo was already leaving, anyway, and Brock was watching her go.

Still, one thought dominated my mind in that moment. *This isn't my body.* It was close, but not the same. I was *not* in that good shape. Not terrible, probably better than average, but a bit pudgy all the same. But now? All I felt was muscle. Even standing and walking around, now that I was paying attention to it, felt different. My legs felt more powerful, my back straighter.

Brock, however, was watching me, looking equal parts suspicious, confused, and amused. "Uh, you alright, there Jacobus? Did you forget what you were wearing today too?" He burst out laughing, but when the echo reached us, he cleared his throat and glanced around the huge room. "Ah, on second thought, maybe we should keep it down. Don't know what else we might find down here."

Filo looked back at Brock's outburst and quickened her pace. As her light faded, Brock snapped his fingers and a similar ball of light floated up above us, following just above Brock's head.

From the way these two treated it, I could tell that magic was an everyday thing to them. But even something as simple as a ball of light was blowing my mind. *Magic exists?* I was still confused about, well, everything, but that was *magic. Real magic.*

Excitement boiled through me as I realized that I could probably do that too. The Truevision thing was cool, but it seemed to have a mind of its own. It was all I could do to just look at the world as normally as I could manage, to stop the power from activating.

I let Brock go ahead of me, then lifted a hand in front of myself and imagined a similar ball of light popping into existence above it.

Nothing happened.

I felt a little frustration but shook it off. Maybe it just worked differently for men and women. I tried snapping my fingers, though, and again, nothing. Brock looked back at me then, but not for more than a second.

It seemed like these two were my friends. Or maybe just companions, considering Filo's temperament. Coworkers, perhaps, but some part of me didn't feel like I could trust them.

Brock, at least, was a little friendly, so I decided to take a chance on him. I ran a few steps to catch up to him. "Hey, uh, Brock. So, uh, we're friends, right?" I felt like an idiot asking, but you gotta start somewhere, right?

He gave me a wry look. "Sure, something like that. So, you really don't remember a thing? Like, not a single detail of your life?" Brock stopped and turned to face me for a moment, letting Filo increase her lead ahead of us. He shot her a suspicious look and then nodded at me, expecting an answer.

I shook my head. "It's probably going to sound stupid, but I don't even know how you did that," I point up toward the ball of light over his head.

Brock breaks out in a derisive laugh. The kind you might make if a kid asked you why the sky was blue. "Oh! Well, shit. You've got a lot more to learn than I have time for, it looks like." His laugh started growing, but when it started to echo, he cut himself off. "Look, you're going to need to relearn *real quick*. Aether doesn't hold on to dead weight."

I held out a hand, stopping him. "Hold on, Aether? Who's that?"

"Uh, not a who, it's a place. Literally the most elite magical university in the world. You were supposed to be this year's most exciting prospect, oddly enough. I guess a lot of people are about to be disappointed, if you can't even conjure a ball of fucking light," he chuckled to himself, looking smug. "At least my spot is safe." He turned and started walking toward the exit. Filo's ball of light was barely visible now as she started taking the steps up to the exit.

I caught up and kept pace next to Brock. Every question he answered just spawned more questions. "Prospect? Was I recruited, or something? And what do you mean about your spot being safe?"

Brock looked over at me and rolled his eyes. "Look, I have a little brother of my own who already asks way too many stupid questions. I'm not going to do this all day, just try to take it easy once you get back to your room and see if your memory comes back. If not... well, I'm sure The Lady will be contacting you soon," his smile took on a devious nature.

Maybe I was wrong to call him friendly.

Just about everything he said just confused me even more.

There was, however, the matter of where I would even go from here. If I was somehow a student at this Aether place, then it dawned on me that I probably wasn't in Rhode Island anymore. But I didn't want to dwell on that right now, I had more immediate worries. "Uh, do you mind showing me-"

"To your room?" He asked, sounding tired of me already. We reached the steps and started climbing up. The equipment that filled the room when I arrived for my shift was all gone, replaced by much older-looking tools made out of wood and crude metal. "Yeah, I figured you forgot that too. Just cool it with all the stupid questions. Especially once we get out of here," he suddenly snapped his fingers. "Shit. I didn't think of that." Brock stopped in the middle of the stairway and turned to face me. "We aren't friends."

"Fine, man, I get it. I'll stop talking to you, jeez."

He grew much more serious then, than I'd seen so far. "No, you *don't* get it. The three of us?" He waved a hand toward the last place we saw Filo's light before it disappeared. "We were given this task together, to scope out this place and your dumb ass couldn't keep your hands to yourself. If The Lady asks any questions, I'm not going to lie to her. They don't like that. And once we're out of here, the three of us can't be seen together. It'll be too suspicious."

"But, why? Who's that lady?"

Brock's eyes widened. "*The Lady* is all you'll call her. Unless you want her taking your tongue. Fuck, man, you really don't know anything, do you?"

I blinked a few times, trying to think of anything that I could say that wouldn't sound stupid. But, yeah. In this place, which I was starting to think was a different world entirely, I didn't know shit.

Brock sighed. "Right. Well, this is the last question I'm answering. Whatever you might remember, you've pledged yourself to the Lord of Shadows and The Lady is, well, our boss. Don't let anyone know about that if you want to stay alive." Then he left me behind in the rapidly diminishing light.

In the shadows that I had *apparently* pledged myself to. In other words, it looked like I was fucked. Either this was a part of some elaborate game, or I just found out that I was basically a fucking Death Eater from Harry Potter.

And if that wasn't enough of a shock, then I stepped outside.

5

THE FIRST THING I NOTICED WAS THE SKY. I COULDN'T believe how many more stars were out. I had never seen the milky way before, so the splash of color in the dark night sky threw me off. It took a few seconds to realize that it wasn't a different sky at all.

This was just what the sky would look like without any light pollution.

Instead of the parking lot I left a few hours ago, we stepped out from some cracks between the rocks into untouched wilderness. There was no sign of Filo, or her light, in any direction, but Brock apparently knew exactly where to go. He immediately set off toward some tall spires that stretched above the treetops in the distance, so I fell in behind him.

It was a long walk and apparently Brock was sick of talking; he didn't say a word.

Meanwhile, I was trying not to freak out.

I had homework due tomorrow that I was planning on doing... tomorrow. In the morning, my Mom was going to be wondering why I hadn't come home. My car was going to have so many tickets by the time I got back to it...

But wait.

If I didn't have my own body, and the one I was walking around in apparently used to know Brent and Filo...

I felt the blood drain out of my face as it hit me. I didn't just invade some dude's body; we traded places! He was probably a hell of a lot more confused than I was, too. I, at least, had a couple people waiting for me, who could answer some questions. Rudely, sure, but it was something.

If what I'd seen here so far was any indication, the other Jake would be in a world full of technology he'd never heard of with a whole host of magical knowledge that wouldn't even work. If these two assholes were his friends, then I figured it was safe to assume he was one too. The guy pledged himself to a dark god, after all.

My Mom could be in trouble if he thought she knew what happened.

But then again, I didn't know shit about this world. And he wouldn't know shit about mine. He wouldn't be able to figure out how to drive, or use Google Maps, he'd never be able to find my house.

As strange as it was, I was in a much better situation than my doppelganger. I knew I had to get home and make sure my Mom was safe, but I didn't think that I could simply recreate whatever body-swap had just occurred.

She would be worried about me, but at least she was safe. I just wanted to check up on her and make sure she knew I was okay.

Then I'd find my way back to this world because I'd need to be a brain-dead moron to leave a magical world behind for the real one. Even if the previous inhabitant of this body aligned it with the Shadow. I checked my wrists and didn't find any creepy tattoos, so maybe they didn't take it that seriously.

By the time we reached the academy, I was able to convince myself that my mother would be safe. For a while, anyway, while I figure out how to make it home. Me, on the other hand? It was too early to tell.

But once I learned how to use the magic this world had to offer, I wasn't sure I'd want to go back.

We emerged from a dense forest into a sprawling university. It was dark, but the night sky seemed to shine brighter here, lighting our way enough to see, even though the moon wasn't even half-full. Globes of light much like the ones Brock and Filo summoned lit the cobblestone pathways of a campus that could rival any in my world. Huge white buildings composed of seamless stone lined the walkways that closed in around a large, square courtyard. Ornate fountains and statues dotted the grounds, but there wasn't a student in sight. Behind the gaudy, vine-covered buildings that lined the quad was what looked like a small village built around the university.

Further into the campus were three silvery spires rising into the sky, starting as individual buildings and twirling together in an image that resembled a strand of DNA. As they cleared the buildings around them, they came together and formed a single gargantuan spire reaching far into the night sky. Even on a clear day, I wouldn't be able to see the top.

"Hey," Brock called over to me and I realized I had frozen in place, taking in the incredible architecture. "Pick up the pace, kid, I don't want to be seen with you." He kept glancing around even though we hadn't seen anyone. Somehow, even Filo disappeared.

"It's fine, man," I swept my hand across the campus.

"There's literally no one here. The sun's rising in a few hours, no one's gonna be awake."

Brock shot me a look that seemed like he was about to call me an idiot again. Luckily, he didn't, because I was about to punch his handsome face in. Sure, he'd probably just snap his fingers and turn me into a muskrat, but that first hit would be *so* worth it.

"The night's not as quiet as it seems, *Initiate.*" The way he emphasized the word made it seem both important and derogatory. I made a mental note to figure it out later. Brock glanced around the quad with suspicious eyes, "There are people in every one of these buildings, dark as they may seem. Studying, running experiments, holding covert meetings, or running dark rituals." He shot me a dangerous smile. "You'll find out soon enough. Come on," he waved a hand lazily and I fell in step behind him.

My new not-friend led me out of the area and into the small town. These streets were lined with far more mundane buildings made of brick, stone, or wood. Many of them shops and restaurants, or housing for students, but some were apparently lecture halls, or headquarters for different departments.

There was a Necromancy building conveniently located near a graveyard, on the other side of which was the also-convenient Regeneration building. I couldn't help but smile at that. These people were nothing if not efficient; it only made sense for the Necromancers to take over where the Healers had failed.

Simply reading off the names of those department buildings got me excited about the kinds of magic that were possible in this world. *And I get to take classes here? Where do I even start?*

My eyes were bulging out of their sockets the entire time, trying to take in every detail of the dark landscape. This place would be far more fantastic in the morning and I couldn't wait to find out what kinds of students walked these pathways every day.

Especially if the girls looked like Filomena. Her haunting purple eyes and perky chest were burned into my memory. Even if she seemed a bit unfriendly, I wasn't about to give up that easily. She might warm up to me, eventually. As Brock led me to my dorm, I kept my head on a swivel but didn't see her deep red hair anywhere.

We did come across a few people though, however badly they seemed like they didn't want to be caught. Every time I thought I saw someone, it was at the corner of my eye and by the time I turned my head, they were gone. There was a strange, secretive air about the place, and the only two students I had met so far, that set me on edge.

Brock finally came to a halt in front of an old brick building. Some of its windows were smashed in, there was graffiti that featured a well-endowed centaur on the back side of the building that Brock sneered at, and a few bricks were missing. "Home sweet home," he quipped, smirking.

"You're joking."

"Not even a little," he gave me a hard slap on the back, his good humor returning. "The school's been expanding faster than it planned, so some of you lucky Initiates get to stay in the old Denavere building."

"That's the second time you called me that. Is the word Initiate supposed to mean anything to me? And what the fuck is a Denavere?" I asked, getting frustrated with the thought of living in the dilapidated building in front of me.

"It's an old, powerful family among the elves," he said, rolling his eyes. "They made a huge donation so that their descendants who attended this school would have a nice apartment in their own building. It's around back, separate from the dorms. No one from their family has been here for the past hundred or so years, so the school stopped using it for a while. Oh, and every new student is an Initiate for their first month. A lot of them die in that time, if not during the exam at the end, so there's really no point in pretending that they're real students. Good luck, by the way!" He shot me a large grin, but the amusement in his eyes was purely malevolent.

"Yeah, thanks," I grumbled, looking up at my new home. "So, can you at least show me which room's mine?"

Brock tossed his head back and laughed. "I keep forget-ting how little you know. You should have a key in your pocket with the room number. Only residents can enter each building after sundown, there are wards in place to make sure of that. Here," he said, walking up to the door. He wrapped a hand around the doorknob and wrenched with all his strength, but it didn't budge. He let go and took a step back. "Now you try."

I walked by him carefully, still not completely sure that this building was even a dorm. For all I knew, this asshole took pleasure in leading new students to cursed buildings that stole their soul or some shit like that. Still, I figured I didn't have any other options.

But when I put my hand on the door and pushed, it flew open as easily as a curtain. I stepped in and glanced around, checking for booby-traps. When no spikes flew out of the wall and no fireballs singed me to ashes, I figured I was safe. For the moment, anyway.

By the time I turned around to thank Brock, he was gone. I could see him walking in the distance, cool and confident like he owned the place. He had the air of a rich kid about him, so for all I knew, he did.

To my relief, finding my room was a simple matter. In that way, this world was just like my own. There was an empty desk by the entrance, as well as hallways leading north and south with a stairway in the middle. The key in my pocket was more of a small metal plaque with "222' inscribed into it. That meant the second floor on the south side, it was easy to notice that the even numbers were strictly in the southern wings.

The relief was short-lived however, because when I opened the door to my room, which seemed to be operated by the same warding-lock as the front door, I recognized it.

From the dream I had last night.

6

A FEELING THAT WASN'T QUITE FEAR, MORE LIKE apprehension, filled me. Being in the exact place from my dream just made it all that much more real.

I thought of the kid in his dorm room being visited by a mysterious, cruel woman. Probably 'The Lady' Brock and Filo kept referring to. Suddenly, the fearful reverence they seemed to put on her name made a lot of sense.

The room was just big enough to fit the bed, desk, a wardrobe, and a trunk that I hadn't noticed before. The bed wasn't scratchy, but it was firm as hell and only had a thin sheet over it. My counterpart apparently didn't see fit to bring himself a fucking blanket.

What kind of psychopath sleeps without a blanket?

First, he pledges himself, *now myself*, to some dark God, then he subjects me to what I can only assume are going to be terrible nights spent on a hay mattress with no air conditioning. I wasn't sure which one was worse.

Jacobus did bring a pillow, at least. Though, on second thought, it was more likely the school provided it. From what

I could tell, he had either just moved in recently or was really taking his time unpacking.

In the dream he was a little too busy groveling on the floor to get anything else done, but I had to assume that wasn't exactly the highlight of his day.

There was a long black staff, made of polished wood, leaning in the corner of the room. I took it into my hands and ran my fingers along its smooth length. It was about as thick as two of my fingers, and surprisingly rigid. As I put it back, I couldn't wait until I finally found a reason to use it.

Next, I searched the trunk, made of old wood so dry that I needed to be careful handling it to avoid a splinter, but only found a few books and a lot of clothing that would make Merlin or Gandalf jealous. Even a few pointy hats that, admittedly, I was excited to wear. If those were considered *in* in this world, then I was all for it.

As I let the lid drop shut, though, I heard a jingling sound. Like keys, or change. I shoved aside all the robes and found a small brown sack slumped and pushed into the corner. Hidden. It was surprisingly heavy as I hauled it out of the trunk and let it fall to the floor with the sound of clinking coins. My heart raced as I realized what must have been inside and untied the top.

A sea of gold looked up at me. Coins of all sizes, from nations of all kinds and in all states of wear. It must have been ten pounds of pure gold and silver in there!

My eyes bulged, and I clutched the heavy bag to my chest before thrusting it back into the trunk. I glanced around the room, suddenly as paranoid as a dragon sitting on his hoard. Just as my eyes fell on the wall opposite my bed, it seemed to fade away.

The next room was shaped and furnished just like mine, but the sleeping guy with short, black, curly hair had apparently brought a few blankets. And a lot more other stuff, as well. Several trunks that were in much better shape, and a pile of books that looked new.

So, apparently, Jacobus totally had the option to bring plenty of supplies and make himself, now myself, comfortable. He just chose not to. *What a dick.*

Suddenly I realized I was watching this random dude sleep and my vision snapped back to normal as if someone had slapped me on the back of the head. There was a soreness that came with using that power that was starting to grow familiar.

Then I noticed that there were a few books open out on the desk. *Lost Artifacts of Old Tris* by Finius Flint. *Pillars: An Examination* with no author listed. And *The Practical Argument for Eradication* by Brother Hulien of the Westcroft Monastery.

In English, I realized with a start. Fuck, I didn't even want to think about how much harder this would be if I had to learn a new language on top of everything else.

They were all open to specific pages for a reason, I assumed, but even though I could technically read them, I didn't understand more than three words in a row at any point. I figured I would have to start them from the beginning and try to figure out what Jacobus was up to, but even the table of contents of *Lost Artifacts of Old Tris* was so confusing that I gave up for the night. I needed a little more experience with this world first.

As much as I wanted to be excited about the magical world I had found myself in, the first night was a pile of shit. Two strangers insulted me as I lost control over the vision in my new body, I didn't even know how to use the magic, and to cap it all off I had to sleep in an uncomfortable bed on a hot, humid night.

But Filo had some pretty nice tits, so that was nice. Magic might still be out of my reach, but the Power I did have was still useful. I mean, what kid never fantasized about having x-ray vision? Sure, I couldn't control it yet, but that would come with practice. I assumed, anyway.

Besides, there seemed to be more to it than just that; I hadn't been able to do it on purpose yet, but when my vision spasmed earlier, it didn't just see through layers, it *zoomed in*. Like a broken camera that wouldn't stop adjusting. At least, even if I couldn't use it whenever I wanted, I was able to be careful to prevent it from happening too much. I didn't know how I'd be able to hide it much longer if I kept tripping myself up because I saw through the floor.

Walking to class was going to be very interesting, though, once I got that power under control. If this school was anything like my own, then there would be no shortage of fine ladies. I couldn't walk to class without passing a few chicks that looked like they belonged in magazines or had tens of thousands of Instagram followers. I'd pass them by with a huge grin on my face and they'd have no idea why.

...In which case I'd just be a huge creep, peeping on unknowing college girls like it was Revenge of the Nerds.

Great. Just great. I can't even enjoy *that*.

A FIST BANGING AGAINST MY DOOR ALMOST MADE ME FALL right out of bed. I caught myself with a hand on my desk and hauled myself out of bed with some difficulty. I pulled back the dark gray curtains to let some light in and lost my breath at the sight.

The campus was hauntingly beautiful at night. Also, strangely silent and empty, but now? It was a clear day, and the sun was beating down against countless students in all kinds of elaborate outfits. My eyes bulged as I noticed some clearly weren't human.

Elves were easy enough to notice, with their slanted eyes

and pointed ears, though there even appeared to be many different kinds of them.

Orcs were another species, though they were much more *human* than I would have expected. Instead of the huge green, ridiculously muscular World of Warcraft type, these were much closer to humans with varying shades of green skin and tusks of many shapes and sizes.

There were others I couldn't even put a name to; purple or blue-skinned people with disproportionately long limbs.

This world might take more getting used to than I thought.

Many wore flowing robes that fanned out behind them as they walked, using their staffs as walking sticks. Others were wrapped in cloth and straps, like they took one long length of fabric and wrapped it around themselves until they were satisfied. There were some relatively normal dresses, though still far more elaborate than the ones in my world, and more pointy hats than I could count!

I could have stood there all day just watching all the different kinds of people walk by, but the pounding against my door took me out of it.

I tore my eyes away and open the door with a sharp, "Alright! Jeez, man, what the fuck could be so urgent?" I was still too exhausted to be very angry, but cutting my sleep short wasn't something I took lightly. Especially when I just got transported to another world and my sleep schedule was about to get all kinds of fucked up.

A small guy, a good half-foot shorter than me, with short black curls pushed to the side that looked like they hadn't been washed in a couple days, stared up at me with fire in his eyes. "Look, man," he started, "I know you aren't here to make friends or whatever, but we're going to be neighbors for a while so cut that I'm-better-than-you bullshit."

I reared back and raised my eyebrows. The guy had balls.

That, and apparently, he didn't get off on the right foot with Jacobus. I rubbed my eyes and gritted my teeth, wondering how many times I was going to have to deal with the consequences of Jacobus's dumb ass. I was still pissed that the guy pledged himself to some dark God and then fucked off to my world, to let me deal with the repercussions, but there was nothing I could do about it at the moment.

"Ah, sorry man," I started, rubbing the sleep out of my eyes and clearing my throat. "Just didn't get much sleep last night so I'm a bit cranky." There was also the matter of the new world I found myself in, but that was neither here nor there. Well, I guess it was *technically* here. Literally, even. "What's up?"

He squinted at me, looking a little confused. "Right. You seem like the kind of person who doesn't get much sleep every day," he grumbled. "But you're missing the meeting. Our whole floor was supposed to come and you're the only one who didn't, so Boba sent me after you. I don't want to keep getting lumped in with some idiot trying to be a rebel, so try to make it on time next week, yeah?"

He turned to leave immediately after that, so I called out to him, "Hold on!" as I threw on all the same black robes from yesterday, not wanting to take the time to sort through the trunk to find a different outfit.

I wasn't sure if he actually stopped until I popped out into the hallway and saw him with his arms crossed, leaning back against the wall. I stuck out my hand. "I'm Jake, by the way. Sorry if we got off to a bad start. I'm really not an asshole. Well, usually."

My neighbor gave me a suspicious look but took my hand. "Uh, Whelan Capri. You said to call you Jacobus before, but I'm guessing you don't remember that because we learned about the meeting at around the same time."

I let out an awkward laugh. "Yeah, sorry about that. Got a

lot on my mind lately. But I guess we're all under a lot of pressure, right?"

Whelan still seemed suspicious but nodded and started walking down the hall. Since I had no idea where to go, I rushed to keep up.

"Got that right," he grumbled. "In a month we'll all have to prove ourselves while they decide whether to keep us around. Or kill us," he shrugged as if it were normal for a school to execute students instead of expelling them.

Meanwhile, I was trying not to freak out. Whelan glanced over at me and apparently noticed my change in expression. "Oh, don't tell me you didn't know that! You know where you are, right?" He added, like he was talking to an idiot, or a child.

I gritted my teeth. "Yes. Aether Academy," I bit out the answer as if I didn't just learn it yesterday.

"Well, then you shouldn't be surprised. Once you're allowed in, you're privy to secrets that they don't want to let out. And if you're too stupid to pass your classes, then obviously they can't trust you to keep a secret, so..." he just shrugged. "It's the best school in the world for a reason. They're strict and expect a lot... but, again, you should know this. Where are you from again?"

The question caught me off guard, but I figured it couldn't hurt to tell the truth. If he was asking me, then Jacobus mustn't have already told him. This world probably wouldn't have a Rhode Island too, so, to Whelan, it would just be another place he had never heard of. Plus, it gave me an excuse. "See, that's the thing. I'm from Rhode Island. *Very* far away, so I don't know too much about this place. But, like you said, it's the best school, so I couldn't turn down an opportunity to come here."

"Right. Still, they should have made all that clear to you before letting you move in. Oh well," he shrugged again, "too late now. You're stuck here with the rest of us," he shot me his first grin and I felt like we might just end up getting along.

Then he turned a right, stepping into a dorm room at the end of the hall that must have been twice the size of my own.

Despite being hit with continuous surprises, I hadn't gotten any better at hiding it. The room was filled with a selection of people, er, *humanoids,* who were as varied as the crowds I saw out my window earlier. Most of them were human, or something close enough, but I also noticed a burly, tuskless orc next to a skinnier one, both males, I assumed, as well as a few of the oddly colored people I noticed earlier. One was a light shade of blue while the other is a new one to me, a dark crimson with small horns jutting out from her forehead.

But my eyes slid right over the rest of them and stuck on a girl that seemed to be hiding in the corner. She was utterly gorgeous and looked a bit terrified. Her dark green eyes were bulging and scanning the room continuously. When they fell on me, they widened further and looked away immediately. It seemed Jacobus had a reputation, and not necessarily a good one.

The girl was wearing a loose white top that clung just below her shoulders, leaving her tanned collar bones exposed. It didn't show even a hint of cleavage, but her conservative outfit failed to hide the fact that she had an amazing body. A green sash pulled tight around her midsection, emphasizing the chest she covered up, and light red skirts ran down to her ankles. She had a small crescent moon-shaped scar below her left eye that was paler than the rest of her tanned body. Thick brown hair set the stage for a light orange witch's hat about eight inches tall with flowers chained together at the base of its cone.

Before I could walk over and join her in that corner, the burly orc spoke up. His voice was rough and deep, and he must have stood a head taller than me. "Nice of you to join us, Jacobus." He pushed off the wall and strode to the center of the room, keeping his arms crossed. "Now that you've all had a little time to settle in, welcome to Aether Academy," he said grimly, "I'm Boba Ports, your residential advisor, so if you have any questions or need help finding your classes, you can fuck right off. Don't ask me until you're at least an Acolyte. For now, you Initiates should be spending all your time studying when you're not in class.

"I'm not going to get on your ass about it, you know the consequences of failure, and I don't care who you used to be, or how you got accepted to the school," he glared at me when he said that, for some reason.

"As of today, you are all equals. Initiates, every one of you. This patch," he patted a large, green-tinted hand over an embroidered globe with three birds flying within, "means I'm a Veteran. You're not to speak to anyone with more than three ravens for now, not if you want to live long enough to die after you fail the exams," that made him grin. It was hideous.

"Just keep in mind the ground rules and stay out of my way until you've passed the entry exams." He held up a finger with each rule, "No magic outside the classroom. No drugs. No parties. No fucking. You can have fun next month, but for now, you work." Then he chuckled to himself, though it sounded more like a rockslide, "Fuck it. Why am I even bothering? You're the ones who'll be punished, not me. Just behave while you're in this building and I don't care what else you do. Now get the fuck out of my room," he nodded his head toward the door and most of the people couldn't scramble out fast enough.

7

I LET THE DESPERATE PEOPLE RUSH OUT FIRST, THEN turned to leave. I heard a whispery, uncertain voice squeak up behind me that made me freeze. The sexy girl who was hiding in the corner was apparently the only one brave enough to ask a question. *Interesting.*

Whelan shot me a frustrated look when I didn't leave the room with him, choosing instead to stay behind and listen.

The girl was clearly intimidated. Her head pointed down, her eyes glanced up at Boba for no more than a second at a time, her arms wrapped around herself like the cloth of those strange outfits I saw earlier. "Uhm. Veteran Ports?" He looked down at her and grunted. "I-I'm sorry, is there anywhere I could get a map of the campus? I don't want to keep bothering you to ask for directions."

"I'd prefer you didn't bother me for any reason," he drawled, leaving it at that as if he had bothered to answer her question at all. It pissed me off.

Why did he need to be such a dick? It was literally an RA's job to help new students and he seemed to be going out of his way to avoid doing it. He was a big guy, but I wasn't about to let him treat her like a nuisance when he should be better than that.

As I stepped up to the two of them, the girl took a careful step back, but Boba stood his ground and glared at me. I met his eyes with a steady gaze of my own. "Look, just tell us where we can find a map, and some people who are actually willing to answer questions. Then we can all just fuck off, as you put it. I don't care if you're a Veteran whatever that means, you don't need to be an asshole, too."

The man's dark lips pursed and curled into a deep frown. "This first month is to weed out the idiots and weaklings who shouldn't have been accepted in the first place. Figuring it out for yourself is the point," he growled.

That's when Whelan rushed back into the room. He patted me on the back in a friendly way and offered, "I'll help you two find our rank building. The one for Initiates and prospective students is just down the street, they'll be able to help you out with just about anything. Sorry about that," he nodded to the orc, who glared without even bothering to grunt.

Then Whelan shot me, and the green-eyed damsel a pointed look telling us to follow him out. Since the big asshole wasn't particularly helpful anyway, I followed my new friend without a word.

The door slammed behind us and the girl jumped about a foot into the air with a squeal rising from her throat. She squeezed her eyes shut, reset her hat's position, and slowly got a hold of herself.

"Are you alright?" I asked, trying to make my voice sound warm and calming. This girl seemed to have more trouble adjusting to her new environment than even I did.

She cracked an eyelid and looked over to me, then nodded. When she didn't say anything, I added, "I'm Jake. And this is my friend, Whelan. How about we all go find that

Initiate's building? I could use a map myself." She nodded again but when I looked over at Whelan, he was eyeing me oddly. "Lead the way," I told him, waving my hand toward down the hall.

I kept glancing behind myself to make sure the girl was following, and even if she was avoiding looking at me, she stayed close. When we passed my room, I popped in to grab a dark, hooded cloak, and black wizard's hat that had a golden strip of ribbon at its base. Seeing Lilly wear hers made my head feel naked by comparison.

When we got outside, her small voice finally spoke up while Whelan looked around. He didn't seem to know the campus quite as well as he thought.

"I'm Lilly," she said, looking up at me through her eyelashes. Whelan was about the same height as her, but she barely reached my shoulders.

"Nice to meet you, Lilly," I grinned, and she returned a weak smile. "You seem nervous, are you *sure* you're okay?"

She nodded, seeming a little more comfortable, but still very tense. "I'm just not used to seeing so many people. And so many *types* of them." She let out a small, wavering laugh, "There were maybe fifty people in my whole town and now I live in a building bigger than any I've ever seen with more than twice that many! It's a lot to take in, and that's without even mentioning that... thing in there," she glanced back at the dorm as we started walking down the cobblestone street and I knew exactly what she was referring to.

"Well, that *thing* is our RA. I don't think he'll be any help so you should probably just avoid him. Seems like an asshole, anyway."

"You two really don't get it, do you?" Whelan said over his shoulder before stopping in the middle of the street. We weren't in the main road, so there were few people around, but occasionally a group streamed by us and Lilly's eyes latched on with shocked fascination every time. "You're at probably the most elite, exclusive school in Miria. They get to pick their students from across the world; everyone wants to go here. You practically have to be such a genius that any other school would hold you back in order to be accepted. Then you have to compete with a couple hundred people who are just as smart and hard-working to make it past the first month.

"If what they say about you is true, you shouldn't have any problem," he glanced over at me and it suddenly hit me that he was talking about Jacobus. I nodded as if I knew what he was talking about but made a note to figure that out later. Such notes were starting to add up. "But you," he turned his gaze to Lilly and his voice softened, "Well, I hope you know what you're getting yourself into."

"I thought I did," she muttered. "But reading about academies like these is a whole lot different from actually attending one."

As Whelan turned and kept walking, I fell in next to Lilly and gave her a nudge with my elbow. "Well, if it helps, I'm just as clueless as you are."

"Really?" She didn't seem to believe me. Her eyes ran down the length of my robes and back up. "Aren't you the one with the Miskatonic scholarship?"

I had no idea what that was, but it sounded impressive. Luckily, Whelan called back with a "Yup," before I had the chance to answer. "He's reminded me of that fact no fewer than five times since we met."

Lilly nodded and looked back at me, clearly impressed. "That must be why Boba didn't snap at you. Magic beats muscle any day, my old teacher used to say. If you're skilled enough to impress even the Miskatonic scholars, then he was wise to hold back."

I kept nodding along as if I knew what they were talking

about. I didn't want to add anything and contradict whatever they already knew about Jacobus. Not yet, anyway.

"You're... different from what I expected." Lilly said eventually as Whelan turned down a pathway that led us to a small stone building about half the size of our dorm. The gray blocks were chipping everywhere and the door we approached was made of a dark wood and engraved with the image of a mountain, viewed from the very base.

"You got that right," Whelan commented wryly. "Practically seemed like a completely different person yesterday."

"Uh, yeah, sorry about that. I was in a bad mood from all the traveling and unpacking. It was a rough transition. Still is," I added and they both nodded their agreement. "Now it seems like everyone has these inflated expectations of me, so I'm thinking I should lay low for a bit."

They seemed to accept that explanation for now, and I heaved a sigh in relief. Too many further questions and my improvised lies would fall apart in a heartbeat.

Whelan pushed open the door and held it as we filed inside. We stepped into a tight hallway with brown and gold tiles covering the floor and seamless stone walls. A staircase in front of the door led up to a hallway that was shrouded in darkness.

"Can I help you three?" a friendly voice called to us from the left. I tried to keep my expression plain while taking in the large orc woman. She was easily as big as Boba, with tusks that curled around her face and almost reached as far back as her ears. She looked so out of place in her little secretary's office.

Whelan stepped forward. "Yeah, can we get a couple Student Handbooks? It seems these two lost theirs."

The woman, who was a much darker shade of green than I had seen so far, glanced back at us with a smile that I assumed was supposed to be friendly, but with the tusks crowding her teeth it just became terrifying. Lilly's eyes bulged but at least she didn't take off running.

The woman nodded and opened a few drawers before finally finding what she needed and sliding two small books across the desk to Lilly and me. "These are our best copies available," she said, sounding proud of herself. "Don't mind the wear, they've been wiped clean and brought fully up to date. You'll find all the functions on the inner cover, and you can add your friends by simply tapping your handbooks together."

Still, they had clearly been passed down between multiple generations of students. The cover of Lilly's copy was covered in half-erased doodles and as I flipped through the first few pages, I saw notes written in the margins by at least three different people, judging by the handwriting. The inner cover she mentioned was filled with icons that reminded me of a smartphone's home screen.

"Uh. Thanks," I said, already uncertain about how much help this 'Handbook' could even provide. At least the map was still legible, but the handbook was surprisingly thin, otherwise.

Lilly repeated my thanks and Whelan led us out. The orc woman called after us, "Oh, and we have tutoring sessions available! If you're willing to risk it," she added playfully. Lilly and I looked at each other, confused, but Whelan just rolled his eyes.

When we got outside, he stopped in the pathway. "The tutors try to kill you," he said, already sounding bored about how much he had to explain to us. "Oh, you learn a lot in the process, but it's only worth it if you stay alive, as well. I'd recommend a lot of studying before you resort to that." He took a glance at our shabby handbooks and added, "They must have a big class this year if that's the best they have left. Mine was brand new," he grinned.

A thought suddenly occurred to me. "Hey, how do you know so much about this place? Haven't you mentioned a few times how secretive it is?"

Whelan grimaced and looked away. His face twisted up in thought for a few seconds before answering. "Right. Ah, well. Shit. Look, you can't tell anyone about this alright?"

I nodded excitedly, but Lilly didn't move. If anything, her expression tightened. I didn't know what her problem was, but I was keen to get my hands on every secret this magical world had to offer!

Whelan pulled us off the path, away from prying ears, and lowered his voice. "My Dad went to school here like fifty years ago, but the place hasn't changed in at least twice as long, according to him. So, he's been spending most of the last few years teaching me all there is to know about the place. Which, considering the school's policies, could get us both punished by death. Letting out any information about how this place works is strictly against the rules, even when it comes to your own family."

"Well, your secret's safe with me," I said. Lilly nodded agreement, looking relieved, as if she was expecting something much worse.

Just as I was thinking about asking the same question, Lilly spoke up, her voice already so light that she didn't even need to whisper, but she did anyway. "Why would they be so strict? Shouldn't they *want* prospective students to know what they're getting into?"

Whelan chuckled and gave her a surprised look, saying almost absent-mindedly, "I never realized how detached from the rest of the world some rural villages can be." Then he gave her a friendly, reassuring smile, "No offence, I kinda figured this stuff was common knowledge. I'm starting to realize how much I learned over the years, despite my efforts to ignore my father's droning.

"Anyway, there are competitions between the schools every year and the rivalries get pretty serious. The highest-ranking students and faculty basically get rented out as mercenaries, too, so every school wants to be known for having the most powerful stock. You might think that each school would end up a recruiting ground for the nation's army, but universities this size are basically nations in their own right. Our student body alone could take on any mage-less army, and that's without even counting the faculty or Post Grad ranks. Think about how serious countries are when defending secrets of national importance," he summed it up and shrugged. "It's the same thing here but covers the entire curriculum and infrastructure."

"Jeez," I muttered, realizing again just how much I still didn't know about this world. Which was basically everything. It was still hard to even accept that I had stepped into an entirely different world, as large and full as my own, but hearing Whelan go into such detail really opened my eyes.

Whelan began eying me suspiciously, but when he opened his mouth to say something, a loud bell suddenly rung out. My new friend's head snapped toward the sound and he said, "Ah, shit. I thought we had more time, come on." He started speed walking along the path, waving for Lilly and me to follow.

He kept speeding up as we passed by other dorms and administration buildings. The mostly open campus was covered with immaculate trees and shrubbery, lining the roads and paths or the bases of buildings. I noticed a few more rank buildings, they seemed to get much larger with each step up.

I caught Lilly staring toward an out-of-place forest as dense as I'd ever seen. My mouth fell open as it dawned on me how huge the trees were. I'd only ever seen pictures of Redwoods, but these were easily as large, though they appeared a darker, almost black brown, and leaves that were as large as my chest and as deep green as Lilly's eyes. The building at the center had an entrance that was carved into a tree that grew through the building, rising far above the others, rivaling even the spire at the campus' center for height. I wanted to stay and figure out what it was, but Whelan kept walking too quickly for me to dawdle.

"What are we in such a rush for anyway?" I said, a little out of breath from our trek across campus.

Whelan shot me another confused look. *What's with this guy?* I wondered but added it to the list of shit I had to figure out later. "We're at a university, remember? Well, we're about to be late for our first class."

❧ 8 ❧

WE ARRIVED AT THE EDGE OF CAMPUS TO FIND A HALF-dozen open-roofed amphitheaters set into the hill that made up the campus grounds. The land was at a slight slant, with these half-bowls of varying size cutting into Earth.

The apparent classrooms were filled with half-circles of stone benches that looked like church pews and were almost completely filled by dozens of students of more races than I could count. I did recognize a few people from my dorm, as well as other faces I'd passed on the street earlier, but the woman they were all listening to was new to me.

A tall, statuesque woman with perfectly smooth, gray-tinged skin stood at a podium in the center of a platform at the front of the theater. She had short black hair pulled into a ponytail, not one strand out of place, and wore a long red gown, the color of blood, accented with black details that were too far away to make out. The scowl on her face, made all the more discomforting by her ruby eyes, was clear, even at a distance. As was the incredible body that she hid under that elaborate gown. She had a full chest and hips that commanded the fabric to flow around them. Something about the look of disgust on the full figured woman just made her look even hotter.

Her voice was pure ice, though, and her eyes pure scorn. "It looks like the lot of you can rest easy," she addressed the already-seated students before turning back to the three of us at the top of the steps, "knowing that there are three students too stupid to make it to the first class on time. Perhaps this year's incoming class is only so large because our standards have fallen so low," she smirked, proud of her insults.

Whelan made an awkward laugh and took on an overly friendly manner. "Sorry, we–"

"I don't care, just take your seats," she cut him off abruptly. "If you can't take things seriously enough to get here on time, then I'll focus my efforts on the students who *can*." Then she shot me a particularly icy look and proceeded to ignore us while returning to her lecture.

Meanwhile, the friendly look faded from Whelan's face and turned into disdain. He clenched his jaw and glared at our curvy professor, though she didn't appear to notice. I tapped him on the shoulder and nodded toward a few open seats. We filed past a few unhappy students before taking the open places with me in the middle.

The long stone benches curved with the shape of the theater. As I sat down, I found that they were as soft as any cushion and smooth, despite their stony appearance.

Whelan tapped the seat in front of him two times and the stone morphed, giving birth to a thin platform that floated out in front of Whelan. It was a sheet of rock floating in place a few inches above his legs. He rolled his eyes and tapped the same spot in front of me and Lilly, a thin desk of rock soon appearing before each of us as well.

Whelan then opened his handbook. When he pressed a finger to the page, over an image that looked like notebook paper, the item shifted within his hands until it resembled the icon he had just pressed.

My mouth hung agape as I turned to my own tattered handbook and opened to a page filled with icons like that. There seemed to be one for every subject; history, the elements, regeneration, etc, as well as some utilities, like the notebook or basic handbook.

I pressed the same icon, as did Lilly, but our notebooks, and the quills tucked into their bindings, were sad, dilapidated versions of Whelan's. Half of my pages were already taken up by a haphazardly written script whose only legible parts were the punctuation. A few pages were even falling out.

Observing Lilly's same disappointment, I nudged her with an elbow and said, "You'd think that if they could make magical shape-shifting notebooks, they'd also make them self-repairing." She snorted a laugh and gave me the first real smile I'd seen out of her. I was surprised by how satisfying that was, and how much cuter it made the already-gorgeous girl look.

It was only then that I was finally able to actually pay attention to what our professor was saying, though her exotic beauty continued to make it difficult.

She was going through what seemed to be a typical college introduction about how much the administration expected out of us, how hard they want us to work, how honored we should be to have this opportunity, blah, blah, blah, etc, etc, so I turned to Whelan. "Hey," I whispered, "Your Dad tell you anything about this lady?"

He pursed his lips and glanced around before giving me a severe look and answering in a sharp whisper. "Professor Doriah's her name and she's like, a thousand years old or something. Literally. She's an elf, so she'll basically live until something deliberately kills her. Father said she was a real hard-ass and I can see why. Can't say I remember much more than that though," he shrugged, "but she's powerful and important so we should probably avoid pissing her off."

So much for that idea. As if we hadn't already screwed up enough, I suddenly realized that the room was silent. And that a lot of the faces were turned toward me and Whelan, while Lilly was laser-focused on the notebook she pretended to write in.

Then my eyes slid over to Professor Doriah. Her arms were crossed, and her cold eyes regarded me with calm fury. "Are you finished?" She spat out the words and waited for us to nod before adding. "If you interrupt my class again, I will have the Morphstone swallow you up to your noses for the rest of the day. Is that clear?"

I started to shake my head, having no idea what Morphstone was, but when I noticed the look of fright on Whelan's face, I thought better of it and nodded along with him.

The professor gave a curt, satisfied nod, then. "I expected more out of a Miskatonic scholar," she grumbled, eying me without anger for the first time, just curiosity. I heard my classmates whispering to each other at that comment. I was getting the sense that these Miskatonic people were powerful in some way. "You will see me after class," she added, then she turned forward, apparently forgetting I even existed.

I took out the quill and assumed it held its own ink as I got ready to take my first notes at the magical Aether Academy. It was such a mundane thing, but it excited me.

"*Anyway*, you should all spend the next few weeks hard at work. Not only because it will set the tone for the rest of your time here, or because you will need to impress your superiors if you ever expect to find acceptance, but because you will need to be strong for the days to come. Not all of you will survive the exams. And it will only get more difficult from there, so consider this your first, and final warning. We do not suffer fools here. You either pass, or you die." She let the words sink into the wide-eyed students around her, glancing around at their reactions with a smug grin.

But she only succeeded in hyping me up. I didn't expect it to be easy, anyway. I'd already felt stupid way too many times in the last twenty-four hours to not realize how far behind I was. Jacobus may have been strong enough to earn that Gin-and-tonic scholarship, or whatever it was called, but I still hadn't even figured out how to use this world's magic and at that point I was a little afraid to ask.

Not that it was embarrassing – not to say it was *not* embarrassing, it just wasn't enough to stop me – but because there was no way in hell someone would be able to make it to this school without even knowing the least bit of magic. It'd be like getting accepted to an engineering school without ever hearing about this thing called math. Or numbers.

Professor Doriah let the silence emphasize her point, seeming like she was looking into every individual student's eyes before finally moving on. She had a slow way of speaking, as if she were laying each word out in front of her in a linguistic mosaic. "Now that we are all on the same page... I am Professor Silith Doriah. I've been teaching at this school since before your grandparents were even a horny, bubbling thought in their parents' minds. I've had a long, illustrious career that the historians would love to tell you about, but that's not what you're here for. I won't brag about myself at length just to earn the respect of a couple hundred Initiates. One of you will step out of line soon enough and give me just the opportunity I need." Her red eyes shifted over to me and squinted with a devious pleasure. I met her gaze without blinking, uncomfortable as I was with her interest in me. "I've been known to execute a few cheaters in my day, so I would caution you against taking that risk. We do not *expel* students. Again, I will say this. You either pass, or you die. There is *no* in between.

"Your first month will be spent with me," she grinned at that like it was a joke that only she was in on. "We will have weekly guest speakers from various disciplines within the school to give you an inkling of what courses you may choose to take, should you pass this preliminary phase. Your ascension in rank will be decided by a round of exams. Part written, based on my lectures, and a part will be a little more... fun. I suggest you all brush up on your combat skills.

"Unless, of course, you wish to spend the next few weeks partying and enjoying yourselves. You may. No one will stop you, despite it being against the rules. But the fun you have will be your last. So, to begin our introduction, get out your history textbooks and turn to the first chapter so that we may get started."

The room filled with the sound of books changing form or popping into existence. Paper scraping against paper hundreds of times became a loud, irritating sound. Whelan showed Lilly and I that if we pressed our fingers to an icon and swiped upward, like a damn touchscreen, the selected book would pop into existence without taking the place of the notebooks we already had out.

What followed was an at least two-hour lecture that brushed over the history of the academy, its founding and a some of its famous former students, who Professor Doriah had met personally, of course. There was a Willem Ballory, who fell into the Shadows and tried to take the entire university with him. She was proud to say that she personally attended that particular execution.

As the professor detailed a few more prominent Shadows, as that was apparently what they called mages who were devoted to the dark god, Vethris, another name I learned today, I took notes on them and it suddenly dawned on me.

I'm one of them.

Whether I signed up for it or not, I was already on the same side as those people my professor hated. A chill ran down my spine as she described another gruesome ending to one of the Shadows, this time a rather explosive death in combat.

My throat felt dry, and my hands were slick with sweat. I'd *definitely* need to keep my secrets close. I'd have to find out if there was any way to sever my ties to this Mothric, but if it was anything like any other cult I'd heard of, its policies probably mirrored my new school's.

In other words, Jacobus signed me up for a whole lot of shit I didn't want to deal with. A school that would kill me if I didn't pass. And a cult following a dark God that would kill me if I... well I didn't really know anything about them yet, but I was sure they'd kill me without a second thought, either.

But all that went out the window as the Professor changed subjects and moved on to our next exercise that she described as 'stretching our magical muscles.' I didn't know what I was in for, but based on the rest of the lecture, and Silith's grim, take-no-shits attitude, I figured it would be dangerous.

And I was all fucking for it.

9

Breathing.

Stretching our magical muscles? Yeah, just a breathing exercise. The professor used all kinds of mystical phrases to make it sound fancy; all about how we were communing with nature and the Gods, letting their energies flow through us, siphoning off a bit of power so that we may bend it to our will.

All she did was take a deep breath.

Of course, I tried it. I was always breathing! She could describe it differently, but that didn't change anything. And yet, everyone around me took the commands in stride. Both Whelan and Lilly shut their eyes and seemed to be meditating, if not sleeping.

I glanced around at the rows of students and tried to mimic whatever they were doing differently, but it didn't help.

My eyes landed on a stunning, pale elf girl with smaller ears than I'd seen on the rest. Her thin, freckled face was scrunched up, focusing hard, her little nose flaring as she sucked in air. Bright pink lips were pursed with frustration, still managing to look plump. A thick mass of pale blonde hair fell down to the small of her back, a few errant strands fell in front of her ears, brushing against her collar bones whenever the wind picked up. My eyes fell to her chest, heaving with deep breaths like she was trying to burst out of the dark blue gown that covered almost as high as her collar bones.

Given that everyone's eyes were closed, I didn't mind staring at the elf girl for a few extra seconds. Hell, my eyes probably would have staged a mutiny if I tried to pull them away.

Suddenly, though, my vision *pushed* through layers of fabric to lay my eyes on a tight body with a full chest held compressed by her gown, and bright pink nipples. Her ribs dipped in and flared out where her hips began.

The power scanned through layers of the girl's skin, muscles, and even organs, until it reached the other side and snapped back to normal. My body felt a little weaker afterwards.

As I blinked my eyes back into focus, I became aware of a devious smile on my lips, and a splash of color above my gaze. It was her eyes. Bright teal, beautiful, and *very* angry. She glared back at me as I was checking her out, and I suddenly felt like an idiot for leering at her so openly.

The girl snatched a dark blue witch's hat from beneath her seat and shoved it over her head, pulling it down so that she could ignore the world around her.

Maybe that was it.

What I was doing wrong all along. I was too focused on the world around me, on what everyone else was trying to do so that I could copy them. Instead, I tried to drown them all out. I closed my eyes and tried to forget where I was, what I was doing, shutting out all sound and sensation. Only breathing.

Suddenly, I became aware of *something. Two somethings.*

One was like a river that somehow felt like it flowed through everything. Me, other students, the plants, even stones and dirt. It suffused all life and matter on Earth and carried them in its flow. I wasn't entirely sure how, but I could tell that I wasn't the only one pulling at that flow of power.

As I focused harder, I could sense many points around me where the other students were siphoning off a small bit of magic as they went through the exercise. I could vaguely sense them around me; who was siphoning the flow and how much. Not that I could tell discrete amounts, but some students were clearly pulling in more power than others.

In the crowded amphitheater, this new sense was overloaded, like a TV full of static, and without any practice, I wasn't able to narrow the sense down to try focusing on a single person.

The other *something* was an ocean, deep and vast. Untapped where the first seemed filled with holes. Something about it was strange and different, dark even, yet still fundamentally the same as the river. They both carried water, or in this case magic, but despite seeming like they occupied the same space, they were distinctly separate.

I wasn't about to pretend this didn't all confuse the hell out of me, but I finally knew what to do. I turned my attention to the river and opened myself up to it, breathing in as if for the first time. Warmth filled my lungs and rushed through me, followed by strength and power.

When I opened my eyes, I was breathing heavily and felt like my body should be glowing, despite its disappointingly normal appearance. Lilly looked up at me with a small smile, but Whelan just looked suspicious of me again.

But I didn't care. It *worked*. Magic was flowing through me. Seeing as no one else was casting spells or anything, I didn't want to draw attention to myself by finding out what I could do. But later... well she did suggest we practice our combat skills, right? I wasn't sure how I could do that, considering that we weren't allowed to use magic out of the classroom, but I could figure that out later.

After a few minutes of just breathing, the professor watching us all along and giving a few tips, she called our attention to her again. "Now, bring forth a small flame and focus all your energies upon it. Feed the power into it, feed your emotions and all distracting thought into it. Let it build intensity and heat without letting it grow."

As she spoke, she held out her left hand, palm facing up, and it looked like a smaller version of the sun popped into existence above her hand. The surface broiled with tendrils of flame, but she kept it contained. "Repeat this exercise daily, pushing yourself further every time, to refine your abilities. It may seem simple, but it is of paramount importance that you master your fundamentals. Great control over the flow of power and its use will pay dividends over the years."

All around me, small flames lit above outstretched hands. They were of many different colors and sizes. One student let his grow a little too big and earned a snap from the professor.

Lilly shut her eyes and a small green flame sprouted above her hand, then she shot me a proud smile. "I used to do this all the time. My old teacher," her smile wavered at that, but she recovered quickly, "had us do the same exercise before every class."

Whelan's flame was a bright orange. "Dad did the same," he said, voice as low as it always was when he talked about his father's lessons.

They looked to me, expectantly, so I held out my hand and hoped for the best. Closing my eyes, I was able to find the river easily enough and open myself up to a small portion of it but wasn't sure where to go from there.

How to actually *use* the magic was such a fundamental question I didn't dare ask it, so I just imagined a flame above my hand, just as I'd seen other do, and cracked an eyelid to check my progress.

A small, yellowish-white flame rose from my hand and swirled through the air like a ribbon. I imagined it turning into a ball like the professor's and it reacted immediately. The result wasn't as impressive as hers, but I was smiling like a kid in a candy store.

I'm starting to get the hang of this, I thought. I played around with it a little, feeling how I could pull more power and feed it into the flame, growing hotter or larger as I saw fit.

We spent upwards of an hour at that same drill before the professor let us out for a break. It was just breathing, letting yourself become an alcove for the river of power as you allowed part of it to flow in and out without using it. It was a bit disorienting after a while.

When I was younger, there were entire days that I'd spend at the beach, playing in the waves. Afterwards, standing on land, I would still feel the push and pull of the tide because my body had grown so used to it. As we stopped the exercises, I felt a bit like that. But it was my core that was drained and pulsing, and I was dripping with sweat, as was Lilly. Whelan, however, was breathing a little heavier than normal but otherwise seemed fine.

The rows of students lethargically rose from their seats and filed out of the theater, some leaving bags or hats behind to mark their places. Lilly led the way for the three of us, but just as I reached the top of the steps, something flicked the back of both of my ears. *Hard.*

Rubbing them, I spun on Whelan, who was the only person close enough to have done it. "What the fuck, man? You keep giving me weird looks and now this?"

He blinked a few times and seemed to come out of a deep train of thought. "Hm? Now what? What do you mean?" My eyes slid past him to the tall elf standing at the front of the class with her arms crossed and deep red eyes glaring at me.

"Fuck," I sighed.

Whelan looked over his shoulder and then shot me a grin. "Hey, maybe she's nicer than she looks. She's an old lady, despite being hotter than most of the girls here." Lilly's eyes tightened at that and she glanced down at herself. Whelan didn't even notice. "Just be nice to her, maybe ask her how her great-great-great-great-great grandchildren are doing. Just turn on that Jacobus charm and you'll win her over in no time."

I gave him a flat look, but that was exactly what I had been planning to do. She might be like a thousand years old, but he was right. Professor Doriah was still as fine as any of the girls I'd seen on campus, if not quite on Lilly's level, or the teal-eyed girl I noticed earlier.

But just imagine the kind of kinky shit a person could get into over the course of a thousand years! She probably had moves most of us had never even heard of! I put on my best smile and jabbed my friend with an elbow. "Watch and learn," I quipped.

He rolled his eyes and took a seat in the back row, Lilly quietly joining him.

"You two can go on ahead, I'll catch up."

"And how would you find us?" he asked with a bit of sarcasm, tilting his head and raising one eyebrow.

"Come on, man," I said, pulling out the handbook and flipping to the map on the first few pages. "Just let me know where you'll be. You can at least count on me to read a map."

"You'd think so, but you've already asked me too many questions that I'd think you'd know the answer to. Especially if you're supposed to be one of the top new students. Look," he leaned closer to me and lowered his voice, "I can get Lilly and I added to your handbook so we can see each other on the map or send messages. I'll set it up while you're talking to Doriah," he held out his hand until I placed the handbook in it.

"This thing's more useful than I thought. How do I get it to show *my* location?"

Whelan didn't look up from the shabby handbook he just took from me, already flipping through its pages until he reached the map. "You just think about it and the map will highlight your spot. The same goes for anyone else you've attuned to it. You know, like literally any other map in the world," he added.

I played it off by turning away in the middle of his last sentence and heard him chuckling to himself behind me.

The professor, however, was not amused. Her appearance was a bit more disturbing up close, but, somehow, no less sexy. It was just that light grey skin and ruby eyes really threw me off, even if underneath it was still a body any guy on Earth would worship. All the different species of people in this world were hard to get used to, even when they were as hot as she.

"Mr. Callidus, no scholarship is enough to give you a ride past the exams. Some of the admissions officers might be persuaded by gifts and fancy scholarships, maybe a powerful relative or two, but once you are a student at Aether Academy, the special treatment ends.

"You're here and you may have thought you were special before, but so was every one of those blossoming young witches and wizards whose time you just wasted by interrupting my class. I've seen too much potential wasted by hubris to let what could have been a powerful mage die young when the world may need them soon. You may waste your own time, *Jacobus,*" she filled the name with hate, "but do not waste that of the class. Go," then she nodded over my shoulder and turned her attention to some papers.

"Well, I think you'll find you've underestimated me," I shot back, fighting down any more insulting of a reply no matter how much I wanted to call her a bitch. That was not the kind of trouble I wanted to bring down on myself, not when my entire life depended on that first month of classes.

Professor Doriah didn't look up or give any indication she had heard me. I ran my eyes down her ornate clothing, weighing her up and checking her out in one motion.

My power seemed to sense what I was doing and took over. My eyes vibrated lightly as the images of her body's layers hit me.

Underneath that dark dress were heavy, oddly dark tits with grey nipples. Her flat stomach, and long, dark legs and the shaven peak between them were all seared into my mind. I was impressed, for someone who seemed to care so little of what we all thought of her, she really took care of herself.

It only lasted a second, though. Her eyebrows drew down almost as soon as my eyes washed over her and when the power deactivated, it left me out of breath. Her ruby eyes shot toward me, no longer angry, just pensive. "What are you doing?" she asked, eying me like a puzzle she was trying to figure out.

I shot her a smirk and said, "Nothing," but I could tell she didn't stop watching me with that curious look as I left her behind.

10

"HOW'D IT GO?" WHELAN QUIPPED AS HE HANDED BACK MY handbook. The first thing I did was flip to the map and think of the three of us. Sure enough, little pinpricks of light showed up at our location, so close that they almost looked like one larger light.

Apparently, this outdoor theater was called the Vixerian Lecture Hall. Donated by some wealthy alumnus probably, like most of the buildings back at URI.

"Well, enough, I guess. She didn't kick me out or turn me into a frog, so it could have been worse."

Lilly's eyes bulged. "Is that really the kind of punishments they give here?"

Whelan cringed. "Oh, they can get a lot more creative than that." I tried to hide my horror at that. I'd just been joking! "One of my Dad's teachers turned him into a clock for an entire afternoon. Said his arms were exhausted afterwards." Lilly's tan face paled and her eyes got wider as I assumed she was imagining far worse things than being turned into an animal or a timepiece.

"Hey," I nudged her slippered foot with my boot to try to

get her mind off of whatever frightening punishment she was picturing. "Let's go find something to eat. This place must have some kind of dining hall, right?"

I turned to ask Whelan and realized I could have saved myself the trouble by checking the map. It was another question I would have known the answer to if I had already been staying here for a few days, as Jacobus had.

But Whelan just played it off, apparently accepting that there was more going on with me than his first impression indicated. He rose quickly and led the way, but it wouldn't have been difficult to find, even without a reference. Students in every direction were flowing toward the same point in the center of campus.

The great white spire's shadow fell over a white-tiled square with a fountain in the middle and tables filled with all kinds of people eating foods that I recognized, as well as some that I didn't. The square had cobblestone streets running out from each side and was otherwise lined with buildings. A few were clearly storefronts or food stands, but most were unornamented.

The place was noisy and crowded, it took some time to find some seats. Professor Doriah holding me back gave everyone else time to fill most of the tables.

I noticed a refined, blonde guy that I recognized and started toward his table. Brock was sitting with some of his friends. They were all wearing similarly ornate, embroidered tunics and looked like they must all be the children of some Lord, or rich merchant. But they barely took up half the table, and apparently no one bothered to fill in the other side.

As we approached the empty seats, Whelan spoke up behind me. "Where are you going?"

"Uh, right here," I said, falling onto a stool at the end of the table and glancing down at the older guys, particularly at Brock, with a friendly nod. Meanwhile, Whelan's eyes kept shifting between me and the other group and Lilly waited a few steps away, her arms wrapped around herself.

Whelan gritted his teeth, and his voice had a tremor. "You sure you don't want to sit somewhere else, mate?" He stared at me as if he was waiting for me to get it, then jabbed his head toward Brock's group.

The bulky blonde rich kid was glaring at me along with his friends. "You lost, there little *shits?*" He called down the table from his seat at the head. Whelan groaned and shook his head, stepping away from the table and shooting me a piteous look.

I guess I was wrong to think the guy wouldn't mind, just because we knew each other. "The fuck did you call us?" I shot back.

Brock's face lost all hint of amusement. He planted his hands on the table, around a porcelain plate with a half-eaten sandwich on it, and slowly rose to his feet. "I called you shit because that's what you are until you've ranked up, *Initiate.* Now go sit in the grass, where shit like you belongs," he nodded toward a slanted hill on the outskirts of the square. It was dotted with faces I was starting to recognize from my class, including the teal-eyed girl who I couldn't help but notice was watching us.

I turned back to the group of guys and counted seven of them, including the noble Shadow himself. Now that things were starting to get testy, I figured it was important to know how many I was up against. Not that it mattered, I wasn't about to back down, but I did like to know what kind of punishment I was signing myself up for.

These didn't look like the kind of guys who would politely line up while I fought them one at a time, and I didn't want to bring Whelan or Lilly into something they didn't start.

I shrugged and shot him a combative look, "I think I'll eat here, actually. Prefer to sit in the shade, myself. Besides, you should get a good look at the guy who'll be outranking you all soon enough. Might wanna make a better first impression, buddy. When I'm your superior, I'll remember this."

He scoffed and laughed like I was a child threatening an adult. And, considering my lack of experience with magic, that was probably an accurate comparison, but I finally knew how to use magic and I was itching to try it out.

Siphon off a portion of the flow and bend it to your will. Seemed simple enough. At the very least, I knew I could shoot a bit of fire at him.

"As if you'll live long enough for that to happen. If you're too stupid to keep your mouth shut, or figure out where you belong, there's no fucking way you'll pass the exams. You're just a piece of shit the academy has yet to scrape off its boot." He calmly sat back down and added, "Why should I waste my time on you when the school will take care of you soon enough," then scoffed and turned his attention back to the sandwich.

That would have been the perfect opportunity to walk away. Or even just eat in silence, but I just couldn't. He'd pissed me off. I didn't care what noble family he came from, how long he'd been studying at the academy, or whatever his rank here was. Brock wasn't any better than me or anyone else here and I figured it was about time he got taken down a peg or two.

Focusing on the sandwich, I thought I'd test out an idea I had earlier. If we could play with fire, then why not the other elements? And this time, instead of the river, I opened myself to the dark ocean of power, figuring that I would see what it was capable of.

I underestimated the difference.

The ocean of power slammed into me like a tidal wave, threatening to throw me to the ground like a physical force even though I knew it was just in my head. Brock's eyes shot wide just before I directed the tide of power into the air between his sandwich's layers and imagined it exploding out in all directions.

The result was a little more extravagant than I had in mind, but it got the message across.

The area in front of Brock became an explosion of bread and condiments. To my surprise, and despair, not only did Brock's food explode in his hands, and all over his face, but the rest of his friends' meals did as well.

They were all covered in bits of food that fell out of their hair, sauces that dripped down their angry faces.

The rest of the tables in the square seemed to fall silent and turn their heads toward us. I saw more than a few horrified faces turn toward Brock and realized that maybe I had chosen the wrong person to mess with on my first day. I didn't, after all, have any way of figuring out how powerful a person was yet, and realized how little I actually knew about this guy.

As with any risk, there was a point where I would think about my chances of winning and decide whether it's even worth trying. In this case, I knew I'd probably lose. Most people would take off running, or just try to avoid those situations in the first place. Unless something seriously pissed me off, I was normally one of those that walked away.

But today? Now that I had this fountain of power at my fingertips, I wasn't going to let some dick like Brock push me around. And in an outmatched scenario like this, I knew exactly what to do.

Okay, to be a little more accurate, I had no idea what to do. But I had seen enough movies to know that a group like this would leave me beaten and bloodied if I gave them even the smallest opportunity.

As the shock wore off and the Brock's group of friends rose powerfully to their feet, I jumped away and tried to toss the table aside, taking the group with it. Since it was the dark, alternative source of power that got me into this mess, I decided to stick with the other one for the time being. The result was a rough, sudden motion as the table jerked a few feet to one side.

It wasn't much, but it slammed into Brock's chest in full force and threw him to the ground, knocking the wind out of him, and taking a few of his friends with him. Two wizard hats, the rest of the group had already taken theirs off, slowly floated to the ground.

The ones that weren't knocked to the ground pulled out wands. One of them grabbed a staff of thin oak that was leaning against the table and turned their fury at me. I focused hard enough to feel the river of power part into four new flows while they flung their attacks at me and cursed myself for being stupid enough to get into such an unfair fight.

Instinctively, I threw up my arms and imagined a wall of air springing up between us that would stop their magic from touching me. While I could feel it start to form, four flows sliced through it and took me in nearly full force.

It felt like getting punched in the chest by a giant. Four times. My breath flew out of me as I was sent flying through the air, spinning so fast that the world became a blur until my body slammed into a table, sending another explosion of food everywhere but mostly on myself.

"Fuuuck," I groaned, rolling over and falling to the tiled ground. I sucked in a deep breath of air.

All around me, other students were rushing away in a surprisingly controlled manner. Some looked frightened, but more looked excited. My chest was killing me, and tendrils of smoke were rising from my back as I crouched onto all fours among the hard tiles.

I ripped the cloak off my back and threw it on the

ground, noticing a large new hole in it where one of Brock's lackeys had apparently tried to set me on fire. I blew out a growl and searched for the blonde asshole among the bustling students.

I found his group pushing through the crowd, Brock at their head with wide eyes overflowing with fury. Well, I had more than my fair share of anger to deal with as well. And who better to take it out on than a rich kid who had everything handed to him?

With no regard for caution, I sought the dark ocean of power and swayed on my hands and knees as it forced its way through me. Then, instead of resisting the tide, I directed it toward my newest enemies and pushed the air between them as hard as I could.

The resulting shockwave sent the rest of the group flying in an imitation of my earlier ungraceful display. They crashed into tables and chairs and only one started to rise. Brock, however, was unfazed, having somehow withstood my attack. *That's something I'll need to figure out.*

A voice bellowed from the far corner of the square, but I paid it no mind. Every face, even Brock's, turned to face it and while I had time to notice the awe in some of their expressions, it had no time to register. Brock was only a few steps away, and distracted, so I tried to siphon power from the river and shove at him, then found a cold sense of emptiness where the source of power should have been.

Brock sneered at me and just as I reached for the other source, the dark ocean, I felt him do the same. His face took on a dark cast and I saw an attack start to form before he gritted his teeth and let it fade away. I figured this meant we were going to duke it out like traditional, non-magical men, so I charged at him, swinging with a hard right hook.

Then I froze in place, about a foot away from the smug asshole's smiling face, my arm cocked and about to unload on him. I struggled and grunted with the effort but couldn't move a muscle.

As I watched, Brock's expression faded into one of subservience. He turned toward the focus of everyone else's attention and bowed his head.

Finally, I figured I should see what the fuss was all about. I looked in the same direction and found a tall elven man, skin as black as night, hair as white as clouds and long enough to reach his waist. A long white beard fell in front of him but did not sway with the air as he walked toward us. His hands were clasped behind the back of his black and white checkered robes. He had the air of a king about him that was emphasized by the bowed heads of every person in sight.

Behind him walked two men in black cloaks that covered them head to toe. Bodyguards of some kind, though I had a feeling that the dark elf wouldn't need them in any case.

He slowly walked up to us and paused, taking in the scene of havoc all around him. Then he clicked his tongue at us. "Boys will be boys, they say." The deep voice carried a weight of experience and power. Black eyes regarded me without a hint of emotion. "I am Headmaster Theid. In the future, when you hear me commanding you, you will do as I say. At once." I would have nodded, but my whole body was still frozen. "Here's your first test. Follow me. Both of you," he added, glancing at Brock, whose face paled a bit.

When he turned away, I found myself able to move again. I stretched my arms and legs, getting all the feeling back as I started to follow behind the reserved Headmaster. Brock fell in beside me, sparing me a cold glance in the process, and the dark bodyguards followed behind.

As I walked through the surprisingly wide field of debris considering the quick fight, I couldn't help but notice the fearful, awed expressions on so many of the student's faces.

And they were all aimed at me.

❧ 11 ❧

HEADMASTER THEID AND HIS MEN LED BROCK AND I directly to the spire. Our march across campus garnished a lot of attention in the process, turning every face in our direction. I got the hint that this wasn't something that happened often. All the while, no one in my little group said a word, or even cracked their grim expressions.

The three bases of the spire were even larger, and more awe-inducing up close. If I didn't bother to look up, the three would just look like tall, individual buildings. The biggest on campus, even before they curled in to connect with one another. They were arranged in a triangle as the road morphed into a wide loop whose center held a strip of green lawn and an amazing fountain that took on the shape of a castle that had water flowing from every orifice.

Two of the spire's bases fell on either side of the circular area and the third, which we entered, held the more important position at the top of the loop. The crystalline buildings sprayed colors in every direction randomly as the sunlight pierced their walls.

The dark, oddly god-like Headmaster held his silence

while leading us to a platform in the center of some kind of lobby that took up the entire first floor of the building. There were a few other platforms spread throughout the large, mostly empty room, but the only other people in sight were sitting in a separate area, behind desks with their eyes on their work.

Theid glanced around himself, then snapped his fingers and, after a brief flash of light that had me rubbing my eyes for a minute, I found myself in a completely different room, that I could immediately tell was high up and lacked a ceiling.

We were at the top of the spire.

Not just that, I realized as I looked out over the edge. We were hundreds of feet *above* the spire's tip. Open air and the occasional cloud were all that separated us from the buildings beneath us.

The campus itself was a blemish on the wide landscape stretching in every direction. Dense forests covered most of the land, with a few towns visible among the expanse of trees. Further off, blurry and small, I could make out what looked like a large town complete with its own castle, and, even further, the horizon ended with mountain ranges.

I had never had trouble with heights before, but I had also never been high enough to kiss an airplane. We had to be thousands of feet in the air! The longer I looked down, over a railing that went no higher than my waist, the harder I was hit by vertigo. My vision swam, and I had to step toward the center of the circular room.

Wind buffeted against me and Brock, but somehow it didn't so much as stir the contents of the room, nor touch the Headmaster and his bodyguards.

As I regained my wits, I finally took in the room itself. It was cluttered with bookcases and artifacts on display. A large wooden desk, ornamented with what I assumed was solid gold, sat halfway between the center and the edge. The very center itself held a staff that couldn't have been thicker than my arm yet stretched several dozen feet in the air and gave off an incredibly bright light from the globe of crystal at its peak. With a start, I realized its length was made of gold and covered in what looked to be a language that resembled hieroglyphics.

This guy's really got a flair for the dramatic. I'd heard of displays of power, of how CEOs would always have their offices on the top floor, but this was a whole other level. Theid wasn't satisfied with the top floor, no, he put himself far higher than that.

I was quickly starting to realize that the man's god-like stature was more calculated than I thought. With his almost pure black skin, voluminous black and white robes, and regal bearing, the guy was a dead ringer for what I would imagine a God's human form would look like! And this office only served to exacerbate that first impression. Looking into those ancient eyes, I had to keep reminding myself that this was just a person. A few-thousand-year-old elf-person whose power made me look no stronger than a blade of grass. For now, anyway.

But I never had much time for Gods in my world; if any existed then they clearly didn't want much to do with us, and I wasn't going to let Theid's appearance intimidate me into groveling before him like some superior life form.

He took a seat at his desk and interlaced dark fingers in front of him before turning his wizened gaze on Brock and me as we took our place in front of his desk. Brock stood with a perfect posture, his jaw clenched, and hands clasped behind his back and chin raised, though he stared off into the distance instead of at the headmaster.

I, on the other hand, couldn't stop glancing around the fascinating room, wondering what kinds of books this guy liked to read, what sort of artifacts he would surround himself with. There was some jewelry as ornate as I'd ever seen that I could only imagine held some kind of enchantment, as well as plenty of weapons.

When he finally spoke, it was over steepled fingers and with a deep voice that easily pierced the howling winds. "Why are two of my most promising students," Brock's face looked offended at being lumped in with me, "trying so hard to reduce the crop of powerful mages that should be coming out of my university? His voice was slow and the way he emphasized every few words gave it an odd rhythm.

"He needs to know his place," Brock spat out. "I don't care how he got here, he's not even a member of the academy!"

Theid nodded slowly, not changing his expression in the slightest. Then he turned his gaze on me and raised an eyebrow.

"Look, I just wanted to eat my lunch in peace. This guy took offence to that, apparently," I said, mildly waving a hand in his direction. Brock scoffed but didn't respond.

"I was informed that you were the one that sent the first shot," Theid replied slowly, his eyes boring into me.

Looking back, I had to admit that that was true, despite the fact that Brock antagonized me into it. I gave a defeated shrug as it became apparent that Headmaster Theid expected something out of me.

"Whatever the case, there is a time and place for that sort of sparring and the dining square is not it. You could have hurt students whose only crimes were sitting too close to you during your reckless duel. Not to mention the wasted resources that will go into fixing the tables you've damaged and cleaning the mess you've made.

"In the future, should you be unable to settle disagreements among yourselves as adults, you may reserve for yourselves a slot in the arena off campus. Once Jacobus passes his exams, of course. As for now," his lips widened slightly into the shadow of a smile. It was deeply unsettling. "I will remind you this one time that the use of magic outside the classroom is not permitted for Initiates. I have just the punishment in mind for you."

His eyes flicked behind us and the bodyguards stepped up to join Brock and me in front of Theid's desk. Brock tried to speak up, but one of the large men slapped a hand on the blonde boy's shoulder and he quieted immediately. I didn't let my eyes linger long, those two black-cloaked men looked about as formidable as the headmaster, but I could tell that the man held a firm grip on Brock's collarbone.

Theid rose from his seat and held a hand up to the bookcase, running it along a few titles on the bindings of the old tomes, until he finally found what he was looking for and plucked it out. Then he took his seat, glanced up at the four of us, and snapped his fingers just like before.

Light flashed again and this time the smell hit me even before my eyesight returned. It was shit and piss, the air musty and wet. I nearly gagged on my first breath, coughing instead. Brock merely sneered, his jaw clenching even harder, but not giving in to the disgusting scent that surrounded us. Theid, meanwhile, didn't seem to notice.

We were in the sewers, likely just beneath the school. Torches lit the immediate area, a long, brick tunnel, darkness swallowing it up on either side. In the dim light, I could still make out the dark, foul river that provided such an overpowering scent.

Theid sat behind his desk still, which was transported along with us, unchanged. He set down his book and walked by Brock and me without a word. As he started down the steps that led into the river of shit, I glanced around me with wide eyes as I expected the other three members of our group to be just as shocked that the Headmaster would wade through his students' waste, which was, oddly enough, up to his waist.

But it didn't touch him. As he stepped into the stream, it flowed right around him. Theid's feet landed on a floor unmarred by the river that covered it just seconds before and he turned to face us with his arms spread out on either side. "Join me," was all he said.

I'd never seen someone as pissed off as Brock looked just then. If I wasn't sure that Theid really meant his command, Brock's expression confirmed it. Resigned, the young noble led the way. When he got halfway down the steps, Theid explained. "Take a close look at what I'm doing, boys. A bulwark of air splits the sewage and protects me from even the slightest amount of splatter. When I step out, you'll notice that not one drop landed on my robes. I'll protect you so that you may get into position, but then you'll be on your own."

Brock hesitated, his foot on the last step before the stairs disappeared beneath the murky water. "For how long?" He grunted.

"I haven't decided."

Brock snorted and shook his head, then stepped down. The waters parted for him, just as they had for Theid. After a few moments, his confidence clearly grew, and he quickly joined Theid in the center of what was now an alley between two walls of sewage.

Then they looked up at me. I bit down a curse and tried to not let on just how deeply I was disgusted by the situation. I barely even understood how to use magic, and now I was going to be pelted with shit unless I could make a shield as well as the Headmaster? He made it look fucking easy, like he was not even really doing anything. As I took a nervous gulp and hesitated on the last step, I noticed a satisfied grin on Brock's face, and it sent a jolt of determination through me.

I could feel that Theid was siphoning power and if I really focused, I could see a faint glimmer against the edge of the oncoming water. Just a hint of the shield of air that Theid conjured, but it at least gave me something to base my own shield on.

As I stepped in to join them, I reached for a small amount of power and started copying Theid's spell, feeling Brock copy my idea almost as soon as I started. The headmaster himself merely nodded as I stepped up beside him.

"Good start Jake but see that you leave no holes. Neither in the body of the shield itself nor the space between it and the floor. And Brock? Ah, yes. Not your first time, indeed," he actually sounded amused.

His shield didn't budge while he left the two of us in there and found his seat behind the desk, taking up the book from earlier. Once he was settled in his chair, feet stretched out in front of himself and crossed, his book open and resting on his stomach, he glanced to the bodyguards who had taken up post on opposite sides of the tunnel near corridors that led who-knows-where, then finally at Brock and me. He was just far enough that in the dimness I could hardly see him, but I swore his lips pulled upwards in the smallest smirk I'd ever seen.

Then, he winked at me.

And the flowing waters crashed against my shield like a charge of cavalry. Brock hardly reacted; it was like the head-master's shield simply shrunk in front of him. But my side? Brown, chunky water leaked under my shield and wetted my shoes. Leaks sprung up in the wall of air faster than I could notice them and it was all I could do to scrape more power into myself and bulk up the shield.

It must have only taken a minute, but it felt like I sat in the middle of that disaster waiting to happen for hours. Once I had it under control, however, it was much easier to hold it together much in the way that Brock was able to from the start.

When I peeked over at him, he was looking as smug as ever. "Having a hard time there, eh? It won't last, but you should be a little proud of yourself. I've never seen someone stop the flow entirely on their first time down here. But it doesn't matter how quickly you learn; your shield will break down soon enough. But not mine," he grinned. "I'm walking out of here spotless."

"Fuck yourself," I said through heavy breaths. Much as the air disgusted me, I couldn't help it. The magic was flowing through me and though I felt powerful, I also felt *used*. Like a sponge that had soaked up water and been wrung out over and over. And the feeling just got worse the longer I held the shield. It wasn't like the burn I'd felt plenty of times from working out, either. It was a full-body exhaustion the likes of which no exercise could match, and I could tell that it was just getting started.

Brock chuckled. "You really are an idiot. I thought maybe you just had a death wish when you stole the Pillar from The Lady, but maybe I was wrong." My eyes darted toward the headmaster as Brock brought up that night, and he added, "Don't worry. Our voices won't pierce our shields, he can't hear us. Besides, what kind of person doesn't know that they should hide their allegiance to a dark God? An idiot, that's who. Sitting at my table, even acknowledging my presence when we have no other reason for knowing each other, is so fucking stupid I can't stand it. I don't know how you got recruited, or why, but if you don't want to get yourself killed, you need to step your game up."

I chuckled, despite my situation, even grinning for a moment before I remembered the shit flowing by me and the tenuous, invisible shield that was barely strong enough to protect me. "And here I thought we were becoming friends.

You know, bonding through this shared punishment and coming out closer because of it."

Brock rolled his eyes. "Definitely an idiot."

"Well, this idiot was wiping the floor with you. And your friends."

His jaw clenched and Brock shot me a furious look. He lowered his voice as if he hadn't just told me that the headmaster couldn't hear us. "That's only because your dumb ass decided to use Vethris' power instead of Pholl's. You're lucky that we were the only ones who could see it, unless Filo was around, but that doesn't mean other people couldn't figure out that you were more powerful than you should be."

A few implications fell into place that I had already started to notice but wasn't sure about. First, the two gods of this world, Vethris and Pholl, were the sources of power. The ocean and the river, respectively, though I still didn't know what caused the difference.

And second, it seemed that anyone who wasn't already aligned with the Shadows would only be aware of Pholl's power, which gave us an advantage. I thought of Pholl's power like gasoline, every car used it and it was the most common source of power. But Vethris' power was rocket fuel in comparison. Dark and vast, those of us lucky enough to be able to access it would be far more powerful than our contemporaries.

It was exciting and tantalizing, but also a tease. I had this bonus power at my fingertips, but if I used it, I would be shining a spotlight on myself for anyone smart enough to figure out that I was a Shadow.

And of course, they wouldn't believe that it wasn't *me* who bonded myself to Vethris, it was the guy who occupied this body until last night. Hell, they'd probably just think I went crazy.

At least I had the other power, given to me by the Pillar.

That didn't seem to face the same restriction. Even as I started to understand the Gods and the magic a bit more, the Pillar remained a mystery. I couldn't control its power yet, but in time, I would find out how to use it to my advantage.

The minutes passed in silence after that. Brock's shield held steady, but he was starting to sweat. I, on the other hand, had a few drops of dirty water on my pants from my barrier weakening. It was a simple spell, basically just holding air in place so that the sewage flowed around it, but the effort added up. It was about as simple as standing in place, but even something like that got tiring after a while.

Meanwhile, Theid barely moved. His feet sat propped up on his desk, crossed, with the book in his lap and a pipe in his mouth.

By the time my feet were aching from staying upright, I was sure that hours had passed. I was breathing heavily, and very carefully, considering the shit flowing around me. My shield was slowly shrinking closer toward me, letting more spurts of dirty water through the cracks and even threatening to burst through from time to time.

Like any dam, eventually I just couldn't hold it any longer. The source of power slipped away no matter how hard I tried to hold on and the tide of waste crashed into me. Much as I knew it was about to happen, and tried to brace myself, I was pushed back and almost toppled over. If it weren't for the set of stairs nearby, I latched a hand onto the corner of a brick for leverage, I would have been swept away.

The smell hit me harder than ever, and I gagged, much to Brock's delight. He looked as tired as I was but grinned anyway. The water covered me up to my belly button and I tried not to think about how long I'd smell like shit after this.

It only took Theid a few seconds to notice what happened. He snapped his book shut and popped to his feet. "Alright, now. Come on out. Good work, Brock. I'm not happy to see you here again, but at least you're getting stronger from all the extra practice. And Jacobus," he summoned a shield in front of me when he saw me surveying the river, trying to figure out how I might cross without slipping, then continued speaking. "Impressive for a new student, but that's to be expected from the Miskatonic boy. Work hard over the next month and I think you could rise far with us. Now that that is settled," he trailed off, glancing back towards his bodyguards, then at the two of us as we stepped out of the canal, and he snapped his fingers.

This time I knew what to expect. A dazzling flash of light stole my vision for a few moments, until I rubbed it away and recovered.

With a shock, I realized that I was standing in front of my dorm building. At night. And alone. I was beyond exhausted and starving but hadn't realized how much time had passed. Theid teleported us all home separately, it seemed.

Now that's a trick I need to learn. Though something made me think it wasn't nearly as easy as he made it look. My stomach growled and I took a deep, delicious breath of fresh air, as I stepped through the entrance with one thing on my mind.

Food.

❧ 12 ❧

I TOOK MY FIRST STEP AND THE *SQUISHING* SOUND IN MY shoes reminded me that, while Theid gave me a ride home, so to speak, he didn't bother helping me clean up.

Alright, maybe shower first. Then food.

If the Headmaster could teleport a group of people to different locations at the snap of his fingers, he could have taken the shit and water, and who knows what other fluids, out of my clothing in the process.

But, no. My pants were just as soaked through as my shoes, and it only took a few moments for the chilled night air to seep through. I stuck out each leg one at a time and shook them, trying not to think about the dark chunks that hit the cobblestone pathway with too many splats to count.

I smelled like shit. Worse, probably, considering the soup I was just immersed in. But luckily, it looked like the campus was winding down for the night and no one approached the building while I made my way inside, leaving a trail of wet footprints behind me.

Remembering the gold sack in Jacobus's trunk, I threw

my shoes in a waste bin just inside the entrance so that I could step more quietly.

This wasn't the time to be meeting new people. *Talk about a shitty first impression.* So, I snuck toward my room, peeking around corners and up the stairwell just to make sure no one was around.

I had to wait while someone stepped out of the bathroom in my hallway and returned to their room, but since my dorm was at the end of the hall, I made it in with my reputation intact. Hell, based on the way some of the other students were watching me as Theid led Brock and I away, my reputation had probably improved! Many were impressed, others fearful, and only a few disappointed.

I couldn't get out of those clothes fast enough. There was a small wooden bin in the corner of the room that I figured was for trash, so I threw them in there and fished through the large trunk for replacements. I eventually found dark gray pants and a loose black shirt with a few buttons under my chin and long sleeves, because apparently this dude had the style of the black Power Ranger.

I didn't find a towel until I checked the wardrobe that I had assumed Jacobus didn't use yet, considering all that I had found in his trunk. But there was a dark blue, plain cloak with a hood hanging alone, then a single towel folded up next to an outfit that must have been Jacobus's, also neatly folded up.

I gave a wry snort at the odd juxtaposition. Everything else was just stuffed into his trunk without any care, and yet he decided to lay out one of his outfits in here, perfectly folded and even perfumed!

Whatever, it was probably the least confusing thing that I had noticed today, so I just scooped up the towel, wrapped it around myself, and headed down the hall. Small globes of light hung freely in the air, lighting the way.

Just as I passed my neighbor's door, it shot open. Whelan stuck his head out, eyebrows shooting up when he noticed me. Then he gave me a confused look and wrinkled his nose. "Fuck, what is that smell? Where have you been, Jake? Lilly and I were starting to get worried when you missed the rest of today's class."

I shrugged and tried to act like I wasn't exhausted, hungry, and admittedly, still a bit pissed off about the sewage canal punishment. "Theid apparently likes to get creative with the way he keeps his students in line. Did your Dad tell you he," I gritted my teeth and glanced down the hallway to make sure no one was eavesdropping, then lowered my voice. "He makes students stand in the sewers and block the waters with a shield of air. Brock and I were down there for fucking hours until I gave out from pure exhaustion and almost got swept away by all kinds of shit. Literally."

Whelan cringed through my explanation, but I could tell he was holding back a smile. "Uh, yeah. He mentioned that kind of stuff. I mean, the exams are a do-or-die situation, the academy isn't exactly lenient with students who don't fit their standards. Most of the punishments are, uh, I'll just say as creative as that, if not as foul-smelling."

I gave a mirthless laugh. "Great. Maybe next time he'll throw me off a cliff and force me to fly for as long as I can. Or drop a boulder on me and see how many times I can deflect it." I let my annoyance seep into my voice a bit.

Whelan shrugged. "They certainly know how to pump out the world's strongest mages, so I guess it's working for them. Anyway, I'll fill you in on the rest of class after your shower. You might need to scrub for a while," he chuckled.

I squinted my eyes a bit. "Oh yeah, keep laughing. Your door's still open, bud. I'll drop this towel and roll around in your bed if you keep it up."

"You wouldn't," Whelan muttered, but still ran toward his

door. When he turned back and noticed that I hadn't moved an inch, he grinned and shook his head.

He disappeared into his room just as I stepped into the bathroom. It wasn't marked as male or female, and when I stepped in the only other person in there was in a stall, probably producing the same sewage that still dripped down my leg.

I gritted my teeth and tried not to think about it. The bathroom was surprisingly modern looking. It had white tiled floors, and there was a line of pale green stalls separated by a brick wall from the other half of the room, where mirrors stood over sinks and another wall blocked off a row of showers on the right.

As I approached the showers, I noticed myself in the mirror and almost dropped my towel in shock.

I was ripped. Not huge or anything, but any morsel of fat that was on my previous body was gone, replaced by lean muscle all over. I'd never had a full six-pack before, the most I'd ever been able to see were two, but the smooth lines of my abdomen would fit in on a magazine cover! Jacobus took damn good care of himself.

I chuckled as I stepped into a shower and swept off the towel, thinking about how frustrated my doppelganger must be back in the real world. His magic didn't work, he didn't have anyone there to guide him, and he was even a bit chubbier than he was used to. Every time I got angry about my situation, I just tried to remember his and imagine all the ways he was struggling. The guy would leave that cavern with no clue what to do next. Even if he were able to get into my car, he wouldn't know how to drive it.

Not for the first time, I thought about how worried my mother must be. She already lost her husband, my father, years ago, and now she'll think she's losing me too.

It suddenly dawned on me that Jacobus could actually get

hurt, die even. If he did, would that mean I was stuck here? Or would we both die? I had to learn more about how this connection of ours worked. I had too little knowledge on this world and how it interacted with my own to even get started on a solution.

It was then that I decided I needed to learn literally everything about this world. Which meant spending as much of the following month at the school's library as possible.

As the hot water poured down my face, I realized three things. One, I hadn't actually done anything to turn on the water. Two, I didn't have any soap. And three, the towel that I was going to dry myself off with probably smelled like shit.

Well, as along as the water worked and was warm enough, which it was, I didn't care how it happened. I noticed a soap dispenser on the wall that looked like a pure white sphere with a small opening underneath. Just like home, I stuck my hand underneath it and a bit of foam spurted out.

A few people came and went as I showered, one even stepping into the shower stall at the other end of the row. His voice rung out as he entered the room, apparently addressing someone down the hall who had the nerve to ask him how late the dining square was open. His gruff voice and rude reply immediately told me who it was.

Our unfriendly neighborhood residential advisor, Boba Ports.

After a long time scrubbing myself down, I pulled back the shower curtain and noticed Boba had left a pile of his clothes on a ledge by the frosted windows, as well as a towel.

Very carefully, I crept out of the stall and took it, replacing Boba's towel with my own. I folded it up quickly and tried to make the orc's bundle look like nothing was touched, despite a few brown stains on the towel that I made sure weren't visible. I wiped myself down and rushed down the hall, half naked, my hair still dripping water, but not wanting to get caught by the huge green man when he realized that someone switched out his towel with one that smelled like a sewer.

Just as I made it back into my room, the bathroom door slammed open, and I recognized his deep voice bellowing down the hall. "Whoever fucking did that is going to be mincemeat when I'm through with them!" I heard a muffled voice ask him what happened, but the orc's only response was a loud growl and a slamming door. I leaned back against my door and let out a deep breath.

I held my own against Brock earlier, but who knew how powerful Boba was. In strength alone, he surely had me. The dude looked like the Rock, or the Mountain from Game of Thrones, so I knew his mincemeat threat wasn't just bullshit.

But if Jacobus took his magical studies as seriously as his fitness, then I figured I could give the orc a run for his money, even if the only thing I had figured out how to do yet was basically just air manipulation. If I could use it to push a table filled with students, then surely, I could toss his big green ass down the hall.

But that would just land me back in the sewers. I didn't even want to know what the other possibilities were, but I knew death was on the list.

I threw on the folded clothes from my wardrobe and hung the towel over a hanger to dry. I tucked a loose-fitting black shirt into snug grey sweatpants, pulled on plain black socks and some dark brown slippers that were extremely comfortable. All in all, this world had pretty decent, soft clothing, even if Jacobus's style was rather narrow.

Then I stepped out to Whelan's room, making sure the hallway was void of any angry orcs, and knocked. His door opened and revealed the smaller guy reading at his desk, the globe of light on the ceiling dimmed to a comfortable setting. I plopped down on his bed, given that these rooms only had one chair and he was sitting in it, then watched as the door shut itself.

Whelan looked up at me and shook his head. "They really don't have anything where you're from, huh?"

I pursed my lips and shook my head. If I could just keep convincing people that I was from this world's equivalent of a one-stoplight town where everyone knew each other because they were all related, then I would be able to ask all the questions that had been burning through my head since I stepped out of the cave with Brock.

Whelan chuckled. "Well, shit. I'm *so* glad I grew up in the city. No offense, of course. I guess it takes a long time for magical advancements like these to reach you guys. So, look," he leaned closer to me and gestured toward the door, "You just gotta think about it, and it'll open for you. It's your room, attuned to only you, so other people can't do it. The lights are the same way, just think about how you want them, and it'll happen. The water in the showers too, but I guess you already figured that out." I nodded, but hell no did I figure that out. Since the shower worked anyway, apparently my understanding wasn't necessary. "Oh, and I bet you don't have any of these," he hopped out of his seat and walked over to the wardrobe.

"Whey, I might be from the sticks, but we have all the basic furniture, I promise."

He shot me an odd look, "Did you just call me Whey? I guess it works. But, no, from the sounds of it, you don't even have the basics." He glanced around the room and scooped some clothes off of the ground. Then he threw them in the wardrobe, that I noticed was empty, and shut the door.

He raised his eyebrows at me and waited a few seconds, cutting me off when I started to ask, 'the fuck is supposed to happen now?'

Whelan opened the door again and, answering the question I didn't get to ask, he said, "This little piece of magic will clean and fold your clothes practically instantaneously. And before you ask, no. I don't know how. Just cause I know about this stuff doesn't mean I know *all* about them." Which was fair enough. It wasn't like I knew how cell phones or computers worked.

I rubbed my chin in thought. "Really wish I had one of those back home. Hey, is that square still open? I never actually got to eat."

Whelan shook his head, but then his eyes widened, and he said, "Oh, you're gonna love this."

He rifled around in an ornate wooden chest that made Jacobus' trunk look like plywood and pulled out two squares of silvery metal about a quarter-inch thick. He placed one on his desk and tossed the other to his bed. "You can use that one if you want, assuming you have some gold?" When I nodded, he took out a coin and pressed it into the center of the silver square. My eyes widened as the gold coin sunk into the metal like it was a pool of mercury. "These little wonders are called Alchemical Chefs," he grinned. "They run on the gold you press into them, then as long as your skin is in contact with the Chef, it will materialize whatever food you imagine."

Whelan leaned toward me conspiratorially and lowered his voice, despite us being alone. "You see, it doesn't *actually* run on gold. The trick is, it teleports the gold to the guild that makes these things, and they teleport whatever it is you wanted onto your plate. Pretty high quality, too. Try it out." He nodded toward the silver slate on his desk.

A part of me wasn't sure whether he was fucking with me or not. Like, maybe once I touched the metal I would turn into a mongoose, or spontaneously shit myself, or something like that. I didn't know what kind of pranks people pulled here. But he had helped me out today, so I decided to trust him. I put my thumb on the corner of the cold metal and imagined a bacon pizza. I pulled away and glanced at Whelan.

"Wait for it."

Then a steaming-hot pizza, already cut into slices, rose out of the metal in the same way the gold sunk into it. It was covered in pieces of bacon, a mix of cheese and all kinds of spices. The smell reminded me of home so much that it almost killed my mood. I was too hungry to be distracted, however, considering that I hadn't eaten all day.

Whelan looked at the food skeptically. "Is that the kind of stuff people eat on that island of yours?"

I blinked a few times before it came to me. "Rhode Island! Yes, oh yeah. All the time, actually, it's a local specialty." Local to Earth, anyway.

"Wow," he said around his first bite, eyes widening at me. "This is amazing!"

"Right? I guess culinary advances like these just don't reach you big city guys."

Whelan rolled his eyes and stuffed his mouth instead of immediately responding.

As he filled me in on the rest of the day's lecture, which was such a basic introduction to magic that he thought it a waste of time, we ended up having the Chef whip up another pizza for us. After a stroke of genius, I had the Chef serve us up a few beers as well. Whelan kept skipping over things that he didn't think needed explaining, until he got tired of me asking questions, and went into full detail from then on.

I was so bubbling with questions that I had a hard time deciding which ones to ask, and which to leave for later. Siphoning off power was simple enough, but it got far more complicated with visualizing what I wanted to happen, and then impressing my will upon reality.

Those were the three key steps, he said, each of which could be improved upon basically forever. A more accurate visualization of what you wanted to happen would use less magical energy and be easier to force upon reality. More practice with siphoning off bits of power would let you use more at a time or more easily wrestle power out of the hands of an opponent. It was a lot to take in, but I learned more from Whelan that night than I did from my Professor.

And that put me a few steps closer to home.

❧ 13 ❧

AFTER HAVING THE ALCHEMICAL CHEF WHIP ME UP SOME pancakes, Whelan and I headed to class early with the hope that we could win back some points with Professor Doriah. There was something kind of hot about the ancient, gray elf-woman, her tight body and even tighter glares, but something told me that she wouldn't give me the kind of *punishment* that I'd be looking for. This might have been a fantasy world, but that didn't mean it conformed to *my* fantasies.

As we were walking down the path, a girl's voice called out behind us.

Lilly, the short brunette girl with the moon-shaped scar on her left cheek and a body that made my mouth water, trotted to catch up to us. Her chest bounced with every step and when I made the mistake of checking her out, I knew exactly what was about to happen.

I felt the strange muscle-spasm in my eyes and my vision slid past each layer of clothing, searing images into my memory that put a grin on my face. But I still couldn't stop it from continuing to see through each layer of skin, muscle, and fat.

As nice an image as Lilly's perky tits were, her insides were disgusting. As before, I saw through every layer of Lilly, front to back, and then my vision snapped in reverse until it was back to normal. At least the last few images the strange power gave me were of Lilly in various stages of undress as her stockings, underwear, skirt, and blouse returned, in that order. It all happened in the span of a few seconds, but to me it felt like minutes.

"Good morning," she said, her voice light as a breeze. "When you didn't answer your doors, I figured you must have already headed to class."

I rubbed the weird vibration-like feeling out of one eye as Whelan and I shared a glance.

"Shit," I started, "Sorry about that. Which room are you in, by the way?" I hoped the question would make her think that we left without her because we just didn't know where to find her. In reality, we forgot.

How I can go even a second without thinking about Lilly's fit, tanned body, though, I do not know. But I didn't want to make the mistake of leaving her out again. She wasn't from the area, like me and my fake backstory, so it made sense that she would latch on to Whelan and me, the first people she had a friendly conversation with.

"201," she said, in her whispery voice. Her moss green eyes shined as she fell into step between us, and a smirk pulled at her lips.

"We'll wait for you next time, Lilly," I put a reassuring hand on her shoulder, the soft fabric of her blouse, and was rewarded with a blush on her face as she thanked me.

"Isn't this place just amazing," she spoke up again with her eyes on the spire, almost tripping over a cobblestone that was a little higher than the rest, but ultimately just stubbing her toe in those light brown slippers. She winced but didn't lose her enthusiasm. "I'm already more powerful than the day we moved in. Professor Doriah is amazing and... a little scary."

We both nodded, though Whelan was a bit distracted. His attention was pulled toward a building I didn't recognize yet, but given its size, I assumed it was one of the academy's major departments.

"Yeah. Those red eyes creep me out. Also the thousands of years of experience behind them," I commented, not adding the part about thinking our professor was actually pretty hot. In a strange, gothic kind of way.

Lilly nodded her agreement. Then she seemed to remember something. "Oh! Whatever happened to you yesterday? I was so concerned with getting out of the way that I barely saw your fight." I deflated a little at that, having hoped that she was one of the students that was in awe of the skills I showed yesterday. "But I saw *the Headmaster* escorting you and that blonde boy away. Did he take you in there?"

Her voice had awe in it that time, but not for me, for the incredible spire that stretched above the clouds. Lilly's dark green eyes widened as they climbed the length of the pure white tower.

With a grin, I nodded. "Hell yeah, he did. Took us right to his office on the top." Even Whelan was shocked to hear that. I had both their attentions, then. "And get this: it's not even attached to the rest of the Spire. It's a platform floating hundreds of feet above the tip! With no ceiling and only half-walls that went up to my waist. I almost gagged when I looked over the edge and realized how high we were. You probably can't even see it from here," I said, trying to make it out above the tall building.

Which was a mistake. Somehow, my power knew to respond to my desire to see something, but I still couldn't stop it. At least when that *something* was Lilly, or Professor

Doriah, my vision had something to latch onto and peel apart layer by layer.

But this time, I was shooting in the dark. My power activated and the sky rushed toward me. I noticed Theid's office at the corner of my eye, but my vision swept right past it and kept going. With no subject to latch onto, I was fed images of clouds, and then space itself. Lots and lots of space, with the occasional solar system and eventually galaxies as I saw all the way to the end of reality, or so it seemed.

Then my vision snapped back just as quickly and with a shuddering breath, I found myself on my newly bruised knees in the middle of the pathway, with a lot of confused faces looking my way.

The two that were friendly helped me to my feet. Despite a good night's rest, I was left feeling drained.

"Uh, what the fuck just happened to you?" Whelan asked. Lilly didn't say anything, but from the look on her face I could tell that she was just as confused and curious. "You just stopped moving and stared into space for a minute. And your eyes were, like, vibrating or something."

"Uh," *fuck.* I knew enough about this world to know that the Pillars, and the powers they granted, were a dangerous secret and I didn't want to pull my new friends into whatever shit Jacobus pulled *me* into. "Sorry, I was just thinking about last night and uh, tripped. The vibrating was just me scanning the sky, trying to spot Theid's office."

"Right. Okay," Whelan replied quickly, nodding, but I got the feeling that he knew I was leaving something out. Lilly kept her mouth shut, but I got the same feeling that my lie didn't fool them as well as I'd hoped. Still, I was glad they didn't pry, as it wasn't something I even knew how to explain to myself yet.

I cleared my throat and tried to pretend that I hadn't just

embarrassed myself in the middle of campus. "Anyway, he just teleported us up there and gave us a few stern words."

When I paused, considering how much detail to give her about my time in the sewer, Whelan spoke up excitedly. He grinned and craned his head, "Oh yeah? Then what happened?" From his tone, I could tell that he was looking forward to hearing about it again.

I shot him a dirty look, but he just barked a laugh. "Well, I guess it'll get out soon enough anyway. I'm sure Brock'll spend the rest of the night telling all his friends about it," I grumbled and turned my attention to Lilly. "I guess Theid likes to dole out punishments that require you to use your power. So, he made me and Brock stand in the middle of the sewage canal beneath the school while we tried to use a shield of air to stop the sewage from hitting us." Lilly's eyes widen and a gasp left her mouth. "Yeah, it was rough." When I met Whelan's knowing glance, I let out a sigh and added the last bit of details to the story. "I, uh, ended up failing eventually, and returned to the dorm covered up to my waist in shit while Brock left spotless," I gritted my teeth just thinking about it.

Lilly's face transitioned from shock, to understanding, and then burst out laughing alongside Whelan. Then she recovered and tried to keep her voice down. "I'm sorry, I'm sorry. That honestly sounds terrible, but I kind of wish I could have seen that walk of shame."

I let out an offended laugh and jabbed back. "One of these days it'll be your turn, Lilly. And when you get back to the dorm covered in mud, shit, or the guts of some creature, I'll be there to help you clean yourself up. At the very least I'll wait until your back is turned before I start laughing."

She rolled her eyes and giggled at that. "Oh, how kind of you. But don't count on it. I expect I'll be too busy with my studies to even think about getting in trouble. I'm already stronger than when I left home, but I still feel like I have a lot of catching up to do," her voice trailed off, her disappointment clear in her tone.

I gave her a nudge with my elbow. "In that case we should be able to help each other out. Whelan might have a step up because of his Dad's lack of respect for the rules," he shot me a dirty look at that, then shrugged it off, "but I've got my work cut out for me too."

Lilly looked up at me, her green eyes wide with disbelief. "You? Jacobus-"

"Just Jake," I corrected her.

"Er, right. Jake. Weren't you the one with the Miskatonic scholarship?" There was that name is again. I'd have to figure out what that actually meant, but for the time being, I just nodded along with her. "Even I have heard of *them*. They almost never do that! Forgive me for being forward, but you must be exceptional already if they were willing to do that for you. This place isn't exactly cheap," she looked away as she said that, as if it shamed her for some reason. I didn't have time to think about it, however, as she was waiting for an answer.

And I had no idea what to say. In which case, something non-committal would have to do for now. "Well, they believed in me. Saw potential that I don't even see in myself, apparently." I shrugged as if I didn't know their reasoning any better than Lilly.

"Well, surely they must have tested you. There had to be a reason they sought you out." *She just has to keep pulling at that thread.*

"I just knew the right people. Honestly, it's not as big a deal as people make it out to be."

Whelan raised an eyebrow at that but didn't speak up. As much as I was glad for that, I wasn't sure if it was out of his own kindness, or just because we'd reached our class. Lilly's further questions were cut off as we found seats, the same ones as yesterday, and got settled in.

Not even half of the seats were filled yet, whereas the full attendance yesterday had the rows overflowing. I gave Professor Doriah a wave and confident smile when she glanced over at me, just to make sure she noticed that we were early.

As the seats filled up and the hum of a hundred conversations died down, a curious-looking man walked down the steps and stopped just next to Doriah and her podium.

His dark tan body was draped in voluminous white robes that reminded me of a toga. They clipped together in front of him and rose over his shoulders in a way that almost made them look like shoulder pads. He had black hair that was so short I could only imagine he shaved it recently, and slanted eyes that seemed to take notice of everything. They were the curious part. At first, he seemed to have no irises, just large pupils. Where the eye's color should have been, it was simply black. It was only when he passed by my row that I could distinctly see that his irises were a pure black color.

When those piercing eyes fell on me, I felt a shiver run down my spine, and out of the corner of my eyes I saw my two friends do the same.

By the time he took his place beside the podium, the only noise was that of his sandaled feet softly hitting the stone. Professor Doriah nodded to him and began her introduction.

❧ 14 ❧

"SOME OF YOU MAY HAVE ALREADY HAD THE PLEASURE, BUT I introduce to you our Head Librarian and first guest lecturer, Octavio Thuvien. Seeing as you'll be needing all the help you can get, I thought it would be a good idea to have him visit us as soon as possible. It would be wise of you all to make use of the library's vast resources over the course of the next few weeks, and you will find that Master Thuvien will be most helpful to that end. Should you have any questions beyond what you will learn from him today, you will perpetually find him, or one of his lessers, in the center of the library's first floor. And, well, I'll let him touch upon the rest."

She bowed her head to the librarian, who returned the gesture as he stepped up to the podium and rested his hands on either side of it. His voice was deep and very smooth. "First of all, I'd like to congratulate each and every one of you for making it here. If the myriad students I've met over the years are any evidence, then I'm sure you all have had very interesting journeys but know this: it is just the beginning. I won't beat you over the head with the same warnings as your Professor here, but you should know that every one of them is accurate. Even if you do live to graduate, the world that you will be thrust into is far more dangerous than the trials you will soon face. Preparation is crucial to survival. And that's where I come in," he broke into a wide grin.

"I've made a life of collecting and disseminating information. I'm proud to say that the library has more than tripled in size since I've taken up my post, and the greater use you make of these resources I've gathered, the more powerful you will become.

"I am also the head of our History and Archeology department, naturally. Should any of you choose that route, then I am sure we will get to know one another very well over the years. Even if you don't, I hope you will feel comfortable coming to my library for any help you should need."

With that, he broke into an extremely detailed overview of the library's different wings and functions. His passion for his work bubbled through the lecture, but the subject matter was just too dull. I ended up struggling to pay attention as I jotted down notes I knew I would never look at again.

After at least an hour, though it felt more like two or three, I let my eyes wander the countryside. The lecture amphitheaters were on the edge of the campus, which was itself set into a hill. Beyond the borders of the academy was a deep and dense forest that stretched as far as I could see.

In other words, it wasn't much to look at. A beautiful forest, sure, but the deep green just reminded me of Lilly's eyes, which made me think of the few glimpses I had of the rest of her incredible body.

I found myself peeking over at her, checking her out at first, but I ended up snorting a laugh when I looked down at her notes. There were some pieces of actual information there, primarily on the subjects of Natural Magic and Regeneration, but beyond that, her notebook was filled with cute or just plain silly doodles. Trees with kind faces looked up at the birds and squirrels that sat on their branches, except for one who frowned at a spot of bird poop on his bark.

But what really caught my eye was her version of the scene before us. In her drawing, even Professor Doriah had fallen asleep, and she was nursing a pool of drool on her shoulder. Behind our speaker, even the trees were getting bored.

Lilly looked up at me with a bright smile when she noticed me admiring her work. She giggled to herself and whispered, "I know I shouldn't be doing it, but I have to keep my mind busy somehow. Plus, it ends up looking like I'm taking notes."

"That's genius. And very good, by the way. I'm a terrible artist."

She blushed. "Oh, it's nothing. And I'm sure you're good at other things," she added, just before the lecturer caught her attention again.

But as I thought about it, I wasn't. I was mediocre at plenty of things, but good at none. I loved my classes back home, and archeology itself was fascinating, but the real-life practice of it was beyond tedious. I could spend all day reading about excavations of old Egyptian pyramids, and the mysteries they continued to hold, but that was only one small part of my curriculum.

As the classes became more advanced, I started to see behind the curtain and realize how much work I never knew about. All the papers my professors wrote, the funding requests, the presentations, the challenges they fielded from colleagues, it all seemed to bog down the work that had seemed so interesting back when I was in high school.

And so, I ended up as a mediocre student and janitor.

This school, this world was my second chance. I doubted these archeologists would have the same hang-ups about the small details, like funding, or personal safety. Since they seemed to be a few hundred years behind Earth in technology, though their magic bridged the gaps in some places, I had high hopes that some spectacular ruins and relics were waiting to be discovered.

The only thing I was sure about was that they'd be dangerous. Ancient peoples booby-trapped the pyramids, and countless other ruins, to fend off grave robbers. In my world, that meant pit traps, spikes coming out of the walls, and maybe some boulders crushing would-be burglars. But now that magic was involved, I was simultaneously excited, and paranoid, to get started. I was going to need to prepare myself for anything.

But first, I had to pass my exams. Which meant going to the library.

As Head Librarian Thuvien finished up what felt like the worlds' longest lecture, our professor took over only long enough to dismiss us for the rest of the day with an assignment. By the end of the week, she wanted us all to check out a book and show it to her as proof. Then by the start of next week, write our first paper about it.

There was a chorus of groans at this first assignment, but to be honest, I didn't mind. It wasn't like I knew very many people or had a hell of a lot to do, anyway. Searching the academy's library for deep magical secrets sounded a lot fucking better than any studying I ever did in my world.

It was funny. To me, this world was new and fascinating. Magic was this entirely exotic force that I was just starting to learn to control, and then there was the power the Pillar gave me, that I still knew almost nothing about. All the other students seemed just as bored as... well, I was in my world. And that was exactly my edge. This world drew me in and begged for me to learn all that I could about it, to harness magical power and use it to bend reality to my will.

If the other students took that for granted, then that was their loss. I had spells to learn and ruins to explore.

LILLY WAS ALMOST AS IMPRESSED WITH THE ALCHEMICAL Chef as I was. Immediately after class, we headed straight to my dorm to use it to summon a pizza, since she had never heard of the food either.

Oddly enough, the exotic cuisine seemed like more of a shock than the literal magical food dispenser. All it took was one bite and it was suddenly the most amazing thing she'd ever tasted. Her big smile and wide eyes as she bit into the slice were extremely cute. Whelan, on the other hand, suddenly acted as if he'd been eating it his entire life.

Then we headed to the building that too many college students never even bothered to enter. The campus library. I could tell that this world wasn't any different in that regard, when the foot traffic around the library was far less than that of anywhere else. A lot of the people I saw were from my class, too, so it was safe to assume that the library's usual daily attendance was even lower. Hopefully good ol' Thuvien didn't take it personally, he seemed the type to care a lot for his work and resent it being wasted.

The building was huge. One of the largest on campus since it also housed the history and archeology department. It was four stories tall and took on the look of a bookcase. The outer wall was made up of unlabeled book bindings with one of the books laying wide open, displaying the library's front door within its pages.

Whelan split from Lilly and me as we made our way to the information desk. It wasn't so much that he already knew his way around, he just didn't really care where he ended up.

"I'll just wander around until I find something that looks

interesting," he had said, clearly just wanting to get his report over with as soon as possible.

Lilly and I, however, were right where we wanted to be. While she ended up in the Natural Magics section, I headed over to Octavio's department.

The History and Archeology wing was split in two parts. The smaller was made up of classrooms and a few lounges for students or faculty to quietly work in, while the larger portion remained part of the library. This area contained books that were relevant to the department, featuring one display in particular that held all of their 'recommended reading.'

I let out a soft groan as I remembered the 'recommended' books that I'd been forced to read over the last fifteen years of my life. But as my eyes ran over the books on display, I realized that there wasn't even a single one that seemed like a chore. They held exactly the kind of information I was looking for.

And yet, I was frozen. I had no idea where to begin. There was something about having so many options that made it almost impossible to choose.

After standing there like a lost child for a few minutes, I heard a deep chuckling behind me. I whipped my head around to find a dark tan man with chilling dark eyes.

"Having some difficulty getting started?" Head Librarian Octavio Thuvien asked with a wry smile. "I had a feeling that you would be one of the students I'd find here."

"How did you know that?"

He shrugged and shook his head in quick, small motions. "I've no idea. Just a feeling, I guess. Maybe something subconscious, like we happened to make eye contact more than most, or you were one of the few that actually tried to pay attention most of the time. Or at the very least, you didn't fall asleep," he leaned toward me with a smirk.

The guy could give an insanely boring lecture, but at least he had a sense of humor about it.

"Okay, maybe you're right. Got any tips?"

"Just one, but I've been saving it for a cute apprentice upstairs," he shot me a wink that sent my eyebrows climbing up my forehead. When I realized what he meant, I barely held back my laughter. We were in a library, after all. He continued his answer after giving a satisfied nod at my reaction. "Really, though, it depends upon where your interests lie. Do you think you'll choose my department? Er, assuming you pass the exams, that is," he added that part with a bit of disdain.

I nodded absently while continuing to scan the area. There were some books on world history, broken down by major continents and the nations that made them up. There was even a world map on the wall, which took a lot of effort to pull my eyes away from. This world was shaped exactly like Earth. All the continents in the same places but broken up completely differently. Miria, which I had heard of before and knew as the place I was in, was the name of our continent, while our nation was Eastern Miria.

The Head Librarian snapped his fingers in a loud pop that pulled my attention back to our conversation and almost made me jump.

"Ah, sorry," I said quickly. "Yeah, I think this department has the most to offer me." And it's the only one that would know anything about the Pillars, or how I could make it home, but I left that part out.

"Anything in particular?" he spread his hands as he tried to get a little more direction.

"Er, ruins? Unexplored ones, ideally, or maybe myths surrounding long-lost monuments that have yet to be found. Got anything like that?"

He grinned. "I know just the place. These are all great

options, of course," he waved his hand over the recommended reading display, "but they are a tad basic." As he led me away, he kept speaking and glanced back every few seconds as if he was making sure I was still there. "This is one of my favorite subjects, myself. Ancient peoples are a source of endless fascination, for me. From what they wore, to what they ate, to what strange discoveries they may have made, that they failed to pass on. Or chose to keep to themselves," he added morosely, during one of his glances.

Being the second day of classes, I didn't expect much, but we walked by several study areas that had students sprinkled throughout. Some read silently, while others shared quiet, yet excited gossip over the books they were ignoring.

The librarian finally led me to a dusty corner about as far from the entrance as possible. The walls throughout the building were lined from floor to ceiling with books of all sizes and colors, and this area was no exception. The tomes in these shelves looked a bit older than the rest, and untouched, judging by the dust collecting on some of them.

Thuvien ran a finger along a row of books until he suddenly snapped and plucked one out. He winced as he got a good look at it and blew off a layer of dust. "Here. The Academy requires all of its students to take some History classes, but archeology is purely an elective to those who don't pursue it."

He let out a sigh and turned his gaze over the rows in front of us. "Turns out, most kids are more interested in the future than the past, these days. But who can blame them? They're just starting their lives, who wants to read about some extinct culture when you could be feeling the power of raw magic at your fingertips. Just this boring old librarian, apparently."

"You're not alone," I grinned. "And I'm fine with that, actually. If I'm going to be delving into ancient ruins in search of powerful artifacts, I don't want competition breathing down my neck, waiting for the opportunity to off me and steal the loot."

The librarian deflated a bit. "That's a good way to get yourself killed, friend."

"Jake."

He nodded. "Good way to get yourself killed. Jake. There are certainly plenty of ruins that are yet to be located, but there are reasons they've been hard to find. They're either in dangerous jungles, unreachable mountains, or something in between. And as for the ones we *do* know about, but haven't fully excavated," he barked a laugh, "well, there's a reason for that too. And it usually involves a mountain of dead, optimistic fools who thought wading through overgrown ruins would be a walk in the park.

"If that's the kind of thing you're looking for, then you had better spend a lot of time studying." He tapped the book in my hands. "Knowledge on ancient cultures will help you navigate their ruins. And you had better be the most powerful mage you know, because that's what it'll take. Unexplored ruins are filled with dangers and even if you make it out, there might be some grave robbers or bandits waiting for you outside.

"Most of those places are old temples or burial grounds for kings. People don't leave their most sacred places unguarded. There have even been rumors of dungeons with minds of their own! With some kind of crystal core in the center that could imbue a man with great power, if only he could make it past the guardians." He shrugged, "But who knows. Could just be rumor. I've certainly heard more reasonable lies before."

I wasn't sure if all that was supposed to scare me off, or seduce me into the program, but I was more hyped than ever to advance in the academy and get out in the world. With the

Pillar strengthening me, and Vethris' power at my disposal as a last resort, I figured I had a few advantages that most thugs wouldn't.

"I appreciate the warning. Sounds like you were there yourself once upon a time." I could already tell that this guy had a ton of interesting stories to share and looked forward to hearing them over a beer one day.

He barked a laugh and patted a large hand on my shoulder. "Oh, more times than I can count. I have a more than a few scars, and less than a few trinkets," he leaned in and whispered that part, "to show for it, too. But all that can wait until you're in my class." He grimaced and added, "Just make sure you pass that exam, boy. Our department's been shrinking over the years. I'd hate to see a promising young mind go to waste."

I gave him a friendly nod. "Well, it's just like you said. I'm going to need to push myself to be as powerful as possible if I don't want to die like all those fools you mentioned." I lowered my voice said in a conspiring tone, "I don't suppose there are any *hints* you could give me about that exam, are there?"

I wasn't being entirely serious, but Thuvien's face darkened. "I'm afraid not, boy. You'll need to prepare for that yourself. Keep in mind that, just like your future in archeology, you will need to rely upon your own power if you hope to succeed. All of your contemporaries will be working their asses off. You need to do the same, and then some. As long as you work harder than the rest, I think you'll find yourself in a good position. Enjoy the book and come find me sometime after you've read it. I'm sure it will raise far more questions than it will answer."

"Sure thing. And don't worry about me. This world has too much to offer to waste it on a short life. I'm going to make damn sure that I'm ready to face whoever and whatever's waiting for me out there."

"I hope so. Take care, Jake." With another pat on my shoulder, and a wise nod, Thuvien disappeared among the rows of books.

I FOUND LILLY AGAIN NEAR THE SAME PLACE THAT WE separated, the information desk. She sat at a polished wood table close by, reading a thick book, and had a few more stacked up next to her. As I walked over to join her, a few strands of her long brown hair came loose and hung over the pages. She swept them behind her left ear and, in doing so, noticed me. It was only a slight change, but she lit up a bit and her lips curled into a small smile that I couldn't help but return.

"I see you found what you were looking for. And then some," I said as I sat down across from her, nodding toward her pile.

"Oh yeah. I couldn't help myself; I've never seen so many books! They must have a copy of just about everything ever written in here."

"And if not, I'm sure they'd pay a pretty high price to anyone willing to help close the gaps in their collection," I mused. Being the first to read through ancient tomes was another perk I looked forward to in my potential career.

Lilly rolled her eyes. "Or... you could donate them to the

school as a sign of your respect and gratitude for their help in making your accomplishments possible." Her hopeful smirk told me that, while she might do that, she didn't necessarily expect it of me.

I pursed my lips in a frown and shook my head. "Nope. All these students pay tuition to be here, and they're risking their lives on top of that! I appreciate the school's help and all, but it's not like they're doing us a favor, or running a charity."

"Good point, but not for you, *Mr. Miskatonic scholar*," she imitated a haughty noblewoman's voice and then smirked.

"Alright, maybe I'm not actually paying tuition, but the point stands." Lilly gave me a sarcastic nod, scrunching up her face a bit. "Besides, I'd rather donate my findings to the people who paid my tuition than the ones who took it." I just needed to figure out who those Miskatonic people were, first.

"So that's your plan then, huh? Archeology? Spending the rest of your life discovering and exploring ancient ruins?"

I nodded. "Yup. That and using what I find to become very rich and powerful in the process. What about you?"

She deflated a bit as the conversation turned toward herself, I noticed. "I'm not sure, to be honest. I definitely want to take some courses in Regeneration and Natural Magics, but I don't even know what I'd ultimately use them for. Rich and powerful sounds certainly nice, though," she shot me a weak smile, then looked away. Her voice lowered as she went, almost as if she were just talking to herself. "My family was much the opposite. Poor and weak, but happy. I'd love to be able to take what I learn here and go back to help them, but..." She just shook her head and I saw tears start to well in her eyes.

Before I could think twice, my hand shot out and closed over hers. She reacted with shock but didn't pull away. I rubbed my thumb over the soft skin on the back of her hand.

"You don't need to tell me if you aren't ready. And, hey, if you have trouble deciding what you want to do, you can always just join up with me. I'm sure I'll be able to use all the help I can get, and an expert in Regeneration sounds like they'd be incredibly useful when I get my dumb ass killed."

Lilly snorted a laugh at that and used her free hand to catch a tear just as it started to fall. "That doesn't sound so bad. Maybe try to avoid actually dying though, resurrection is the kind of thing that even our Professors would have trouble with."

"Hold on, that's actually possible? I was just kidding."

Lilly giggled. "Well, sure. I mean, like I said, it's not easy, though. It's literally one of the hardest spells anyone has ever performed, but there are a select few who have managed it, without any... er, side-effects." She grimaced as she added, "Necromancy, on the other hand is much easier. As it turns out, if you don't care about the bodies you're dealing with, or the people that inhabited them, it's not that difficult to turn corpses into puppets."

"I take it you're not a fan?"

Lilly pouted and shook her head. She wanted to look mad, I imagined, but only achieved cute. Her voice sounded like she was personally affronted. "I can't believe they actually teach that kind of stuff here! I mean, I get that we might need to know something about it in case we end up fighting a necromancer one day, but *training them?* We may as well just start recruiting for," she glanced around and lowered her voice before finished her sentence with, "*Vethris*, himself."

My eyes bulged before I could get them under control.

"I know, even hearing his name makes me uncomfortable," she added.

"Uh, right. Yeah, definitely. I mean, what kind of person would become a Shadow?" *Certainly not me, at least if I had a choice.*

"The same kind that would become a Necromancer," she added matter-of-factly, and I had to nod at that.

It was a bit strange to reconcile the juxtaposition. When was the last time a necromancer, in literally any story, ended up being the good guy? Still, I had to admit that power over the dead was a bit tempting. Especially if I was going to be finding myself in ancient tombs; I had no doubt that skeletons and mummies would be just one of the many dangers. Maybe if I had some understanding of the magic, I could cancel it out without actually using it myself.

Not wanting to dance around the topic, I let the conversation die there. By the way Lilly brought it up, and almost seemed afraid to even say the dark God's name, I could tell that it was a sore subject with her.

Coming from my world, it was hard to take it completely seriously, to be honest. It was not like Satanists were actually aligned with the devil, or planning to take over my world, but with Vethris and his Shadows, that was quite literally case.

I had spent so long being an atheist, that it was hard to get used to a world where the Gods took an active part in its development. And yet, if I looked for it, the evidence was all around me, in the magic itself. I could close my eyes and sense the two sources of power, but it was still tough to accept that those came from the Gods themselves.

After asking Lilly to watch over my book for a bit, I asked the information desk for some help finding a book about theology. The woman I spoke to led me to the second floor before handing me off to one of her underlings.

It was a girl I'd met before and had been looking forward to seeing again. But from the way her eyes shot fire at me, I didn't think she felt the same way.

Filo's purple eyes bore into me as her boss introduced us and explained my request. Her look only grew more suspicious when she heard about my interest in Theology. She wore a loose white shirt with its long sleeves hiked up to her elbows. Her long red skirt rested on her hips, low enough that when Filo moved *just* right, a bit of skin peeked out.

"Come on, then," she rasped. Her fiery red hair flared out around her as she turned and took off. I had to speed walk just to keep up with her, but damn did her angry walk look good. My eyes kept returning to the small of her back and the smooth skin that kept showing as her severe steps shook her shirt out of place.

Filo led me to a remote corner of the library where there wasn't another student in sight. Then she opened a door and pulled me in.

To a janitor's closet.

"Hey, I'm down for anything. But when we're done, can you still help me find that book?" I quipped.

Filo gave me a flat look. Which was an improvement, considering it lacked her usual ire. "I have no use for *you,* whatever-your-name-was."

"Jake," I offered.

"Don't care," she dismissed it with a wave of her hand, then got serious. "Who sent you here, and why? The Lady expects a lot out of me already, and I can't be wasting time like this."

"Look, Filo, it might be hard for you to understand this, but the world doesn't revolve around you. Maybe I just wanted to do a little light reading!"

"On *theology?* You're telling me that wasn't some veiled threat to remind of who I've sworn my allegiance to?"

"Yes," I sighed, "That's what I'm saying. And I gotta be honest, this is the worst conversation I've ever had in a broom closet."

Filo looked around as if just realizing where we were and then scoffed as she pushed her way out of the room. Then slammed the door behind her, right in my face. I gritted my teeth and pushed the door open. There was still no one around, so no one saw or heard us, which was a shame.

All it would take was one gossipy girl to see the two us of heading out of a closet all hot-and-bothered and the rumor mill would begin. I'd love to see Filo's face once that one got back to her. It was almost enough to make me consider spreading it myself.

She was a short way away, standing between two rows of bookshelves with her arms crossed and a foot tapping. When I joined her, she just held up one hand and jabbed it toward the books on her left. "Please. Knock yourself out," she said tiredly, and walked away.

"Hey Filo." She stopped at the edge of the bookshelves and turned to face me with a sigh, then raised her eyebrows, waiting. "Thanks." I tried to offer her a friendly, even charming, smile, but it was powerless. The red head rolled her eyes and stomped away.

Chuckling to myself, I let my eyes run along the shelves. I was looking for something basic, some sort of overview of the Gods and everything we knew about them. But as I was searching, some of what Filo mentioned stuck out to me.

The Lady expects a lot out of me already.

I couldn't help but wonder what she was referring to and worry about what the mysterious Lady might expect from me.

With so many options, and only the titles to judge by, I settled on a book named "Gods and Godly things," by the oddly named Villip Weizse, but then again, all the names were a bit strange here.

Not more than a half hour could have passed by the time I returned to Lilly, and for all that I could tell, she hadn't moved a muscle. When I set the book down, I noticed her eying it, nodding slightly. "That's not a bad idea. The more you know about *Vethris*," she whispered the name again as he might overhear us talking about him, "the less scary he'll be. Let me know what you think of it and maybe I'll check it out when you're done," she said, referring to *Gods and Godly things*.

"Will do. And you'll have to let me know how," I craned my neck to look at her book's binding, "*A Passing Conversation on Muscle Regeneration* is..." Though considering how thick the book was, I didn't think the name was being completely honest. Either way, it wasn't a conversation I was particularly interested in. "Okay, on second thought, how about I just look over your book report?"

Lilly lit up, "You'd do that? That's just perfect, Jake, we can be each other's proofreaders! Like our own little study group."

"That's exactly what I had in mind," I lied. "While the rest of those idiots are only out for themselves, we'll work together and be better for it. You and I are gonna get through that exam with ease, Lil."

She beamed at me with a wide, beautiful smile. "I'm a little less nervous already."

❦ 16 ❦

LILLY AND I DECIDED TO PART WAYS ONCE WE GOT BACK TO our dorms, but not before she asked me to have the Alchemical Chef conjure up another pizza. She took a few slices and then froze in my doorway, looking back into the room with a slight smile.

"You want another slice?" I asked, assuming she was looking at the pizza.

Lilly shook her head. "No, I just wanted to thank you for going with me today. I know I've already mentioned it, but this place is pretty scary for me. I had never left my village before coming here, and it's just nice to have someone in the sea of strangers that I can trust. Especially these days, when it seems like Shadows are lurking around every corner. Anyway, I'll see you tomorrow, Jake."

"See you," I called after her, willing my voice to sound normal, despite my heart going into overdrive whenever someone mentioned Shadows or Vethris.

I couldn't help but laugh at myself. Lilly was just a simple, sweet village girl, and she *trusted* me. What would she think if she found out that I was a Shadow? Sure, it wasn't by choice, but who would even believe my story? I know I wouldn't. People didn't just find themselves in the body of a doppelganger in another world, at least not without copious amounts of drugs. I dabbled, sure, but not with anything *that crazy*.

There was clearly some kind of struggle going on between the Gods and their followers and I was already on the wrong side. The ability to use Vethris' power was great, its boost set me above people who might normally squash me like a bug, especially since I didn't even know how to utilize the magic I had. It would be invaluable for the exams, and the trials that I knew would come afterward, but I also ran the risk of being discovered, and executed for it. Not to mention the expectations Vethris's people would have for me in exchange for this power, or their likely fury when they realized that Jacobus stole the Pillar that they were saving for someone else.

It was only a matter of time before they came for me, and I had to be prepared for it. I spent the rest of the night with my head buried in *Gods and Godly Things,* devouring page after page.

Ever since my Mom stopped forcing me to go to church with her every Sunday, I'd had no interest in religion. No hate for it either, it just wasn't a part of my life. In direct contrast to that apathy, I was completely enthralled by this world's theology.

My biggest shock was that, not only did the Gods definitely exist, the people didn't even know *how many* of them there were. My mind immediately thought of them all as sources of power that I could add to my own, though I didn't know if that were even possible yet.

Pholl and Vethris weren't this worlds' only Gods, they were simply the major Gods of this continent. Though minor ones were likely here too, they were less prominent. It seemed that every major landmass, even some large islands, were inhabited by different gods whose strengths ranged greatly. And they were always trying to expand their territory.

It wasn't nearly as simple as the Earthly God and Devil dichotomy.

As far as I could tell, Pholl was one of the most benevolent, though the author knew less and less about Gods of increasingly distant lands. Whereas Pholl made himself available to all the mages of his continent, which was part of how he was able to dominate the area, that was a rare choice.

Vethris's method of doling out power only to those who served him was much more common. It was his methods that made him evil, though, not some intrinsic unwavering hatred as I imagined the Devil had. Vethris's philosophy, evidently, was to win power through any means necessary, and he awarded his followers who exemplified the same ideas. Cruelty and deception were just part of the game, even toward each other.

I made it probably a third of the way through the book and couldn't decide whether I was more comfortable with this world, or less, afterward. I was caught on the wrong side of a war that happened behind the scenes and didn't know what to do about it.

Except lie my ass off and hope it didn't come back to bite me.

OVER THE COURSE OF THE NEXT FEW DAYS, I FELT LIKE I was really starting to get used to things. I thought less and less about my old home and became fully enthralled in the new one. There was an entire world's worth of thousands of years of history here that I was eager to sink my teeth into, and the Theology book was just the first step. An appetizer, basically.

I was also shocked when I noticed that their names for

the days of the week were the same. It quickly subsided as I realized that I probably should have had that epiphany sooner. They spoke English, oddly enough, with no out-of-place words from what I could tell, why would the days be any different? It also seemed to imply that this world and my own had a greater connection that I first thought.

I finished *Gods and Godly Things* on the third day, having little else to do, really, and immediately got started on my report.

When I showed my choice to my professor the morning after I checked it out, she arched an eyebrow and cryptically said that she was "looking forward to my thoughts on Filn." I played it off as if I knew what she was talking about, but only learned the next day that it was one of the foreign Gods of lesser power.

Filn apparently ruled some unspecified islands off the coast of the eastern continent, where she manifested herself physically and made the islands' inhabitants worship her. Instead of her own power, she rewarded loyal servants with favors of a more... sexual persuasion. Needless to say, I had a few questions about this female God, such as: *Where is this island?* And *how exactly do I win her approval?* And perhaps the most important, *is she hot though?*

By Friday, I had finished my paper. I headed to the library with Lilly after the day's class so that we could look over each other's work.

The little brunette wore her usual blouse and long skirt combination with a sash tight around her stomach where the two met. Today though, she donned her witch's hat. It was a cute, light orange, floppy hat that she angled down over her face a little bit to block out the sun. The top of the hat's cone was flopped over and around the base was a string of yellow and white flowers.

Any university, magical or otherwise, was filled with hot

young women, but Lilly was beautiful. Shy, sweet, and even pretty funny. As we spent a lot of time together, I could already feel myself developing feelings for her. And if the smiles and looks she kept giving me were any indication, I thought she might be doing the same.

We took seats at a table on the fourth floor of the library. Each floor held fewer students than the last, so we chose the top, which was veritably silent. It was less distracting in other ways too, given that there were always interesting-looking people walking around. And no, not just attractive ladies; I was still having a hard time not staring at the orcs and elementals that were so commonplace. Their colorful skins and different clothing styles never failed to grab my attention.

Lilly smirked as she sat down. "Now, keep in mind, this is just my first draft so take it easy on me," she joked. Then she reached into a knapsack and pulled out a heavy stack of papers that she dropped in front of me.

My eyes bulged as I picked up her report and flipped through it. She had really gone all out! There were at least a dozen pages, both sides, of handwriting so neat it could have been typed. I was almost embarrassed to bring out my few pages of words that I could barely even read. *And I wrote them.*

Lilly scrunched up her face as she looked over the first page and I cringed inwardly. "Uh, did you write this yourself?"

"I know it might look like a dog wrote it, but yeah. My handwriting sucks, I know."

"Well, yes. It does," she offered me a kind smile to ease the pain of her words. "But that's exactly my point. Why did *you* write it?"

I blinked a few times, trying to puzzle out what she meant. Then it dawned on me. I lowered my voice a little, despite there being no one else around. "Oooh, you *cheated*?

Just let me know who wrote this for you and I'll throw them some gold to take care of mine too."

Lilly's jaw dropped and she immediately looked offended. "I would *never*. Jake, in a place like this *cheating*," she whispered the word in the same way that she said *Vethris*, "is punishable by expulsion. And you know what that means?"

"Death?"

"Yup. Or worse. If you're too useful to get rid of, they'll find a way to make their investment in you worth it. You know those bodyguards that follow the Headmaster around?"

"The silent ones in the black cloaks?" They certainly creeped me out when I met with Theid.

Lilly nodded and gulped. "I overheard some people talking when they lead you out of the dining square. They're *former students*, Jake. The girls I listened to didn't know how it happened, but they clearly recognized one. It sounded like it was one of their former boyfriends, but they said he would have never just followed someone around like some mindless slave. I swear, this place is getting more terrifying the more I learn about it."

As Lilly hands started to shake, I reached over and held them still. I turned her soft hands over in mine and said, "We'll just have to make sure we don't get caught then, eh?"

She snorted a laugh but shook her head. "More like: We'll just have to study so much that we don't *need* to cheat."

"Alright, alright," I said with feigned reluctance. To be honest, I kept my mind open to the idea, anyway.

Getting caught cheating might mean death, or some kind of magical enslavement, but failing my exams wasn't any better. In which case, I guess I didn't really have many options, did I? Cheating wouldn't be my first choice, obviously, but it was a tool that I wasn't willing to disregard. Yet.

Lilly looked back down at my paper and exclaimed, "Oh,

right! You didn't answer my question though, why did you write this by hand?"

By hand? Is that what she was asking? "Is there another way?"

Lilly scoffed and looked at me like I was stupid for a few seconds, before forcing a sweet smile. "Jake. Don't you have an Auto-Quill? I know the school doesn't provide them, but practically everyone has their own anyway."

The name was easy enough to figure out, it had to be some kind of pen that wrote for you. "I mean, of course I have an Auto-Quill. Who doesn't have an Auto-Quill? I just... thought they would want us to write it ourselves, is all." The lame excuse was all I could come up with at a moment's notice.

Lilly reared back as if she hadn't thought of that. "I guess I can see why you might think so. The academy is pretty strict in most regards but..." she pursed her lips, and glanced back at my handwriting, "in your case, Jake, I think you should just let the Quill do it."

We spent the next hour reviewing each other's work. Lilly clearly had a hard time, as she kept bringing the paper closer to her face to read it, and several times asked what a certain word actually said. A couple times, I couldn't even tell, myself.

Her paper, on the other hand, read as if it was its own textbook. It was perfect and I learned a lot, even if it wasn't exactly entertaining. *A Passing Conversation on Muscle Regeneration* was apparently a biology textbook, or at least this world's version of it. Specific and deep anatomical knowledge made Regeneration much more efficient, so most of Lilly's paper, and probably the textbook, was just about the muscles that made up the human body. How they grew and deteriorated, best methods toward healing them, stuff like that. Most of it went over my head, but it definitely gave me a better understanding of Regeneration magic overall.

When we were both finished, I had no notes to offer. It was far better than any paper I could ever write. Which Lilly would certainly agree with, considering her lengthy list of changes I should make.

"It isn't bad, exactly. Just needs some work," she offered kindly, before outlining exactly what that work would entail. It was another grueling hour of rewording sentences, and restructuring the entire thing, but by the time our stomachs started to growl, I was far prouder of my work.

"At this rate, I think you're as good a teacher as any professor here," I commented as we were packing up to leave. "It's not like Doriah was willing to help any of us."

"She will be, after this month. The school just doesn't like to waste resources on us Initiates, sadly. But, as long as we make it through, we'll have full access to the most amazing magical minds and textbooks that the world has to offer," her smile grew, and she looked mystified at the possibilities. "I can't wait," she practically bubbled over with excitement and I couldn't help but smile back.

Just as we left the fourth floor, though, I noticed that we weren't alone. Lilly and I took a table in the middle of the fourth floor since the rest was seemingly empty. But in one remote corner, I caught a glimpse of a girl with slightly pointed ears. Her arms were crossed, and she looked down angrily at a mess of papers on her desk. An Auto-Quill was furiously scratching out words and rewriting them as she watched. Her breathtaking teal eyes flashed up at me and glared.

Putting on a charming smile, I waved to her. We were in the same class, after all, even if we hadn't spoken to each other.

But the extremely attractive girl just snorted and turned her attention back to her work.

"Who's that?" Lilly's voice rang out when she realized I had stopped.

"I dunno."

"Ooh, I've seen her. Nice legs," she commented, staring at the girl just as openly as I was. The teal-eyed girl wore a long dress that parted just above her knees and the skin that it revealed was pale and flawless. I turned a confused look on Lilly. "What? A girl like that can turn even a statue's head. Her skin looks so soft, I don't know how she does it." From the look on Lilly's face, and the way she bit her lip, I could tell that there was more than just admiration on her mind.

"I'm learning more about you every day Lilly Oakheart. Who knew we had the same taste in women?"

She giggled and jabbed me in the ribs as we started walking again. "Hey, if there's a beautiful painting near me, I'm going to look at it. And maybe kiss it, if it'll let me," she sent me a wink. "I don't care who painted it, or what they painted; I admire beauty of all kinds." She eyed me up and down as if to emphasize that her attraction wasn't limited to other females.

My first thought about that was, *Oh, hell yeah*. As long as I made it through these fucking exams, I could tell I was going to have a lot of fun with this girl.

❧ 17 ❧

BY THE TIME I WAS BACK IN MY ROOM AND LILLY HAD LEFT for hers, I was mentally exhausted. My brain felt like its wires had been fried from a long day of thinking too hard. Lilly really took me to task over my paper, but even I had to admit how much better it was afterwards.

Earlier in the week, I purchased some more comfortable bedding from a textiles store, and they were already making my life in this world more bearable. New sheets made the scratchy mattress smooth, a new pillow replaced the lumpy one Jacobus brought, and a soft blanket worked with everything else to make this bed almost as comfortable as mine at home.

But if I thought that it would mean uninterrupted sleep, I was sorely disappointed. But mostly just sore. Because in the middle of the night, I awoke to what I at first thought was a nightmare.

The first thing I felt was pain. Before I had even opened my eyes, pain pulsed through every vein of my body like my blood had been switched out with fire. A scream wrenched its way out of my throat, but it didn't even reach my own ears.

When I finally did open my eyes, there was a familiar dark portal on the opposite wall and a figure standing in the middle of the room.

My eyes burned as they fell on her and moved away by their accord. The Lady's head was shrouded in an unnatural darkness deeper than the rest of the room, and the rest of her body was draped in an ornate, glossy black gown.

My muscles spasmed as I fought for control, but they swiftly carried me to the floor in a kneeling position with my forehead pressed to the tiles. *Now I know why Jacobus was so pissed off that first night.* My breaths came ragged and rough, but the woman's voice was clear as day. It was also haughty and derisive.

"I gave you one job. Confirm the location of the Pillar. That was all you had to do, but no! Your worthless, greedy, selfish, stupid mind chose to take it for yourself. And now it'll be a year before anyone can take it back, so congratulations. You just became my slave for an entire year." She let the words sink in while she stepped over me and sat on my bed, then put her feet up on my back.

This bitch thought she could treat me like trash. And as much as I wanted to do something about it, the pain made it impossible to focus on anything else. I couldn't tell if she was actually forcing my teeth to clench, or if I was doing that myself. All I could focus on was getting through the next moment of indescribable pain. Even her light feet pressed against my back felt like blows from a hammer.

Fighting against Brock was one thing, but this woman may as well have been a God in comparison to me. I could still sense Pholl and Vethris' power, within reach even, but my ability to reach for them was overtaken by the only sensation I could feel at the moment. Pain.

"I like what you've done with the place," she added. I heard her lift a book from the desk next to my bed and make a tsk sound with her tongue. "*Gods and Godly things*? Phaw! They have you reading that sort of trash these days? Villip held Pholl's favor, sure, but so does any mage who steps on this continent. What would a man like that know of the world? Hearsay and rumors, the lot of it. Now, I have a *real* book of consequence that I want you to acquire for me."

And there it is. Filo's not the only one with expectations to fulfill. I'm starting to see why she's so angry.

"As an Initiate, you may not be aware that the library has more floors *below* the ground than above it. Don't worry, I won't be sending you to the bottom... yet. The book I need is on the third level below ground, in a hidden office belonging to a certain friend you made recently. Octavio Thuvien." The way she said his name made it clear that they knew each other. Hated each other, probably. "Somehow, that man has come into possession of a copy of the *Iterad Virtutem*. I don't care how you do it, but you *will* bring me that book and you *will not* read it. Understand?"

A flash of pain ran down my back when I didn't move, so I bit out a word. "*Yes.*" I could hardly believe how hoarse my voice sounded.

"Good. You will have one week. If it is not in your possession by the time I return, then you will find that the pain you've experienced tonight was actually quite pleasant." Then she planted a foot on my back and used it to step over me. From the top of my vision, I saw her step into the portal and turn around. "Do not be so foolish this time. Vethris may be satisfied that one of his followers captured the Pillar, even if it was not me, but I am not nearly as forgiving. Do not fail me. Do not betray me."

The portal closed in upon itself and the pain slowly subsided. Planting my hands on the cold floor, it took all the strength I could muster just to get myself back into bed.

I didn't know whether that bitch was crazy, or stupid, or

what, but how could she even expect me to pull this off? If the school didn't tell Initiates that the basement floors *existed*, then how was I supposed to get access to them? Never mind stealing a book from the office of the Head Librarian himself.

Still, it didn't seem like I had a choice. As much as I wanted to flip the script and have that woman kneeling before me in pain next time, I doubted that a week would be long enough to close our gap in power. As much as I hated it, maybe I could use Thuvien's friendliness toward me to my advantage.

The only thing that kept me from tossing and turning all night was the pain that spiked through me whenever I moved. After endless minutes of trying to come up with a plan, sleep finally came.

And so far, I had nothing but hopes that tomorrow would be better.

Nope. Not feeling better at all. Worse, actually. I stifled a long groan as I got out of bed, woken up by an incessant knocking at my door. Whelan's voice leaked through. "Come on, man, I let you skip breakfast, but you can't sleep all day!"

I scrunched my eyes and glanced outside. Oddly, even the light hurt. My head, and everything else, felt like I had gone through a grueling full-body workout yesterday, then got black-out drunk. The headache was worse than any hangover I'd ever had, though, and I had to squint my eyes even after I pulled the curtains closed.

I wanted to thank God for not having classes today, but I wasn't sure which one to choose.

"Alright, jeez. Just keep it down a little bit," I said to Whelan as I opened the door.

Even his normal voice felt like it was pounding in my

head. "Well, you look like shit. Did you get in trouble again last night?" A jolt of panic shot though me as I thought he knew about The Lady. "Theid make you spend a few more hours in the sewer?" I held back a sign of relief.

He doesn't know. No one knows or is even suspicious. How did Filo or Brock even manage to function when they had such a deadly secret hanging over their shoulders all the time? Someone like The Lady might be powerful enough to kill anyone who found out she was a Shadow, but the rest of us had to hide in plain sight.

"No. No, I just drank too much. Way too much." I figured that excuse was the most believable. The headache and light sensitivity should count in my favor, and hopefully prevent Whelan from thinking too hard about my full-body soreness.

He held his hands out to his sides, "You were in here getting drunk all night and you didn't even think to invite me? You're not the only one with a bit of stress, mate. I was working on my paper for hours!"

"And how would being drunk have helped?"

Whelan rolled his eyes. "Because it gives you a different perspective on things. An idea that seems great while sober might seem terrible once you've had a few drinks, or the other way around. If someone else is going to be reading the paper, then it helps to alter your own mind a bit before you read it over. Helps you see it the way another person might. See what I mean?"

"I guess."

"Whatever, man. You wanna get some food? On week-ends, the dining square has a pretty great all-day breakfast. And uh," he rubbed the back of his head awkwardly and stared at the ceiling while he continued, "I was wondering if you and Lilly might be willing to take a look at my report. You know, the whole different perspective thing I mentioned."

I snorted a soft laugh. My voice rose with sarcasm. "Oh really? Mr. My-Dad-Taught-Me-Everything-There-Is-To-Know-About-This-Place needs my help? What made you change your mind?"

Whelan cringed. "Look, I'm not trying to join your study group or whatever you call it, but that doesn't mean we can't help each other out from time to time. I just don't like going to the library."

"Well, if you want our help, that's where we'll be," I shrugged.

"Fine. But can we be in the dining square first? Cause I want another omelet."

AFTER AN ADMITTEDLY GREAT MEAL, WHELAN AND I MET Lilly in the library. As we walked through the first floor, I kept my eyes peeled for stairs that led down but didn't notice any.

The soreness throughout my body was fading more quickly than I expected it to, down to a dull throb now.

Lilly was just as disappointed as Whelan to find out that I was drinking in my room without them. "I mean, we were together until pretty late. I just don't see why you wouldn't have shared, is all," she said as we were getting settled into our spot on the fourth floor.

The entire time, I kept a closer eye on my surroundings as I was on the lookout for anything that could get me into the basement. The teal-eyed girl was there again, as well as a few other students I didn't recognize that were each studying alone in quiet alcoves. The girl looked up at me curiously, before returning to her work. Strange, but better than the glares I got before.

"Sorry," I shrugged, turning my attention back to Lilly and going along with the lie, "You two just seem pretty straight-edge. I don't want to get you in trouble or distract you from studying, or whatever it is you do when no one's around." Lilly blushed at that for some reason, whereas Whelan rolled his eyes.

"Jake, I had my first drink like ten years ago at a ball in New Tris. They're usually gross, but I'd never turn down a drink. Pholl knows we have enough stress to deal with these days, I'm sure we could all use some relief," he grumbled.

I peeked over at Lilly and thought about the relief we might be able to give each other. Maybe with a hand wrapped in her long brown hair while I bent her over my bed. My eyes vibrated and, knowing what was about to happen, I braced myself for the images I knew were coming. Lilly's clothes, skin, and flesh flashed through my mind in the way I was starting to get used to, even if I still couldn't control it. At the very least, I could enjoy the fleeting view it gave me of her perky chest and pink nipples.

Lilly suddenly cleared her throat and I realized that I was an idiot. Just because people didn't know that my power saw through layers of clothing, didn't mean that they wouldn't know if I was blatantly checking them out.

Which I was. And she was blushing an incredibly deep red, despite a small smile on her face that sent some of my blood rushing south. "Whelan's paper, Jake?" She said in a reprimanding tone.

"Ah, right." But I glanced once more at the modest amount of cleavage she was showing, remembering the view my power gave me, before taking up one of the two copies Whelan brought for us.

We ended up spending the rest of the day there. While Lilly and I went through Whelan's paper, he read ours, and we ultimately all ended up making some changes to our work. Lilly's was still more than twice as long as either of Whelan or I's papers, but I was happy with the final product regardless. The sun was almost going down, and with the work completed, our group had grown quiet.

Just the opportunity I was waiting for. I knew I would have to be a bit vague but had to fish for clues somehow. "Do either of you know anything about the basement floors of this place?" I asked openly but figured Whelan would be the one to know anything. Sure enough, he paled a bit. Lilly scrunched her eyebrows and shook her head.

Whelan seemed like he was forcing the words out. "We're supposed to learn about the lower floors when we sign up for our next round of classes. We don't get permanent access or anything, but we can request it as long as we have a good reason. Why?"

I shrugged innocently. "Maybe I have a good reason." Whelan gave me a flat look. "Alright, maybe I'm thinking that there are some books down there that could help give me an edge for the exams. That better?"

"More honest, anyway," he grumbled. "But I don't see how you could get down there, anyway. Even Acolytes get a library assistant to chaperone them down there. It's straight to the book you need, and straight back."

An idea started to form in my head. "But the library assistants, they get permanent access?"

"Well, sure. They work here, they'd need it."

"That's all I needed to know."

❧ 18 ❧

WHELAN AND LILLY MIGHT HAVE BEEN WILLING TO BEND the rules enough to drink, but my plans regarding the library's basement floors were thankfully too risky for either to want to get involved. Lilly even tried to talk me out of it, so I promised to give it some more thought.

In reality, I stayed behind when they left because I already knew who to turn to. She might not be happy about it, but from what I had seen, she never was anyway.

I waited for her to walk around the corner of a bookcase, then clamped my hand over her mouth and pulled her into the same janitor's closet she pulled me into a few days ago. And she repaid me with an elbow to the ribs.

"What the fuck are you doing?" Filo bit off as she whirled on me. "If you *ever* touch me like that again, I'll cut your hand off."

Rubbing the sore spot on my ribs that already felt bruised, I shot back in a similar tone. "Jeez, fine. I just didn't know how to talk to you in private, since you clearly don't want to be seen with me." She crossed her arms instead of responding, and I resisted the urge to look at the way she compressed her cleavage. "Look, I need you to help me get a job here."

"What?" Her purple eyes bulged with the fury that she always seemed full of. "First of all, why? And second, what makes you even think I can do that?"

"You aren't the only with a job to do," I said, lowering my voice to a threatening level and hoping she understood what I meant. Her eyes widened, so I went on. "I need to get to the third sub-floor and I'm sure you know how impossible it is for an Initiate to do that. So," I shrugged, "I need access, somehow."

Filo shook her head and stared back at me for a minute. "Library assistants don't just automatically get access to the entire place, *idiot.*" She held up her right hand and pointed to a white orb that hung from her bracelet. "See this? White means that I can only access the first sub-floor. Green lets you in the second, blue the third." She let out a deep breath and seemed to calm down a bit. "Look, I can put in a good word for you but can't promise you'll get a job. And either way, you'll need one of those blue spheres to get down there, so it looks like you'll need to steal it. And before you ask, fuck no will I help you. I'm already putting myself at risk by just associating with you."

"I know, I know, and you have your own shit to deal with. At least now I know I'll need to steal one of those things and replace it before they find out. Thanks, Filo." I held out a hand, hoping to settle our differences so that I could get on the path that led down her pants. Instead, she slapped the hand away.

"First of all, *no*, you *can't* return it. There are forensic scryers here who can look into magical objects' pasts and figure out who used them. You'd get caught. Easily. And second, don't thank me. You owe me, *idiot.* And you're damn right I have my own shit to do, so when I figure out how you can help me with it, you can bet your dumbass is going to be seeing me again. Got it?"

Her hands flung out to her sides and clenched into fists while she took a threatening step toward me. Filo's tits pressed into my chest, but I didn't let her force me backward. To be honest, I kind of liked it. The tussled red hair, angry purple eyes combo really did it for me. Not to mention the tight body she hid under that proper librarian's uniform.

I leaned my head close enough to smell the mint on her breath. Just another couple inches and I'd be kissing her. She didn't back away either. In fact, it was dark, but I could have sworn I saw her blush.

I squinted and bit off the words, "Got it." And as soon as they were out of me, Filo burst out of the room.

Now all I needed was a plan.

I headed back to the fourth floor to think it through. As much as I would have liked to have Whelan and Lilly's help, I didn't want to risk pulling them into my mess. So, I opened up the first of the Jacobus' books that I had been meaning to get to, *Lost Artifacts of Old Tris,* and pretended to read while trying to come up with ideas.

But all I achieved was dozing off.

A sound pierced my half-asleep ears and my eyes cracked open. The sound repeated. A sharp, "Hey!" that made my head throb. I rubbed my temples with two fingers each and tried to shut my eyes so tight that no light could get through.

Then something slammed on the table with such force that the wind flipped my book's page. The thunderous sound pounded in my eardrums and felt like I'd been punched in the back of the head. *And here I thought a nap would help me feel better.*

When I peeked an eye open, I was very confused by the beautiful, albeit angry, teal-eyed girl before me. She had a two-inch long silver wand hanging down from a loose necklace that settled between her breasts and was wearing the type of long navy-blue gown and matching witch's hat I'd seen on her a few times. Today, however, the dress was disheveled a bit and one side was hanging lower than the other, giving me a nice view of her ample cleavage. It gave me the motivation to open both eyes, just so I could get a good look at her.

As I should have expected, my power activated and scanned through the girl. Luckily, even in my present condition, it didn't hurt. The vibration still felt strange, but less so. I tried to ignore everything but the first few images it sent me of the girl in a corset and stockings, then nude, and my jaw practically dropped.

I had already seen it before, from afar when my power activated in class one time, but up close was an entirely different story. The clothing she wore compressed her curvy, fully figured body into one that was still impressive, if less *accentuated*. The corset served to downplay her chest, but once I saw through it, I could tell how badly those puppies wanted to break free. I bit my lip and sucked in a deep breath as I resisted the urge to keep staring long after the images ceased.

"Hey!" One last time, she called out, louder than before. "Don't just stare right through me like I'm not even worth your time. I don't care what kind of scholarship you have, if you keep getting in trouble the school will still expel you. And you know that doesn't just mean they kick you out, right?" She crossed her arms and rested back on her heels, looking down at me imperiously.

"I'm sorry but if you don't want me staring at you, at least point your, er, *assets* toward someone else. My willpower isn't that strong," I admitted, openly glancing down to her chest.

When the girl did the same, her face took on a deep scarlet and she hastily pulled her dress up by a few inches.

She let out a disgusted sound and said, "I hope you focus on your studies more than you do on the women in class."

"I do, usually, as long as I keep them separated. Or at the very least, fully clothed." She blushed again at that and I couldn't help but grin. "Why do you care, anyway?"

She stared back at me for a moment before answering. "I've heard about you, you know. A lot of people have been talking about the Miskatonic scholarship like it's some big deal, but I'm on to you." The way she squinted her eyes made my heart skip a beat.

Could she know I'm a Shadow? As far as I could remember, I didn't make any mistakes, so I didn't think so. She stared me down after her accusation and, instead of opening my mouth and possibly incriminating myself, I let the silence stretch on. She never did answer my question.

Eventually, she continued as if she had never paused. "If you were really as good as I've heard, then you wouldn't have needed the slacker and that rural girl to help you. But today's your lucky day, because I've decided to offer my assistance."

My eyes widened. *That's not where I thought she was going with this little conversation at all.* As much as I loved being around any beautiful woman, I couldn't help but think that there were strings attached. After all, she just came up out of nowhere and rather aggressively offered her help. Unusual, to say the least.

I leaned back in my seat and crossed my arms, giving her an appraising look. "You haven't even told me your name."

"Haether."

"Well, Heather–"

"*Haether,*" she said, louder than before and a little frustrated.

"Uh, yeah. That's what I said."

She shook her head and closed her eyes as if she had this conversation all the time. "You know the school's name?

Aether Academy? Say Aether with an 'H' in front of it, and that's my name. Not the purple flower. Haether is bioluminescent and only grows in areas of extremely high magical concentration. It's a rare and beautiful flower with all kinds of useful properties!"

"Alright, *Haether*," I rolled my eyes and emphasized her obnoxious name just to rile her up. It worked, but I talked over her interruption. "You're a rare and beautiful flower, I get it. But I can also see that for myself," I sent her a grin as she blushed even deeper. "Look, I don't mind if you want to join us. People seem too concerned with competition around here, but I just want to make it through alive. You don't have to be so pushy," I added.

"Right," she nodded with a sigh and fell into the chair opposite mine. "I'm sorry. I mean, the work we put in during this month is literally life or death. I knew what I was getting into, but I had no idea how anxious the constant pressure would make me." Then she reached into a silk sack that I didn't notice she had already placed on the seat next to her and pulled out a small stack of papers. Haether pushed it toward me, expectantly.

I scrunched my eyebrows and looked down at her report, and suddenly it all clicked.

She didn't come over here to offer her help, *she came to ask for mine*.

Just in her own roundabout way, apparently. I chuckled a bit and realized that I was way out of my depth as soon as I read the title. *The Efficiency of the Multiple Enchantment Method.*

I pushed the papers back across the table and deflected. "Sorry, but I'm pretty burnt out from a long day of too much reading. Hence the nap I was taking when you tried to get my attention."

Her eyes bulged and she laughed a little. The way her smile lit up was just gorgeous. "You were *asleep?* Here I thought you were just ignoring me. But, fair enough, I guess. It is getting late. We must be two of the last students here. Well, if you're all done here anyway, mind walking me back to the dorm?" She asked with a surprising meekness to her voice. Her arms wrapped around herself. "The city I come from is too dangerous to go out alone at night, and I'm still not exactly comfortable with it."

"O-of course!" I stuttered, surprised by her request, though not disappointed. Haether's teal eyes were captivating and her usually severe face took on a vulnerable look that could have made me walk through fire if she asked. I wouldn't even think twice for a girl like that, particularly after seeing her smile.

As soon as our initial confrontation was over, Haether lightened up and quickly grew more friendly. We packed up and headed out of the library. I kept an eye out for stairs down, but again didn't notice anything.

Keeping in mind my conversation with Filo, I also paid keen attention to the information desk on the first floor and the several librarians at work with it. A few had their orbs on display, but none better than green. Still, now that I knew what to look for, I could start thinking about what to do.

Later, anyway. At the moment, I had a gorgeous girl to walk home.

The cobblestone pathways were lit by the occasional floating balls of white fire about the size of my palm. They sat at the top of lamp posts but hovered just above them without any apparent support. Despite all that I'd experienced, even that simple bit of magic was still enough to impress me.

The campus wasn't empty, but the students we passed were few and far between.

Haether threw on a thin cloak as we got outside. It was a lighter shade of blue than her hat or dress and clasped together at her collar bones. She wrapped it around herself and a shiver ran down her spine as she glanced in every direction.

"Where do you come from, anyway? And why's it so dangerous?" I asked, picking up our conversation from earlier.

"Well," she started, her eyes still darting around, "being so close to the border, whenever tensions rise between us and Central Miria, we end up with a sudden influx of criminals. My father thinks that Central keeps emptying their prisons and just sending them all over to Calich. That's the city where we live, along with most of my father's family. We are a, uh, minor noble house, and I'm not skilled enough with magic yet to fight off a group of thugs, so I'm the perfect target," she seemed a bit ashamed to admit it. Haether sighed and shook her head. "I'm sorry I had you do this. It's so stupid. I know the campus is safe and all, I just can't shake a feeling like I'm being watched. And I hate those damn statues and fountains all over the place. They're too lifelike, especially in the dark."

I followed her eyes as they darted from one statue to another. She had a good point; the campus was practically littered with the things. Whereas I was impressed by the apparent craftmanship that magic could produce, I definitely got a creepy vibe now that Haether mentioned it. Like looking into the eyes of a doll and immediately wanting to burn it, just in case.

I leaned into Haether a little bit, nudging her to take her attention away from the sinister statues. "Well, if they all spring to life, at least you won't die alone," I grinned.

She barked a surprised laugh. "That *doesn't* make me feel any better." But she was smiling, so I wasn't sure I agreed.

I shrugged as if it didn't matter. "Oh, we'd put up a good fight, I think. Maybe even turn a few of these grey bastards to rubble in the process, but there's just too many of them.

We'll need a few more members before we can take them on."

Haether looked up at me and chuckled. "It's a good thing you let me join your little study group, then. You never know when they'll declare their war on the living, but when they do, anyone fighting alone may as well just give up."

"Exactly. Except Theid and those bodyguards, I get the feeling they can hold their own."

"*Headmaster* Theid," she corrected me, "could probably take them all alone, from what I've heard. My father used to say that when the Headmaster wanted to, he could cut off the entire campus from Pholl's source. Even working together, the entire student body couldn't wrestle it back." Then she gave a light shrug, "Probably just an exaggeration, but still. He is like three thousand years old, so I'd expect him to be pretty powerful."

I pursed my lips and nodded. "I guess that's the plan then. When the grey uprising occurs, we'll gather the group and make for the spire. I'm glad we did this, Haether, I'm feeling safer already." She shot me a sweet smile but didn't say anything. As we walked the rest of the way, though, she was no longer glancing around nervously. In fact, half the time we passed a statue, she would just smirk.

When we got to the front of the dorm, Haether thanked me again and headed off toward the side of the building.

"Where are you going?" I called out, pointing to the only entrance I was aware of.

"Oh," she let out a nervous laugh, "my dorm's much closer to the side entrance."

"Huh, alright well I'll just head in that way with you."

"No! I mean, it's just that... it's an emergency exit, so I'm not really supposed to be using it and I don't want you blowing my cover."

I chuckled. "Alright, fair enough. At least I'm not the only person around here willing to break the rules a bit. By the way, Lilly and I will probably be back at the library tomorrow, if you wanna join us."

Haether smiled, nodded, and waved, then disappeared around the building. I watched her go, though my eyes mostly rested on her perfectly round ass. I'd never seen someone so flawless and after a bit of a rocky start, she was actually pretty cool.

And just like that, our 'little' study group became a little bit bigger.

19

After lunch the next day, Lilly and I headed back to the library. Whelan, on the other hand, had a couple of friends that were Acolytes who he wanted to delve for information about the exam.

Before we even reached the stairs, Head Librarian Thuvien called my name and pulled me aside, so I told Lilly I'd catch up with her. Thuvien grabbed me by the arm, seemingly angry, but was just very focused.

"So, I heard that you have some interest in working for the Library? Good, good. We aren't the most popular department these days. When you can apprentice with a necromancer, librarians hardly seem up to chuff," he rolled his eyes and shook his head. "But I can at least be proud that the students we do attract are always the most studious and hardworking. It is the library, after all.

"Filo said you'd do just about anything to start and, while we usually don't hire Initiates due to the, uh, nature of the exams, there are certainly a few things you could help out with. It won't be the most exciting work, but you'll be doing the library a valuable service by taking the more, shall we say, tedious jobs out of the hands of the more experienced faculty. How does that sound?"

He never did actually say what I'd be doing, but I figured that I didn't have much of a choice. It was the only lead I had at the moment, and if I was going to get my hands on one of those blue orbs, well, I'd need a reason to get close enough to someone who owned one. Someone like Thuvien, I assumed.

So, I pretended to give it a bit of thought, and then nodded, sticking out my hand. "When do I start? And what does it pay?" The dark man cringed at that.

"Err, I assumed Filo was upfront with you about this being more of an internship, than an actual job. As your ranking within the school increases, I could set you up with something more official, but at the moment, you being an Initiate and all, this is the best I can do." From the way he looked at me then, I knew he expected me to change my mind.

When I didn't, he was positively ecstatic. "Fantastic, my boy! I think you could be a great asset to our department one day, and this is the first step. Tell you what," he ran a hand over his chin in thought for a moment and stared off at nothing as he continued, "meet me at the information desk after your classes on... let's go with Tuesday. And I'll get you started. After that, you could come by and help out whenever you want. Sound good?"

Considering the deadline, I was on, that wasn't ideal, but I considered myself lucky to get this far and didn't want to push my luck. I'd have to thank Filo, somehow, without pissing her off.

By the time Thuvien let me go and I made it up to the fourth floor, Lilly and Haether were already chatting at our table.

"I see you two have met. Sorry about that, but you're looking at the newest, and dare I say best, library assistant on campus." Lilly softly clapped her hands and let out an impressed sound while Haether just smirked. "Thank you, thank you," I added, with joke modesty.

"And how did you manage that?" the more cynical one asked, her teal eyes weighing me up.

"It's all about who you know, my elven friend." She blushed at that, so I quickly added, "I mean, you are an elf, right?" I ran a finger along the curved tip of my right ear to emphasize how hers were pointed.

"Half-elf, actually," she corrected me, sounding a bit embarrassed.

"Fascinating." The word left Lilly's mouth in a whispery breath. "Sorry, it's just that in my town the most exotic thing I'd ever seen was an imp my teacher summoned, and it ended up taking a leak on my shoes," she grimaced at the memory.

A number of questions popped into my head about Haether's mixed race, but I also didn't want to put her on the spot, considering her withdrawn reaction. Instead, I decided to wait for an opportunity to ask Whelan what he knew about elves.

I changed the subject back to class and the paper due tomorrow and noticed Haether immediately relax as the topic moved away from her background. Lilly and I, but mostly Lilly, tore through Haether's paper with a litany of questions and suggestions, and by the time we were finished, Haether was looking a bit shellshocked. She ended up with far more ideas than she had time to explore and had to take the rest of the day to get the paper finalized. While she worked, Lilly and I took out books to read.

Well, Lilly read. I just pretended to, while I admired the women before me. Both were among the most beautiful I'd ever seen, as well as smart, funny, and hard-working. The half-elf was the taller of the two by about a half-foot, with more slender limbs and a fuller chest, but Lilly had a sexy tan, and a fit body that growing up on a farm resulted in.

And, unless my radar was far worse than I imagined, they both kinda seemed into me. Not that I even had to yet, but I had no idea how I could choose between them. I hardly wanted to pursue both of them at the same time and make things awkward for all of us, but if I rejected one and chose the other, then that would be just as bad.

Well, there was no use in overthinking a problem that hadn't even cropped up yet, so with an enormous effort, I tried to ignore the girls at my table so that I could read uninterrupted.

Even the way they worked was distracting. Lilly's plump lips silently mouthed words out as she read through the Regeneration school's recommendations. Haether's face scrunched into a focused expression that almost looked like she was angry at her Auto-Quill, while murmuring to herself. They were both too cute to ignore and I just found myself staring at the pages of *Lost Artifacts of Old Tris* without comprehending a single thing.

The next day, a long line of students handed in their papers, creating a large stack on the professor's podium. If I focused hard enough, I could see the flows of magic that she was using to prevent the stack from falling everywhere. It was something like what I did to Brock and his friends. Except where I grabbed hold of air, so to speak, and then *pushed*, the professor just held.

She sat nearby and nodded to students as they added their reports to the pile. Then we were treated with another guest speaker.

From the Necromancy department.

Lilly bristled immediately, shifting in her seat and grimacing. Haether joined our group this time, taking the seat on my left since Lilly was on my right, but she didn't seem to mind the dark magic.

Whelan, on the other hand, seemed excited. After a brief introduction to Haether, he noticed Lilly's expression and said, "What's not to like about using dead things to get the job done? You stay out of harm's way and, well," he shrugged, "they're already dead anyway."

Lilly scoffed. "And how would you like it if some necro-mancer used your body? Sure, they just seem like zombies but what if you're actually resurrected into a body you can't control? And then he makes you do terrible things?"

Whelan's expression slowly darkened with each of her questions. "Well... I mean, I don't know," he grumbled. He looked up at us from his slightly lower seat in the next row, "That's not *really* how it works, is it?"

Haether and I shrugged, but Lilly pursed her lips and nodded.

Whelan squinted, not ready to give in quite yet. "How do you even know this?"

Lilly cringed and her face turned a deep red. "I just do, alright!" She fired back.

"Fine, fine," Whelan reared back and put his hands up in defeat, more shocked by Lilly's outburst than anything else. And so was I, I'd never seen her angry before. I knew she had strong feelings about necromancy, but I suddenly realized that maybe she had a good reason for it. The way she shut down after that made me certain.

When a pretty woman, who couldn't have been more than thirty, approached the podium, the amphitheater grew silent. I had been expecting a wrinkled old man who looked close to being a corpse, himself. The woman had dark red hair and purple-tinged skin that was a new one for me. I had seen many shades since coming here and assumed she was some kind of elemental, but her clothing was different from the wrappings they wore. I could only refer to it as a sundress, but there were clear differences. The light-green, floral dress reached her knees and was held up by thin straps. It had built-in pockets and several loops around the waist in which the woman carried a very thin sword on one side, and a wand tied to a loop with a strap of leather on the other.

In other words, she was about as close to the exact opposite of what I was expecting as possible. She practically bounced up to the podium with a big smile on her face.

"Hello everyone! I'm High Necromancer Willow Waterdeep." She sounded like a sorority girl, or cheerleader giving a speech to their new recruits. Far too perky. I was almost expecting her to go limp while the real necromancer controlling her crawled out of the shadows. "It's always exciting to meet a new crop of students and start getting an idea for who might be joining my department next month.

"Now, I know some of you might have some preconceived notions about necromancy, so I'd like to get those out of the way quickly. Yes, it has been considered a dark form of magic at times, but these days, what hasn't? I know a lot of you aren't old enough to remember our last war with Central Miria, but I saw a hell of a lot more fireballs coming at me than zombies. And by having knowledge of the necromantic arts, I was able to put my enemies' armies of the dead to sleep without so much as swinging a weapon. If kings can send thousands of men to their deaths on the battlefield, how is it worse to send the dead instead?"

She paused at that and looked around the room, as if trying to make eye contact with anyone who still might disagree with her. Lilly was visibly uncomfortable, but I found myself having a hard time disagreeing with the purple woman. At least dead soldiers wouldn't be sacrificing their lives for a leader who would never know them.

But if Lilly was right, and those zombies were resurrected

along with their souls, just to be turned into locked-in puppets, well, I couldn't support that either. I would need to learn a lot more about necromancy before I could even decide how I felt about it.

When no one spoke up, Deepwater continued. Ultimately, most of her lecture was a list of selling points for anyone considering her classes. She tried to focus on unique applications of the magic, but it didn't make her look much better, in my eyes anyway. That is, until she reached a pivotal point that she, for some reason, saved until the end.

"And it is my belief that it is only within the necromantic arts that one may find the ultimate answer toward cheating death," she paused as that point sent up a murmur among the students. "That's right. We speak of control over death itself. Not just in the dead, but in the living. Death may creep up on us at any point. If you were to die unexpectedly, those at the Regeneration school would only be able to help if they were there when it happened. Oh, they would mourn you and give you every burial rite your culture demands."

Then she took on a devilish grin. "But if you make the *right* choice, the school of Necromancy would have you rejoin our ranks. Not as a mindless zombie, but as your former self. My very own research has resulted in that particular breakthrough. I, myself was present for the first true resurrection of a man whose heart and brain had ceased for over an hour. With a few of us working together, we were able to bring him back with *almost* no side effects! The possibilities are limitless, and I hope you'll explore them with me as we continue to push the bounds of what is possible. Thank you." With a wide grin, she stepped aside, bowed to our professor and gracefully hopped up the stairs that led back to campus.

After being dismissed for the day, Lilly was in a terrible mood. Her pout was obvious, her footsteps were more like stomps, and her jaw kept clenching and unclenching. She walked next to Haether while Whelan and I were a step behind. Always good to leave a little space between yourself and an angry woman.

"She is so damn smug," Lilly bit off as we left class. "Not to mention full of shit. She's really enticing people with *immortality* as if such a thing were even possible! And notice how quickly she swept under the rug the side-effects of that supposed resurrection? The poor guy probably tried to eat her brains or something, but no! He moved on his own and made his own decisions, so *clearly,* he was fine. Ugh," she let out a frustrated groan while the rest of us allowed her to talk herself out. Whelan rolled his eyes after a while but didn't speak out.

"I must agree with you," Haether said, to Lilly's surprise. "That woman was *oddly* vague about her greatest achievement. She never did mention how long the man managed to survive, or quite how lucid he actually was. It reeks of a story whose negative details were left out." Lilly nodded as if that were exactly what she was thinking as well.

Then they both shot glances backwards. I threw up my hands, "Oh, don't worry. It's not like I'm thinking about pushing Whelan out a window just to get some practice in." He shot me a look, so I added, "What? I said I *wasn't* about to do that. I might like to learn to dispel a necromancer's control but wouldn't go any further than that." Lilly's nod told me that was good enough.

Whelan, however, cringed through his answer. "Alright, look. I just don't think we should completely rule it out. Yet! Sure, she left out some details, but we can't just go jumping to conclusions and decide that she left out anything incriminating." He snapped his fingers suddenly, "I know! You guys are always at the library, anyway, see if they have any records on Deepwater's resurrection. If it was really that groundbreaking, then you can bet your collective asses that someone wrote a book about it."

While Lilly and Haether nodded and gave that some thought, I took an opportunity during out lull in conversation. "What, er, *was* she, anyway? I mean I've seen elementals, but not purple ones."

Whelan shot me an incredulous look and burst out laughing. "Really, man? I thought Lilly was from the middle of nowhere, but you must have been raised in a damn cave. Oh, don't look at me like that, you ask almost as many questions as he does! Do *you* know what she was, smarty pants?"

Lilly glared back at him. "As a matter of fact, I do. I'd never seen a Fae until I got here, but I can certainly recognize that purple skin anywhere."

"Maybe you're not as bad as I thought," he quipped. "You, on the other hand," he turned to me and gave me a sarcastic pat on the back. "are hopeless. You ever see orange or purple tinted skin, they're Fae. Or that battle dress she was wearing, though those are becoming popular among all kinds of people these days. Fae aren't exactly common, but they're around."

"Why's that?"

He shot me another look and sighed. "Well, I guess if you didn't even know about them, you wouldn't know that."

Haether spoke up as Whelan took his time insulting me. "They're from the Eastern continent, for one thing, and persecuted for another. They're the only race that is inherently magical. They don't need any Gods or sources to use magic, they each come with their own, albeit small. So, for probably thousands of years, they've been seen as a threat by the other races. In some cases, they were, and are to this day, enslaved."

"Well, shit."

"Shit, indeed." Haether added. "Furthermore, even the Gods hate them. For the most part, anyway. Since they don't need the Gods' power, they don't worship them as the rest of us do. As you can imagine, Gods don't like that." Whelan chuckled and Lilly shook her head regretfully.

"Now, this one knows what she's talking about," Whelan chuckled, jabbing a thumb toward Haether. "Why'd you link up with us, then?" He joked.

"Lilly and Jake happen to be the only students I found at the library as often as myself." Then she shot him a sarcastic glare, "You, I wasn't aware of."

"Ouch. But fair enough. See, I've-"

"Been given insider information that'll help him basically cheat his way through the exam," I butted in, getting a laugh out of Lilly and Haether.

"I'd rather describe it as being well-prepared," he corrected, then jabbed me with an elbow. "Speaking of which, my friends wouldn't say much. Apparently, the test isn't always the same. There's a written portion and a combat portion, but the rest of the details are always changing. Even if the punishment wasn't so severe, they wouldn't have much information to share anyway," he shrugged.

"Combat, huh?" Lilly groaned. Haether only glanced back for a moment but she didn't look any happier about it.

"Yup. They're not joking when they say not all students survive this phase."

The girls shared another anxious glance, so I pushed myself between them. "That's exactly why we need to keep spending so much time at the library," I said, ignoring Whelan as I left his pessimistic ass behind. He was funny, and an alright dude, but not helping. "You said it yourself, Haether, most of the other students aren't putting in as much time as we are. That's exactly what will give us the edge we need."

She nodded quickly, but the tension wasn't gone from her face. Lilly was much the same. And as we reached the library,

Whelan broke off as usual as he started talking to himself about what the dining square was serving today.

The rest of the day was quiet, but no less tense, as the girls mostly kept to themselves. I made it through some of *Lost Artifacts of Old Tris,* and as fascinating as it was to read about the fallen nation, my interest was dampened by the girls' attitudes.

It may have only been the start of the second week, but the pressure was slowly getting to us all. And on top of that, I had a job to do for The fucking Lady by the end of the week.

We'd make it through the exams, I was sure. Lilly and Haether, though, grew more anxious by the day. Somehow, I would help them. The two beautiful women just entered my life, and I wasn't about to watch them die.

I just didn't know what I could do to stop it.

20

PROFESSOR DORIAH LOOKED OUT OVER US WITH A HINT OF what I thought was pity as she began the next day's class. "Now that we've covered the fundamentals, we'll be moving on to another unit. As I stated before, each week will cover a different topic.

"This week will be Magical Defense. Of course, depending on what school you choose when the month is over, you will be entering years of training during which you will become an expert. But for now, we do require a certain general level of aptitude from our students. Even if you do not plan on facing combat, you can never guarantee that it will not seek you out. Whether as a soldier, or a civilian, you will need to know how to defend yourselves. And if you don't, then it will look bad on all of us who hail from Aether Academy.

"I know you must all be itching to train or duel, but I encourage you to hold off for just a bit longer. I'll be teaching you the most basic forms of protection that will be utterly invaluable in the days to come," she paused and glanced around the room ominously.

Sounded like Whelan was right about combat being a part of the exam, not that it was much of a surprise. I, for one, was pretty psyched. After a week of plain, if still interesting, lectures, we would finally be getting to the actual *use* of magic, instead of just discussing what it was or how it worked.

After a few more vague warnings, Doriah spent some time talking about one's greatest defense, if it were available. And that was running away, according to her.

"The only fight you can always win is the one you avoid. Don't put yourself at unnecessary risk," she had said in a tired voice. If she'd been teaching here for as long as it seemed, then I was sure she had seen a lot of stupid mistakes and students killed before their time.

But, given that the school was the one putting us all at unnecessary risk, it seemed a bit unfair. It wasn't like the exam was something we could just run away from. I didn't have much time to dwell on that though, as she finally got to the good part.

Bidding us all to watch closely, she siphoned a bit of power from Pholl and held a hand out in front of her. She moved it in a circular motion and spoke, "Now, as I create a shield of air, what I'm doing with my hand isn't strictly necessary. I could stand still and do just the same thing, but perception is of utter importance. This motion *feels* right to me. It *seems* like it should help me create the shield, and so it helps my mind form an idea of what I am trying to do. In turn, that improved mental image makes the shield more effective.

"In time, through repetition and training, you should all gain the ability to see magical energies in use, but for now just try to focus on the air in front of my hand. Not every mind sees it in the same color, but the air that I am touching should be tinted. Someone like Headmaster Theid would see the shield as clearly as any a soldier carries. The shield is the focus of today's class, but the ability to see magic in use is arguably as important to learn. You cannot avoid a trap that you don't even know is there."

She kept weaving in bits of wisdom like that as she showed us multiple ways of shielding ourselves. Each time, she asked us to focus on the air in front of her, but I was hesitant. The last few times I tried too hard to focus on something obscure, like air itself, my Truevision ended up zooming through what I could only assume was the end of the universe. Still, since I wasn't seeing any colors in her shield of air, I knew I had to practice. It would be good to get the strange power under control, anyway.

Professor Doriah stopped and moved on to a shield of Earth next, as Air and Earth are the two elements most readily available to us, she explained. She held her hands out in front of her at waist height, then planted her feet and suddenly jerked her hands upward. A wall of dirt half a foot thick rose and quickly towered over her.

As I focused on it and felt the vibration in my eyes that always preceded my strange power, I tried to fight it. It must have looked ridiculous, but luckily everyone was paying more attention to the lesson. I squinted hard and tried to focus on the space between myself and Doriah's wall of Earth while slowly moving the focal point of my gaze closer to the wall. The vibrations slowed and as I looked at the dirt, I felt myself push through layers of soil and saw within.

I let out a soft, surprised breath at finally having some semblance of control over it... and lost the aforementioned control immediately.

My vision pushed through the dirt and kept going as I gripped the armrest of my chair tightly to avoid falling forward. I was rewarded with a vision that passed through the Earth itself. I was looking down from the top of the amphitheater, after all. The first object in my line of sight was the ground.

I saw dirt and darkness, until it suddenly burst alight as I reached the Earth's molten core. Much as I tried to shut my eyes against the brightness, nothing helped. It was like staring into the sun but thankfully only lasted a few moments before my vision was plunged back into darkness. Just as I pushed through the other side and caught a glimpse of nothing but void, my vision snapped back through the layers it just showed me and was normal again.

By the time it was over, my eyes were aching, and I was breathing heavily. Lilly tapped my right hand and quirked an eyebrow at me. I was gripping the armrest so hard that my knuckles were white and when I let go, my fingers were stiff. She looked at me a few moments longer before turning back to our professor, but I could tell I was going to be getting some questions later.

It might have been nice to confide in someone, but I didn't know how to explain the strange power without also going into a lot more details that I wasn't ready to share.

I was from another world.

I was technically a Shadow. Not even technically. Literally. Especially now that I was planning on going through with the job The Lady gave me. Somehow, I would need to steal one of those blue orbs.

And all of that information was tied to the power I continued to keep secret.

Professor Doriah swept a hand down and her wall of dirt returned to the Earth. "Air and Earth are all around us. Beneath our feet. At our very fingertips. Water is as well, just not in the same way. While we can control the air around us directly, if we wish to use water, we must extract it from the atmosphere."

She glanced in my direction and took on a derisive tone.

"That's just a fancy word for air. Water, in the form of vapor, is all around us. You can collect it by pushing your magical will into the air around you and visualizing the water within gathering together. Start with that, practice, and soon you will be able to do it much more quickly."

As she went through her explanation, she held a hand in front of herself, palm up, and moved it in a small circle, while focusing on the air above it. Slowly, a globe of water grew about a foot above her hand until it was about the size of her head.

"Now that I have the water, there are innumerable applications, but for now I will focus on just one. A shield. Just like before with air and earth." She swept her hand down suddenly and it looked like the water splashed against an invisible wall, then froze in place. "Now, there are times when this sort of shield is ideal, but you'll notice that it involves much more work than air. Instead of simply commanding the air to hold its position, you must extract the water, shape it to your will, and expel its heat. All of this requires magical energy. The result is far less efficient, as you can see."

Professor Doriah stepped out of the tiled floor, picked up a small rock, then returned and tossed it against her ice wall. Despite putting almost no force behind it, the wall shattered. She pointed to the empty air with one hand. "See that? Walls of earth or air would stop projectiles far more easily, but ice or water could save you from other things. For example," she smirked and then drove one hand upward, until her palm was pointed above her head.

Flames jutted out from her hand in a cone toward the sky as some students gasped. My eyes definitely bulged, and my heartrate picked up with excitement. It might take some practice, but I could do that too! Everything she was showing us was actually possible, it was still hard to believe that I wasn't just watching illusions, but actual *magic*.

The professor then closed her hand into a fist and the flames formed a shield. She moved her hand down and the bulwark of flames followed her motion. "Fire does not exist all around us, but heat does. And that's all you need. I take heat from the atmosphere and concentrate it into fire but do keep in mind that you can freeze yourself to death if you rob the air of all its warmth.

"This sort of shield, much like that of ice or water, is not full in an ice a shield, that is. The rock would pass through this more easily than even the ice, but a *man* could not. Watch closely," she focused on the flames as they roared to life. What was a wall of orange and deep red grew brighter and brighter until it was a pure white that I needed to shield my eyes against.

"A white-hot barrier will stop anything living. Hot enough, and even arrows will turn to ash as they pass through. But stop something like a rock or boulder with this sort of shield and you'll find that the molten rock that reaches you will be far deadlier."

Her hand fell away, and the fire winked out. "As you can see, the elements all have their own unique uses. This is as true for offense as it is defense, but you will learn more about that next week."

"FINALLY GETTING GOOD, HUH?" WHELAN CLAPPED ME ON the shoulder as we left class. I couldn't do anything but nod, still in awe of what I'd seen, and that was pretty basic. I couldn't even imagine what the upperclassmen dealt with in their classes.

Whelan whirled a hand in front of him and then pushed. A little column of air flew toward Haether and sent her perfectly straight, long hair, flying in a thousand different directions.

The blonde girl let out a yelp as she fought against the column of wind, clutching her dark blue hat with one hand and a knapsack that rested on her hip with the other. After it passed, Haether collected her mess of disloyal strands and tucked as many as possible behind her ears.

Then her cold stare turned Whelan's laughter into cringing silence. He slowly settled down and suddenly coughed.

"At some point, just when you think everything is going right for you. I'll get you back for that."

Whelan took a nervous gulp and faked a laugh. Then as soon as Haether turned back around, he leaned in to my ear. "You wouldn't let her kill me, right?"

"I'm not sure I could stop her," I quipped and then burst out laughing as my friend paled. Haether shot me a smirk as Whelan walked away, leaving us to our studies as he usually did.

As we walked into the library, I noticed a girl that I had seen before, but only just realized what I was looking at. Her orange-tinted skin and what was apparently called a battle dress marked her as Fae. Short black hair barely reached her ears, and she definitely had a tom-boy kind of look going on. She was barely over five feet and moved with a smooth grace.

The girl managed to close the distance between us before I even realized what was happening, and cut me off from Lilly and Haether, who hadn't even noticed.

"Like what you see? I can hold still for a while if you'd like to commission a painting. It'd last longer," she leaned in and squinted sarcastically. The short, orange girl planted her hands on her hips as she ran her eyes down my body, measuring me up. "Aren't you the guy that fought with Brock last week?"

Caught off guard, I didn't have time to make up an excuse.

"Sorry, I've never seen a... one of your kind before. But yeah, that was me."

She crossed her arms and met my eyes. "Well, now you have." Then one of her hands snaked out and ran up my inner thigh. It was such a shock that I jumped, and the girl's laughter rang out.

Then she pushed by me. She stopped for a second and turned back to say, "You're too easy, Bumpkin. There's a big world out there full of people much more exotic than myself who would do things much more... interesting," she smirked, "to see people like you jump and squeal like that." Then she turned on her heels and started walking out.

I called after her, "I did *not* squeal!" But that just made her laugh.

She was a thin little thing, and confusing, but *damn*. I watched the way her dress clung to the soft curves of her ass until she was out of sight.

Then I ran a sobering hand across my face. Girls could wait. It was my first day on the job and I had a lot to learn.

❦ 2 1 ❦

THUVIEN WAS WAITING FOR ME BY THE INFORMATION DESK, having seen everything that just happened. He held on to a wide grin and tapped the back of his hand against my chest as I reached him. "I see you've met Pixie. She's an interesting one. Probably as driven and intelligent as any this academy has ever seen. Shame she only cares about one thing."

I quirked an eyebrow at him. "And what is that?"

After a second, he shook his head. "You'll have to ask her that yourself. Said too much already, I have. Anyway, I think you've met Ruthie over here," he indicated the disorganized woman who managed the information desk.

We'd been introduced briefly during one of the many times I'd approached the desk for help. She was shuffling through some papers and mumbling to herself until Thuvien cleared his throat and got her attention. Her eyes snapped up toward him and squinted. "They're on your head, Ruth," he said in a tired voice.

The woman reached up and tapped a pair of glasses, then laughed at herself and put them on. "Ah! Oh, of course they were. Nasty little buggers, always getting away from me. Did you need help finding something?" She directed the question at me.

"No, no, he's the new Initiate I told you about. Starting today?"

"Oh! Yes, yes. I didn't know it was you, Jake. Good to see that some of our newer students still value this old place. Is that girl, Lilly, going to be joining you? Such a sweet kid "

"No, just me. I might be able to convince her to help out though, once the exams are over."

"Well, we can always use an extra pair of hands," she said with a smile, then nodded to Thuvien and returned to her work.

"Whenever you can't find me, you just go see Ruthie. She's the second-in-command around here but is probably more important to the library's daily operation than I am." She blushed a deep red at that but didn't look up from her mess of papers. "She'll keep you busy, should you finish your work. Come on," he waved for me to follow and I fell in beside him.

"For now, you'll be doing the grunt work. It's not the most entertaining, but we've all been there. Even I spent some time restocking these bookcases. I can't even tell you how many paper cuts I've had over the years."

A sudden realization dawned on me. "You mean, you can't do this with magic?"

"Oh, you could! Certainly. If you don't care about the books, which of course isn't the case. Wrapping the books in air is easy enough, but it's also far more abrasive that just your hands. The covers degrade much more quickly, pages fray, the binding loosens. Reduces the lifespan of the book, to put it simply. So no, we do all the handling by, well, hand."

He pointed to a room in the corner of the building, just to the right of the entrance. Once he was sure I noticed the room he was indicating, he started leading me upstairs. "Over there will be your main hub. There's a slot to return books just on the other side of the wall that you may have noticed. Whenever you come in, you'll head over there, grab a cart, load it up, and go. Over time you'll get better at knowing which books to grab together to make it easier on yourself, so, for now, you'll just be tagging along with one of our aides." I nodded along and as we stepped out of the stairway, into the second floor, Thuvien froze. He scanned the floor, clicking his tongue in thought, until he finally found what he was looking for. "And here she is now."

We stepped around a bookcase and Filo's bright red hair popped out immediately. She gave Thuvien a surprisingly genuine, not to mention beautiful, smile, that faltered for just a second when she saw me. "So, you decided to take him on, after all, huh?"

"That's right," he chuckled. "It's like you said, why turn down a pair of hands just because they might not be here for very long. Besides, I think this one might have it in him to pass the exam. Should be an interesting show, anyway."

"We'll see."

"Right, well, you take good care of him. Don't let him slack off too much or get distracted by his lady friends on the fourth floor."

Filo's eyes tightened at that. "Oh, don't you worry about that," her voice lowered, "I'll make good use of him."

As soon as the Head Librarian was out of sight, Filo's veneer of friendliness disappeared. All warmth left her voice. "Well, there you go. You're welcome. There's not a whole lot to explain, just put books away. Each section is organized in alphabetical order, by author, then title. And everything on the cart is from this section, so knock yourself out."

"Nice to see you too," I chirped. Filo just snorted and grabbed a couple books from the cart. I did the same and started scanning the shelves. "You don't have to be so cold, you know. We *are* on the same side, after all." Her jaw clenched, but she otherwise showed no reaction.

After finding a few books' homes and grabbing more, I tried again. "Did you ever figure out a way I could repay you?"

She let out a huff and rounded on me. Her purple eyes rolled, and her red hair bounced lightly as she shook her head. "First of all. *Shut. Up.*" Then she took a deep breath and lowered her voice. "How you were allowed to join us without having it drilled into your *dumb* head that you need to keep it a secret, I'll never know."

I walked to either end of the alley between bookcases and glanced around. Filo stopped working and watched until I returned. For her sake, I whispered. "There's no one close enough to overhear, even if we didn't bother lowering our voices. It's fine, Filo. You're safe. These books won't betray you. I won't sell you out. Hell, even if you told most of the Initiates that you were Vethris himself, they'd all be too concerned with the exam to care."

"Well, you may not take this seriously." Then she stepped so close to me that her boobs brushed against my chest. Just like in the janitor's closet last week. I didn't budge. "But *some of us* know people who screwed up. And do you know what happened to them? Seriously, do you? Because they disappeared and I never saw them again. My own brothers," she caught herself and pursed her lips. Her purple eyes scoured my face and she let out a huff, then went back to work.

"I'm sorry. I didn't know."

"Of course, you didn't."

I stepped up next to her and pretended to be looking through the shelves. "Well, look, I wasn't just teasing you when I offered to help. And it's not just because I owe you." She glanced over at me and, for the first time, I didn't see any anger. "I want to help. Just let me know what I can do for you. You're not the only one struggling with this secret. It's actually kind of nice talking to someone who already knows."

Filo blinked at me a few times, then nodded and looked away. "It's just... My task isn't quite as simple as yours."

She thought stealing a priceless book from the Head Librarian's office in a secret, secure basement that no Initiate was even supposed to know about was a simple task? The hair on the back of my neck stood up as I asked, "What is it?"

Her eyes flicked over to me and she was silent for a minute. Clearly thinking it through. Finally, she shook her head. "I just can't risk it." I waited for her to add something, anything, but she stayed silent.

After a little while, I wanted to give her some time to calm down, I spoke up again as we both grabbed from the cart at the same time. "Hey, something I've been wondering. How do people even get to the basement? The only stairs I've noticed lead up here."

Filo snorted, "That's because they don't use stairs. You know the janitor's closets? Like the one I pulled you into? If you have an orb with you and just think about which floor you want to go to, when you open one of those doors it'll lead there." After a minute, she added, "How're you gonna do it? Steal an orb, I mean."

I flashed her a smile. "I was actually hoping you might help me out with that."

Despite the flat look, the groan that accompanied it, and an insult or two during my explanation, Filo agreed. *Maybe she doesn't hate me as much as I thought.*

Once we'd finished with the cart, we headed back downstairs. While Filo grabbed another load of books, I approached the information desk to put my plan to action.

The disheveled Ruthie looked back at me with a smile. "How are you enjoying your first day? Exciting, isn't it? Seeing what the library is like behind the scenes," she was practically bubbling.

"Uh, yeah. I'm definitely learning a lot. It's a shame how many of these books I'll never actually get a chance to read."

"Oh, I know! I think about that all the time. If only I were an elf and had their lifespan. Then I wouldn't be rushing around all the time, trying to get everything done at once!" She let out a soft sigh and for a moment reminded me of my grandmother. The kindly woman shook her head, "So what's up? Did you run out of work, becau-"

"No!" I interrupted her before she could get distracted, "I actually wanted to ask you something. I was waiting for Filo to get back and I found this book wedged between some cushions," I held up an old tome whose binding was almost entirely ripped off. I felt terrible about doing that to an antique, but it was the only way. I felt even worse at the horrified look on the woman's face, but I didn't let it enter my voice. "I thought you might like to repair it before I actually put it back."

"Ugh, I just can't believe how little value some people place in knowledge." She gingerly took the torn book from my hands, "Yes, thank you for bringing this to me. Actually... yes, come with me. I'll show you how to use our rebinding tool. This one looks to be in good enough condition to be repaired completely, so it's the perfect opportunity."

A minute later we stepped into a small room that mostly held filing cabinets and cupboards, but also a cart filled with damaged books. Ruthie clicked her tongue upon seeing it. "I see Filo has been slack with her duties. It's a good thing you joined us. Anyway, to the reason I brought you here," she placed the book in the center of a flat-topped wooden podium against the wall opposite the door.

Then she shot me a grin, "Octavio, er... Head Librarian Thuvien came up with this little gadget himself. Now, I don't want to tell you how many years have passed since I was a student here, so I'll just say that it's enough time for the curriculum to have changed substantially. I'm not sure whether they've taught you about Imitations, yet..."

When I furrowed my brow, she continued. "I suspected not. Well, I'm sure you have used them, knowingly or not. Think of the floating lights or the Auto-quill all the kids use these days. You can think of them as a specific feat of magic captured so that it may be reproduced. Outside of the simplest applications, like those lights, they are extremely difficult to make.

"This here," she tapped the podium, "happens to be the only one of its kind. I call it the Invisible Binder," she grinned, proud of the name. Then it was replaced with a grimace. "Thuvien isn't a fan, he prefers to call it the Repair Station, or the Rebinding Tool, but he never did have a flare for the creative. All you need to do is place a damaged book on the platform, siphon a bit of power, and feed it into the Imitation. The *Invisible Binder*," she added with a wink.

As she did so, the book slowly rose into the air. The torn pages mended themselves and a nearby drawer opened on its own.

The word, "Amazing," leaked past my lips as what could only have been glue flowed out in a thin stream and lathered the inside of the book's binding before it pressed back into place. No more than a minute could have passed by the time Ruthie was taking the book back into her hand.

"And there we are. Good as, well, not new, but as good as it was this morning. In the future, as you find these books, you can just keep them with you until the end of the day and bring them to this room all at once. At some point, I'll assign you in here. But for now, I'm sure we both have work to do, so..." she held out a hand toward the exit and with the other one, gave the book back to me.

"Right. Thank you," I glanced behind myself and saw Filo in position. I shot her a wink, and she just rolled her eyes. *Good enough*.

I opened the door and backed out of the room as if I was about to ask Ruth another question, but just as I did so, Filo ran into me with the cart of books.

Harder than she really needed to, I might add. It rammed into my right ankle and hip, crushing me against the door-frame and then into Ruthie. We both went tumbling to the floor in a mess of limbs and grunts.

"Oh, *sugar*," she uttered the word like a curse while I apologized profusely and climbed off her.

Filo stuck her head in, "Jake? Oh Ruthie, what did he do to you?" she called out and grimaced at me as she pushed me aside to help up the older librarian.

"What did *I* do? You ran into me with a load of books!"

"Well, the least you could have done is fallen in another direction," Filo shot back.

"Come now, you two. No damage done," she said, checking out the recently repaired book before even thinking of herself. "It was an honest mistake. But do be more careful to watch where you're going from now on. Both of you," she added and trotted back over to her station.

With one hand rubbing the injured hip, trying to keep my weight on my left side because my right ankle was screaming, I glared at Filo. "You really had to hit me that hard?"

She grinned, as happy as I'd ever seen her. "Yup. Oh, and don't worry about paying me back for this one. I was glad to help. Did it work?"

"Yeah, I bet you were," I grumbled, reaching into my pocket. I pulled out a small earring, from which hung a light blue orb and struggled to put on a smile. "But yes, it worked perfectly."

22

I SPENT THE REST OF THAT NIGHT PLANNING OUT EXACTLY what I would do.

Filo didn't know where Thuvien's office would be, given that she'd only been as low as the first sub-floor. Since I only had a couple days left, I had to run with the plan I had and hope it would be enough.

The entire following day, I couldn't focus. I kept running through scenarios of what might happen. For all I knew, the orbs knew who they belonged to, and I'd be setting off some silent alarm by even stepping through the basement door-portal. Or maybe the place was guarded by ghosts or monsters or some shit I couldn't even imagine.

I barely paid attention in class, could hardly study afterwards, and didn't even pay much attention to what Lilly and Haether talked about. They were worried about the exam, but my life would end much sooner if I failed to steal that book.

As soon as I stepped into the library, Ruthie's face killed me. She was in tears at her desk, struggling to keep herself together, shuffling through papers and folders or rushing around the first floor in what I could only assume was an attempt to retrace her steps.

I spotted Thuvien, who shook his head sadly as he watched the woman panic and I avoided them both as if my life depended on it.

Which, in a way, it did.

But I still felt like shit. The woman's only priority in life was this library, and from what I had heard, she did a great job. And now she thought that she had lost her most important possession, one entrusted to her by Thuvien himself, whom she practically worshipped.

All because of me.

But I had to bite that down. If I didn't steal it, I'd be dead soon. It was my only option.

When the library was closing down, I followed Filo into the book returns room as she put the cart back and closed up. She handed me a spare key to let myself out and then lock myself in after the job was done.

"Good luck," she muttered when she pushed the cart into just the right place to block view of me from outside the room. And she actually meant it, from what I could tell.

Warmed by some of the first nice words Filo had ever said to me, I laid on the floor and waited. For hours.

Any time I considered slinking out of the room, anxiety would spike through my chest and encourage me to wait just a little bit longer, despite it being a long time since I'd seen or heard anyone. Eventually, I just had to do it.

As quietly as possible, I unlocked the door and stepped out into an eerily dark and silent library. I froze and even tried to breathe quietly as I scanned the floor one last time. It was empty. I stalked toward the janitor's closet.

I took a deep breath, put my hand on the doorknob and thought of the third sub-floor. Then pulled.

Instead of a dark closet filled with cleaning supplies, the

room I stepped into was dimly lit by blue slats of light on the walls. To either side was a hallway that ended in darkness. As I took my first steps, choosing the right side arbitrarily, I braced myself against the likely alarm or motion-activated lights.

When nothing happened, I wasn't relieved in the slightest. It just had me thinking that the trap, or alarm, or guardians, were always around the next corner. Even after a few minutes of nothing, I couldn't fight down that feeling, but eventually I found Thuvien's office.

And I passed more than a few interestingly named rooms in the meantime. As much as I wanted to know what the Starlight Project was, or the Gray Man Protocol, I wasn't willing to waste any time.

I muttered an aimless prayer, not sure whether I should be thanking Pholl or Vethris, when the office door opened easily. The dark room looked like a principal's office. A large desk near the back wall, bookcases on one side and cabinets on the other, and even a potted plant by the door. What really drew my eye, though, was the comfortable armchair in one corner of the room and the small table in front of it.

The table held several books, half of them left open. They were clearly ancient. As I touched one, the pages were surprisingly brittle and cracked under my fingers, so I set it back down as carefully as possible.

I siphoned a bit of power and forced heat to collect into a single point. A small globe of white light appeared over the table, just as I'd imagined, and a brief jolt of excitement ran though me.

I can bend reality to my will. Sure, only in minor ways for now, but I'll only keep getting better.

As I looked for the *Iterad Virtutem*, it became clear that the rest of the books that sprawled over the table were just as valuable. Whatever The Lady wanted out of this book, others might want out of the rest of them. Or they could contain the kind of information that even a higher servant of Vethris would be willing to kill for...

Well, it was not like I could fit them all in my pockets anyway, so started checking them out. Most were actual books, if clearly old, but there were even a few scrolls and one thick stack of papers that was clipped together at one corner. Oddly enough, that haphazardly thrown together stack was the *Iterad Volume*. Clearly a copy, while some of the other might have been originals. I discounted any that were too fragile to take with me and when I read the remaining titles, the choice was clear.

The Multiverse and its Implications.

Another anonymous tome, but the title drew me in immediately. All along, I wasn't sure whether these people even knew about my world, but these few words changed everything. As I picked it up, I realized something else.

If my world and this one coexisted, then how many *others* were there? It did say the multiverse, not the two universes, after all. But that thought would have to wait for later.

I tucked the two books under my arm and stalked out of the room, more desperate to get out of there than anything else.

That's when I heard voices.

They were angry and getting closer. Around a corner, I saw a light growing brighter as they approached, and panicked.

"She is, she really is. But I just don't know anymore. It seems like she's misplacing more and more important things more and more often. And now look at what happened! Our lower floors infiltrated for the first time in twenty years!"

Thuvien.

This place was basically his kingdom, of course he would know if some shady shit was going down! He wasn't alone, either, though I didn't recognize the voice. I was too busy looking for a way out. As they rounded the corner, I desperately reached for the closest door that wasn't his office and threw myself inside as quietly as possible.

It was a janitor's closet.

As I brushed aside a broom to make space, I cursed myself for an idiot. That was my way out! All I had to do was think of the first floor and I would have been there by now. But no! The damn Head Librarian had to come at the worst possible time.

I held my breath and listened with every fiber of my being. A door opened and closed. Seconds later, it opened and slammed shut.

"Where is it," he growled.

"They couldn't have gone far," a woman's voice said. "We can still catch them."

Their footsteps grew louder until they stood just outside the door. My heart stopped and felt like ice. My lungs burned from holding my breath for too long, but I dared not make a sound. Clutching to the two stolen books, I gritted my teeth and prayed that they would just move on.

But then I heard the doorknob turn, saw the door open, and looked right into Thuvien's furious eyes.

"Let's go," he said to the woman behind him, then stepped into the room.

And vanished.

I saw the woman just as she crossed the threshold but had no idea who it was. She was dressed like an elemental, but I couldn't see any further detail than that. Then she vanished as well, and I took the deepest breath of my life.

I'd never felt so relieved or been so close to shitting my pants. *They didn't see me. All they saw was whatever floor they were going to.* For a minute, I couldn't stop laughing. I thought I was a goner! But instead, I held two of the most obscure texts I'd ever known and was itching to get back to my room so I could go through the *Iterad Virtutem* before The Lady returned Friday night.

But first, I let an hour pass. Or something like that, it was dark, and I had literally nothing to do but wait. When I was finally satisfied, I cracked open the door and stepped out. Then turned right back around and made for the first floor.

As soon as I stepped through, I realized I wasn't alone. But it wasn't Thuvien. Whoever it was, didn't want to be seen. I only caught a rush of movement from the corner of my eye and by the time I turned, it was gone.

As curious as I was about who else would be sneaking around the library at that hour, and why, I couldn't risk it. Didn't want to risk it. It would have been stupid. But then again...

Fuck. I need to know.

But as I rounded the corner, a ball of flame was already heading in my direction. I threw myself out of the way, back in the direction I came. The heat hit me as it passed by and crashed into a bookcase with a loud explosion.

The bookcase was wide and long, weighed down by hundreds, if not thousands of books, but it toppled as easily as a house of cards. The old paper caught fire immediately.

I knew I couldn't have been the only one who heard it, but would Thuvien get there in time? Or would the whole place be up in smoke by the time I was hiding under a table?

Fuck. Fuck. Fuck.

All I wanted to do was steal a tome of ancient knowledge without getting killed or caught in the process, was that too much to ask?

Thinking about the lessons earlier that week, I drew from Pholl's power and turned all my attention to the growing flames. I tried to simply put them out, pushing the magic into them, but nothing happened. I envisioned the process of pulling water out of the air and actually managed a trickle, but it died in the face of the inferno.

Then I remembered what my professor did to *create* fire. It was just gathering heat. Simple as that. So, I did the opposite. I drew as much power as I could and threw it into the flames, then spread it out as much as possible. The entire room must have risen ten degrees, but the flames disappeared, their heat dissipated entirely.

Feeling as tired as if I'd ran a marathon, I made my walk over to the book returns room as quickly as possible and locked myself in.

Then I crawled beneath a table and didn't move. Didn't sleep. Didn't even think. I just listened toward the door.

And cursed myself for being dumb enough to go along with this.

23

"WHAT THE ABSOLUTE FUCK DID YOU DO LAST NIGHT?" THE pure anger in Filo's voice was a contrast to the way she calmly closed the door.

"You're late, you know," I quipped, "And it wasn't me."

"Yeah, well, when the library almost goes up in flames, it kind of throws off my schedule. Thuvien's pissed. Hell, everyone is! Except Ruthie, she's just a mess. And if it wasn't you, then who? Why would anyone even do that?"

"First," I said, holding up a finger but keeping my exhausted eyes closed, "I don't know. Didn't get a good look at 'em. Second, well, they were trying to stop me from following them. To be fair, it worked. I was too caught up putting out the fire to see where they went and by the time it was out, I was just desperate to get back in here."

Filo put her hands on her hips and looked down at me, inspected me, weighed my words. Then, finally, she nodded.

"I believe you. For now. I know you're an idiot and all, but even you wouldn't risk getting caught like that. Look, the library is closed for now, so I'm going to need to sneak you out when no one's looking. But right now? Everyone on fucking campus is looking. So, sit tight."

Filo glanced behind herself, through the windows next to the door. "Thuvien is furious. Ruthie is beside herself. Ugh. What a mess." Then she grabbed the book cart and whispered, "See you soon."

By the time the door was shut and locked, I was asleep.

SOME TIME LATER, THE OPENING DOOR WOKE ME UP AGAIN.

I rolled over and cracked my head against the leg of the table I was laying under. While rubbing it, I croaked, "I really hope that's you, Filo."

She sighed and said, "It is. Sadly, I'm about as caught up in this as you are. You realize you owe me, like, half a dozen favors by now?"

"Yes, and you refused to cash in on 'em so far."

"Well, it's not my fault you're useless."

I shot her a glare and pulled the *Iterad Virtutem* out from behind my cloak. "I think The Lady would disagree. Unless you actually finished that job you don't feel like telling me about?" When she didn't answer, only deepened her frown, I pursed my lips and nodded. "That's what I thought. Besides, you could always ask *Brock*. Seemed like you two got along, well, terribly in that cavern, but something tells me you aren't the type to work well with others."

Filo glared at me for a minute. I kept waiting for her to say something, and raising my eyebrows every few seconds, but then I just felt awkward as she stared me down.

Then she shook her head and sighed. She pushed by and started loading up the empty cart. "Library's open now, by the way. Leave whenever you want."

But as I watched her from behind, something about her

made me feel like I should stay. Maybe it was the sad tone in her voice, or something about her posture, but as much as I wanted to get out of there and devour the *Iterad Virtutem* before The Lady returned for it, I suddenly found that I couldn't.

Instead, I stepped up next to her and started loading the cart too. Filo's purple eyes glanced over at me, but she took her time responding. "You have class today, you know."

"I do." I nodded but kept grabbing books. "She's covering magical defense this week and, considering the night I had, I think I've learned enough."

Filo snorted. "Well, the least you could do is get rid of that cloak."

"What do you mean?"

She reached behind me and pulled some of the fabric over so that I could see it. It was charred and torn in several places. She didn't say anything, didn't need to.

"Well, shit. I guess that fireball came closer than I thought." *Maybe I do need those defense classes after all.* But something about Filo was different today. The anger that always seemed ready to boil over had a particular sadness to it, now.

Or maybe it always did, and I just didn't notice.

Now that I thought about it, I didn't think I'd ever seen Filo anything but alone. Most of that had been at the library, so she was working, but even around campus, she was always walking alone. There were no friends walking with her to the library, no visitors trying to break up the boredom that was her job.

She didn't have anyone. I was always complaining about having no one to open up to about being a Shadow or being lost trying to complete the job The Lady gave me, but at least there were still people that were there for me. Even if I wasn't willing to tell them the truth.

Maybe if Filo wasn't so lonely, she wouldn't try so hard to

push me away. Even though she was silent most of the time, I could tell she appreciated the company.

Filo wasn't lying when she said people were angry. As we rolled the cart through the first floor, I noticed half a dozen librarians shuffling around the ashes of a burnt bookcase. They were trying to recover whatever they could, picking up charred books and flipping through what pages they had left, only to throw them down in frustration more often than not.

Meanwhile, Thuvien stood over them, talking quietly but clearly in anger. His arms were crossed, his face red, head shaking.

And then there was Ruthie. The kind older woman who reminded me of my grandmother had tears rolling down her face as she watched from afar. She kept glancing over at the carnage from her information desk, insisting all along to her nodding apprentices that she had no idea what had happened to her orb and that she would never forgive herself.

Which, of course, made me feel like shit. But what could I do? It's not like I could return the blue orb to her. As Filo said, they would just hire a forensic scryer to figure out who last used it. Then I'd be as good as dead.

I couldn't even go over there and comfort her. Wouldn't be able to trust myself, I knew too much about what happened last night, and too little about what information had already gotten out. All it would take was one little detail I wasn't supposed to be aware of and, again, I'd be as good as dead.

All I could do was look on as if I had no idea what had happened.

The next few hours were among the longest of my life. Tediously grabbing book after book and finding where they belonged, it wasn't exactly distracting. If anything, it just forced me to keep my own mind occupied, else I would die from boredom.

My mind was racing anyway, so it was good to have that time to wind down, even if I was constantly anxious that Thuvien would pop around the corner of the bookcases at any second and ask to speak with me.

All the while, a copy of one of the world's most sought-after ancient tomes, was waiting for me on the first floor. I had until tomorrow night to get through it, so I was sure I had enough time, but not being able to read it yet was killing me.

After agonizing over it all week, and almost getting myself Prince Zuko'd in the process, all I wanted to do was head back to my room, away from all the prying eyes that felt like they knew too much.

But it was hours before I felt safe leaving. Nothing could seem out of the ordinary or I'd be putting myself in danger.

The sun was starting to set as I finally left the library behind. Filo didn't say much, but she smiled a little bit when I said I'd be back on the weekend, so that was enough for me. It was progress, anyway. The feisty redhead had a temper and a penchant for insulting me, but I liked her anyway. Almost as much as Lilly or Haether, which wouldn't make choosing between them any easier.

There I go getting ahead of myself again. As if any of them wanted anything to do with me. As if I'd even survive the next few weeks.

I carried my bundled-up cloak under my left arm and tried to walk at a normal pace back to my dorm, even though I wanted to run. It felt slower than ever. Every statue I passed felt like their gray eyes were staring at me. Through me. Like they knew what had happened and would pass it on, given the chance. It just made my heart beat faster as I willed my legs to match the speed of traffic. *Were people walking slower today?*

When I finally made it back to my dorm, I could have kissed every inch of it. Like getting back on dry land after years of being at sea, I was overjoyed to see the place I had taken for granted.

But almost as soon as the door closed behind me, someone was knocking.

"Hey!" Whelan called out as I opened the door. "I thought I heard someone go into your room. Glad you're alright, but you might not be after tomorrow. Doriah was not happy to see an empty seat among our little group. She didn't say anything, mind you, but she did glance over like a dozen times with a deeper frown each time. Even the girls are annoyed at you, so watch out! That Haether is... a little scary."

Wait til he meets Filo.

"I get Doriah, but why are the girls pissed?" Frankly, I wasn't sure who I should be more afraid of. If her threats were at all accurate, I had an afternoon up to my nose in concrete to look forward to. But if I couldn't rely on Lilly and Haether's help over the next few weeks, I would be in even worse shape than that.

Whelan shrugged, "They just said some stuff about how if skipping class was even an option, then you aren't taking this as seriously as they thought. I tried to stand up for you, mate, but they're a strict bunch, apparently."

"And now I won't be at the library with them today, either." I mumbled, thinking. Then I shook my head, "It's not like they care about you skipping out on all our study sessions. Missing one day isn't so bad."

"Right? I mean, this first month of stuff is more basic than I expected. I haven't even been studying," he chuckled. "I'm sure you'll be fine."

I nodded. "Well, thanks for the heads up."

"Sure thing. And hey, I'm heading down to the Salty Scryer if you wanna join. Gonna have some drinks with those friends I mentioned."

"No thanks, I've got some reading to do." I glanced over at the bundled-up cloak on my bed to make sure the books weren't peeking out. They weren't.

Whelan rolled his eyes. "Jeez. You three. Always reading or studying. You gotta enjoy life sometime! Especially since it might be over soon," he gave me an encouraging, though sarcastic, tap on the arm.

"Thanks for the tip," I shot back. "Oh, and if you die during the exams, I'll be sure to have Deepwater resurrect you. As a zombie, of course. Not that it'd be much of change."

"Yeah, yeah. You have fun with your best friends, Ink and Parchment! I'll just be down at the tavern picking up girls all night. If you need me, maybe try *not needing* me. At least til morning. Might have some visitors in the room tonight, wish me luck!" He called over his shoulder as he left my room and strolled down the hallway.

"Good luck maintaining your self-esteem after getting shot down all night!"

Whelan shook his head and waved a nonchalant hand over his shoulder, but I distinctly heard him chuckling.

Finally. I closed the door, opened the curtains, and settled into my bed with the *Iterad Virtutem*.

24

THE PATH TO POWER.

That was what Iterad Virtutem meant. As for why the writer didn't just title it that, I had no idea. But it was still, easily, the most interesting book I'd read so far. By the time I was too tired to keep going, I had made it about halfway through.

Some chapters were incomplete and the book itself was missing about a third of the original's contents, but it was still more than enough information to be useful.

It all focused on ways of becoming more powerful, as the title implied. Starting with simpler, less potent methods, and growing more of both with every chapter.

The first few detailed simple exercises. Basically meditation. The idea was that you would focus on your source of power, siphon off as much as you can manage, and then slowly release it. Like the breathing exercise from the first day of class. By taking in as much as you can over and over, you would increase how much you could hold at any given time. Just like working out a muscle.

Similarly, you could work with a specific spell over and

over to slowly become more proficient at it. Simple enough. Practice any skill and you'll get better at it.

But then came the juicy stuff.

Some of it I was already aware of. Like seeking out foreign gods and gaining their favor, but it went into further detail. Just like people, Gods varied in power and had their own specialties. It didn't list those specialties out or give ideas toward which Gods were worth seeking out, instead referring the reader to a theologian

While I definitely planned on doing so eventually, I didn't exactly have time to go searching for new sources of power.

There was one option that really caught my interest, however. All it required was a few close friends. *Very close.* As it turned out, people found a way to mimic the connections that humans formed with Gods. It wasn't exactly the same, but similar enough and it certainly sounded powerful.

The result was a bond between every person who took part in the ritual. As the bond strengthened, it let you not only speak into each other's minds, but even fuse your powers together. One person would be able to pull power through the others, basically multiplying their strength by as many people as they bonded with.

All you needed to do was repeat the ritual, and the bond grew stronger.

Oh yeah, that ritual? It was sex.

As excited as I was, as much for the increase in power as for the ritual that it required, I didn't know how to even bring it up without sounding completely full of shit.

Guys had been lying to get into girls' pants, probably since the day pants were invented. 'We'll be able to pool our strengths and read each other's minds,' just sounded as lame an excuse as any. And as much bullshit but given how much importance The Lady put on this old book, I had no doubt that it was accurate.

Then there was the issue of how I was even aware of the ancient ritual, considering that I couldn't tell anyone but Filo about the stolen book. As much as I seemed to be wearing her hatred for me down, I was pretty sure I had a long way to go before she warmed to the idea of hopping into bed with me.

Which left Lilly and Haether as my only options, not that I was complaining.

Lilly was short and sweet, with a fit, tanned body that could have been a swimsuit model in my world. Haether, on the other hand, was more severe and striking. Her more serious mindset put her one pair of glasses away from looking like a sexy teacher or librarian. And as much as she tried to cover it up, she had an amazing body. Both of them did. I'd consider myself beyond lucky if even one of them believed me, never mind both.

I did have a bit of fun with my imagination though, at that idea, just as I was getting ready for bed.

Whatever the case, I still had two weeks to become powerful enough to get through the exams. If I couldn't form the bond with at least one of them, then I'd need to get studying.

And if I could? Well, then we'd need to repeat the ritual, thereby solidifying it, as many times as possible before the month was over.

As many times as possible. I liked the sound of that plan far more.

I WAS *NOT* LOOKING FORWARD TO THAT MORNING'S CLASS. Professor Doriah had already threatened me about arriving late. Not going at all hadn't even been in the conversation, but I knew the punishment would be worse.

The girls were already there by the time Whelan and I

approached the amphitheater. They ignored my "Good morning," as I walked by. I wasn't even able to make it to my seat before the professor called me down to her with a crook of a finger.

Now, I didn't want to lie to Lilly or Haether any more than was necessary. But Doriah? I'd been cooking up that one all night.

I coughed a few times as I got close to her, exaggerating them as much as possible and making my voice sound a bit hoarse. "I'm so sorry I wasn't able to come in yesterday. I was lying in bed all day, switching between sneezing and coughing most of the time. My head and throat are just killing me, I hope I didn't miss too much."

My professor looked surprisingly sympathetic. Given that she was like a thousand years old, I didn't have much hope for tricking her, but it seemed like it worked. "You poor thing. It's a shame. I can't redo an entire day's lecture for one person, so you will have fallen behind a bit. But... I believe what I have planned for today will fix that right up. I'd been planning on taking volunteers from the class, but since you are already up here, you might as well just stay."

She left it at that and walked by me to approach her podium. Then she looked back and waved a hand, indicating for me to step up to the side of the platform and wait. Anxiously. Whatever she had planned, my mood darkened as soon as she opened her mouth. Her voice was altogether too... happy.

"I have a special treat for you all today. I know how tedious these lectures can be. After all, how much can you learn about magic without ever actually using it?" She shot me a grin that could only be described as ominous. My heart sank. "And luckily, we have a volunteer. So, give Jake a hand, because he's going to have a long day ahead of him."

She was *not* exaggerating.

We started with testing out each of the shields she had covered. Doriah asked me to form a shield of air in front of myself and hold it as long as I could. Then she proceeded to harry me with hurricane-level winds, trying to push me around while I tried to protect myself. It didn't take long for her to get through my shield and send me flying into the grass nearby.

With a grunt, I pushed myself to my feet and checked my limbs for any breaks. Sadly, there were none, so I had no excuses. Gritting my teeth, I walked back over to the lowest level of the amphitheater.

"Feeling alright? How's your head and throat?" She asked in an almost threatening way.

But I was at least as pissed off as she was. "Doing just perfect. Is that all you've got? If you wanted to blow me all you had to do was ask." Her face darkened at that and I immediately regretted it.

"Very well. You want a challenge?" She brought one hand up beside her. Just above it floated a fireball the size of a base-ball. "Water," she called out and sent the ball of flame hurtling toward me.

Panicking, and getting a flashback to my night in the library, I resisted the urge to just jump out of the way and quickly opened up to Pholl's power. I focused on the air around me and pulled as much water out of it as I could, concentrating the clear liquid just where I expected the fire-ball to hit.

It crashed into my shield, if you could even call it that, and sizzled away. Steam rose from where the water used to be, and I shouted in triumph. "Ha! Better luck next time, Professor."

She quirked an eyebrow at me and pointed toward my left sleeve, which was getting pretty hot now that I thought about it.

Because it was on fire, of course.

Another, less triumphant, shout came out of my throat as I started waving the arm around frantically. I threw my shirt off, luckily it wasn't the only layer I wore that day, and stomped it out.

Meanwhile, Professor Doriah couldn't stop laughing. Most of the students even joined; Lilly, Haether, and Whelan included. Louder than anyone else, they were.

"Now, who can tell me what he did wrong? There's more than one answer, by the way." She smirked, looking happier than a dog in a meat shop.

No one raised their hands, in typical college fashion, so she had to pick on someone.

"Andrith?"

A short guy with black hair and dark tan skin that reminded me of the Head Librarian looked up from his notes. His dark eyes were wide, and I noticed a nervous gulp. He was only a few rows back, but I could barely hear him. "Uhm. Yeah. He threw the shirt on the ground instead of just putting out the fire by dispersing its heat."

"That's right," she nodded and shot the boy a smile, but he was already looking back at his desk. "Anyone else for the second part?"

Haether raised her hand, with a smirk on her face. Our professor nodded toward her. "He panicked. So instead of forming a shield, his water took the shape of a... well, a sort of shapeless blob."

"Exactly. Panic out there in the real world and you'll find yourself burned a lot worse than that. Now," and her eyes shifted back to me, "Earth!"

She cocked back with both arms and summoned a fireball the size of a basketball this time.

I gritted my teeth and forced myself to stay calm. With as much power as I could muster quickly, I thrust my hands down and then swept them up. A wall of dirt rose from beneath my feet. It shoved me backwards and rose in front of me just before the fireball crashed into it and both exploded. Bits of dirt and rock rained over me as the smoke dissipated.

"As you can tell, some shields work better than others. Whereas the water countered the fire perfectly, resulting in mere steam, the shield of Earth exploded. Both dirt and flame could have struck out at those nearby, especially if this were a battle. In closer quarters and desperate situations, you need to come up with the perfect counter to any attack, else you'll be putting your companions in danger. One last demonstration," I was already siphoning power as she turned toward me. "Fire!"

Assuming that she would say the last element remaining, I was ready for it. Heat coalesced in front of me and burst into flame while my professor held out her hand and shot a stream of water at me. It met the wall of flame, but unlike her previous two attacks, this time she kept up her assault.

The air around me grew cold as I collected more and more heat and fed it into the flames. But the water kept coming. The resulting steam made it difficult to even see and as the air became colder, it grew more difficult to squeeze any last bit of heat from it.

The steam, however, was scalding-hot, so I turned my attention toward it instead of the air. It turned back into water as I pulled the heat away and I actually saw Doriah nodding. But if she was even the slightest bit proud, she had a shitty way of showing it. The stream of water doubled in size quickly and punched through my shield.

It felt like being hit by a linebacker. The column of water crashed into my chest and sent me sprawling to the floor. Soaking wet and exhausted.

In the past hour, I'd used myself as conduit for more magic than I had the rest of the time I'd been here. For something that seemed completely mental, the toll it took on me was surprisingly physical.

My arms ached as I pushed myself to my feet. This time, I knew better than to take off the wet clothing. Despite the dull aching in my head that cropped up as I pulled more power, I pulled the water out of my clothing and hair, and let it go over the ground nearby.

"Very good. See? Now you've had more practice than any of them," she said, her dark red eyes brimming with delight. "You can thank me later if you pass your exam.

"Now, as for the rest of you. I'd like you to spend the rest of class practicing your shields. You may find a partner and take turns attacking and defending, but keep in mind that we have not yet covered magical offense. If you do decide to try it, take it easy. We don't want any of you killing each other. But, it happens," she shrugged as if it were inevitable. "And do stay within eyesight of the classroom. I'll be wandering around with pointers and at least that way, if one of you does get singed, I might get to you in time to help."

25

THE ROWS OF STUDENTS STARTED TO RISE IMMEDIATELY, AS did the dozens of excited conversations.

"You might want to sit this one out," Doriah said, still grinning. "You're probably not used to such exertion."

Breathing heavily as I was, I tried in vain to hide it. "Not at all. I learned more today than I have in the past two weeks." She arched an eyebrow at that. "I think I'll just join up with my friends, if you don't mind."

"By all means," she swept a hand toward the stairs as if giving me permission. "Oh, and Jake. You see that boy?" She pointed toward the one she called Andrith earlier and I nodded. "You would be wise to associate with him. For both your sakes. Strong allies will be invaluable in the years to come." And with that, she turned and left.

Andrith was standing alone, at the edge of the spread-out crowd of students who were too busy arguing which one of them would attack first. He didn't move anything but his eyes as a thick wall of Earth burst out from the ground in front of him. A few students nearby gasped and re-situated themselves a bit further away.

As I got close, he watched me approach and looked around himself as if I couldn't possibly be looking at him. His eyebrows scrunched down further the closer I got. "Uh. Hi."

"Hey," I nodded my head a little in greeting. "I'm Jake. That was impressive. At least twice the size of my own."

"It's not all about size, you know." I resisted the urge to make a crass joke and just let him go on. "If you practice, you'll be able to sense the makeup of the ground beneath your feet. Then you can sense for what the wall will be made up of. Stone, raw metals. It's not as easy as dirt, but offers much better protection."

I nodded along. "I'll have to keep that in mind. You wanna join us?"

His eyebrows shot up. "You want to practice with *me*?"

"Yeah," I shrugged, "why not?"

"You already have friends," he protested, glancing toward Whelan, Lilly, and Haether just as the girls decided to team up on him. A very nervous-looking Whelan was barely holding off two small jets of water. I couldn't help but laugh.

"Sure. Doesn't mean we don't have room for one more. Besides, you seem to know what you're doing. Come on," I nodded my head toward my friends and just started walking. Sure enough, I heard him follow.

The girls let up their attacks as I drew close, and Whelan looked at me like I'd just saved his life.

"Whelan, Lilly, Haether," I gestured toward each of them as I called their names, "this is Andrith. And I think he might just be smarter than all of us combined." There must have been a reason, after all, that Doriah called on him, and then suggested that I seek him out. *Maybe she doesn't hate me, after all.*

Lilly was the only one who seemed to take offense to that, but they all greeted him in a friendly manner.

"Why don't you pair up with me?" Whelan suggested

quickly. "Jake could use a break, I think, and the girls should really learn to defend themselves." Lilly shot him a glare and Haether scoffed.

Despite talking big with Doriah, I was happy to rest for a bit. I took a seat on the field nearby, leaving a good amount of space between myself and the two pairs.

Whelan, as it turned out, wasn't as full of shit as I thought. He rarely joined Lilly, Haether and I to study because he already felt like he was ahead of everyone else. All due to years of training with his father, that apparently paid off well because he was able to fend off most of Andrith's attacks with ease.

I was also finally starting to see the magic in use around me as a pale blue light. It reminded me of pictures of the aurora borealis; soft waves of neon undulating through the sky. Shields of air glowed a soft blue, that grew slightly darker as my fellow students poured more power into them. Otherwise, if they were using fire, water, or Earth, I would see the air in front of them start to turn blue just before their chosen element took its place and drowned out the color.

Andrith was the only person whose wall of Earth was suffused with enough power to take on a blue cast, to my eyes, anyway. As the professor had said, other students might see it in a different color, or not at all yet.

Whereas Andrith's assaults with the other elements seemed weaker, his attacks with Earth were levels above anyone else. Just like the thick shield he summoned a few moments ago, his projectiles were larger and heavy than anyone else's and they punched right through Whelan's shields, no matter what they were made of. After dusting the dirt off himself a few times, Whelan insisted on switching roles.

Not that he was any better at getting through Andrith's shield of dirt and stone.

Lilly and Haether were a similar pairing, but Lilly appeared to outshine our half-elf friend in every way. Hardly what I'd expected. Haether always seemed more serious, calm, and confident while Lilly was the meek, small-town girl who hadn't seen much more of this world than me. And yet, Haether was clearly struggling on both sides of the duel, if you could even call it that.

Lilly broke through the other girl's shields easily and defended with as little effort while Haether grew increasingly frustrated. After struggling for a while, I offered to take her place, but she refused.

Eventually, Professor Doriah reached our group as she made her rounds. I couldn't hear much of what she said, the numerous mock battles going on around me filled the air with small explosions or shouts every few seconds. I did see her nodding as she spoke to all but Haether, who she spent some extra time with before walking over to my place on the ground.

"Decided to sit out after all?" She said, standing over me.

I shot her a grin. "Just figured they could use some practice before pairing up with me."

Doriah snorted. "You may be better than average for this year's students, but I have seen plenty during my tenure that would put you all to shame. As well as some who threw their lives away by coming here before they were ready." She took on a somber tone and seemed to be looking over at Haether as she said that.

And I had to admit, seeing her struggle made me nervous. I didn't want to lose any of these new friends, never mind one that was hot as well. I was already forming small hopes that we could be more than friends one day, but it was hard to think much about that when the threat of death was constantly looming.

After a minute, Doriah spoke up again. "You sure you

don't want to get some practice in? Initiates don't get these opportunities too often. We'll do something similar next Friday, but you should still take advantage of this opportunity."

She was right, given that Initiates couldn't use magic outside the classroom, I wouldn't have many chances to practice. I nodded and got to my feet, "Alright, but this time, I'm on offense."

Doriah burst out laughing, so hard that I couldn't help thinking that she just wanted to hurt my feelings, and nodded. "Sure, sure. Good luck, boy." Then she slowly walked away until about ten yards separated us, and said, "Come on, then. Let's see what you can do."

Then she pulled a book out of an unseen pocket in her robes and started reading.

"Really?" I called over to her, but she just smirked.

Siphoning every bit of Pholl's power that I could, which wasn't much since there were a couple hundred other students doing the same, I started with fire. To burn those pages in her hand.

I shot a ball of flame straight for the book. Smoke rose from the projectile as it raced toward Doriah, who couldn't possibly look less worried. She didn't even look up as it struck a shield of air that appeared as suddenly as it disappeared. There was only a flash of blue as the fire dissipated.

And she smirked a little bit wider.

Alright, then. If that's how she wants to be, I'll have to start trying.

Taking a different approach, I shot water at her this time. Except, as it got closer to her, I also started collecting a globe just above and behind Doriah's head. There was no way she could have seen it. Just as my first shot hit her shields, I dropped the mass of water down on her from behind.

But just like the fire before it, it struck an invisible wall and fell away.

She did look up that time though. "Better," was the only word that left her mouth before she returned to her reading.

Gritting my teeth and determined to at least get the hem of her robes wet or singed, I wracked my mind for something else. I could try coming at her from even more directions, but that would just result in each individual attack being weaker. So, the same fruitless outcome.

There was, however, another card I could play that no one knew about. That they wouldn't be able to sense if I just used a little bit to bolden my attacks.

Again, I pulled in as much of Pholl's power as I could, but I also made myself aware of Vethris. His dark ocean of power reared up before me in my mind and offered more than Pholl possibly could. After all, there were hundreds of students siphoning off of Pholl in this area. Even a dozen would have been enough to start cannibalizing each other's power, according to what I'd been reading.

Vethris, on the other hand, was untapped. Even if anyone sensed it, it wasn't like they could call me out without revealing themselves as a Shadow as well. It was a risk, but a minor one, in my mind.

I started with some wind, that Doriah didn't even bother to defend against. She just gripped the book a little tighter to prevent the pages from whipping around. Then I threw a few balls of water into the breeze, hoping it would help them move faster and potentially catch her off guard, but those splashed against her shield just like before.

I threw a few more but added a stream of water infused with Vethris' power to the assault. I had to brace myself against the kickback of both the dark source of power, and the empowered stream's force, at first shocked at the torrent that flew toward Doriah.

Unlike my other attacks that hit her shield and failed, this one held up. A jet of water connected us, from my hand, pummeling into her shield, which held constantly now, a darker blue than I had seen thus far.

After a second, her eyebrows scrunched down, and Professor Doriah looked up at me. Not impressed or angry, just confused. Her mouth fell open slightly and she tilted her head to the side as she inspected me from afar. Then I felt her wrenching power from the hands of dozens of students close by as she took in such an impressive amount that I could barely hang on myself. The small blue shield erupted and engulfed her entire body in a dark blue cloud that seemed to be leaking into the air above her.

Suddenly, my jet of water started to freeze. It started at just the point where it met Doriah's shield and slowly climbed up toward me. I realized that most of the class had stopped what they were doing to watch the two of us and it dawned on me that this was a terrible idea.

Too many eyes on me. Too many chances for someone to realize that I wasn't using Pholl's power at all anymore. That something was wrong here, and I shouldn't be able to do what I was doing. As the ice reached the midway point, I let it fall away and I collapsed to the ground along with my attack.

If exhausted was how I felt before, I wouldn't even know how to describe myself now. I couldn't even stand. And instead of one headache, I felt two distinct bundles of pain in the back of my mind. I didn't need to read it in some old book to know that I had strained my connections to both Gods. It would be sore for a bit, but, like any muscle, would be stronger for it.

As it was, I could barely move.

Doriah walked slowly over to me as the rest of the students returned to their practice and gossip. More than a few still watched me as they talked.

"It seems you are more capable than I thought. What you were able to do with so little power is... interesting. Are you fully human? No elemental blood in you? No Fae?"

"Uh, not that I know I of," I offered, hoping that would be the end of the questions. *She knows something is up, but not what.*

"Hm." Was all she said, nodding to herself and inspecting me as she stood over me. "Don't die, Jake. It will be interesting to see where you go from here, if that is your starting point."

With that, she turned and left me alone. I didn't bother rising until class ended, around an hour later. Even then, I could barely keep my feet under me.

One ache in my head subsided, but the other... the constant reminder of the dark power I was foolish enough to use today, lingered for far longer.

26

I REJOINED MY GROUP OF FRIENDS AS WE ALL LEFT THE field just at the edge of campus. Andrith thanked us briefly for including him, then headed back to his dorm, declining offers to study with us.

As we walked down the path silently, Whelan was the first to speak up. "So, did no one else notice how amazing our boy Jake was back there? I mean, I thought I had a head start, but that jet of water you shot at Doriah probably would have blown a hole straight through me! How the hell did you do it?"

I shrugged awkwardly and tried to think about possible excuses. I'd watched a decent amount of anime and read plenty of books to pull from, so I went with a classic explanation. "I guess I just got angry. Seeing her toss my attacks aside so easily, while reading a book, no less! I hated that smug look on her face and wanted to wash it off."

Whelan burst out laughing, "And you nearly did! I couldn't believe it. Doriah's stronger than I would have guessed, too. Did you see that aura around her near the end? Speaking of which, can you guys see that yet? Mine's green."

"Yellow," Lilly called over her shoulder.

"Pale blue," I said.

Haether, however, seemed like she was trying to shrink in upon herself. When she saw the rest of us looking at her, she let out a huff. "Ugh, fine! I can't see it yet, okay?"

"Alright, it's fine," Whelan said, putting his hands up defensively. "We all move at a different pace. Nothing wrong with that."

"Except in my case It means I won't live longer than a couple of weeks," she grumbled.

Lilly reached out and grabbed her friend's hand. She stopped walking, so suddenly that Whelan almost crashed into her, then she pulled Haether's hand close to her chest and wrapped it in both of hers. "Don't say that," she plead. "I know you're struggling, but we'll make it work! Somehow... we'll practice outside of the school grounds, if that's what it takes to make sure no one finds out." She glanced at Whelan and I as she added, "These days, you three are all I have. I left my family, everyone I ever knew to come here, and I don't want to lose any of us!"

Haether gritted her teeth and forced a nod. "Alright. You're right, I can't give up now. It's just... l-let me wait until we're alone," she said, waving a hand toward the traffic of students passing us by. "I want to tell you all something. In private."

"Of course," I said, stepping up and putting a hand on her shoulder. "Whatever it is, we've got your back." I couldn't imagine what she had on her mind.

I had a few secrets of my own I wasn't quite willing to share yet, and one in particular that I thought might help us all. Well, Lilly, Haether, and I. If Whelan was too confident to study, then I was all too happy to share the bond with only the girls. Especially considering the awkwardness of adding another guy to the *ritual*.

We walked in silence until we reached our table on the fourth floor. I swept through the area just to make sure no one was close enough to listen in, then we all gave Haether our undivided attention. Lilly took a seat to Haether's right, while I sat on her left. Whelan sat on top of the table and rolled his eyes at Lilly when she asked him not to.

Then Haether took a deep breath and began. "My full name is Haether Denavere." Whelan perked up at that, but it didn't mean anything to me. "My father is older than our professor. In fact, he's never even told me a number. Apparently, it's rude to ask an elf how old they are, even within your own family," she added, grumbling. "He's very... pushy. He's a powerful mage, as many on that side of my family are, and doesn't want any of us to tarnish his reputation. So... he was able to pull some strings to get me admitted to this school earlier than I should have."

"Okay," I said, being the first one to speak up. "That doesn't sound so bad. How early are we talking?"

"Well, you know how humans don't fully develop magically until they're eighteen?" That was news to me, but I nodded as naturally as Lilly or Whelan anyway. "Elves, being much longer-lived, don't reach that same point until they're *two hundred years old*. Mixed races like myself are kind of an unknown. It all depends on what you're mixed with, and how much." She gritted her teeth and forced the last part out, "But as you may have already guessed, I haven't gotten there yet." Her eyes were glued to the table, unwilling to meet any of ours.

Luckily, Whelan asked it before I did. "So, and I know you just mentioned it's rude but now that we're talking about it... how old are you?"

Haether cringed, "Eighty-two."

Three pairs of eyes bulged, though Lilly and I were able to control ourselves quickly enough.

"Holy shit," Whelan muttered. "And you have no idea when you'll be as developed as any eighteen-year-old human?"

"Right."

"But your father forced you to enroll anyway," I added.

"Right," she repeated herself, sounding more down-trodden this time.

"Haether, that's terrible." Lilly grasped our friend's hand just like before. "Y-your mother couldn't stop him?"

Haether muttered "She was human.

Lilly paled just as the realization hit me too. If Haether was eighty-two, then her mother was...

"She died about fifteen years ago. All the cousins I grew up with are old and decrepit by now. That side of the family barely recognizes me, they're an entirely new generation. And I'm..."

"Caught between two worlds," I muttered. *Kinda like me.*

Haether nodded, her teal eyes looking into mine, glossy with unshed tears.

I shook my head, "I can't imagine how hard that is for you." Then I reached over and grabbed Haether's other hand. I let out a sigh and decided to tell them all about the bond. I still didn't have a proper excuse lined up for how I knew about this, and I didn't want to tell them I learned it from a book that I stole from the Head Librarian's office, but I had to help.

And at least if I told them about the ritual while I still had the book, I'd be able to prove that I wasn't lying.

"I think I have an idea that could help us all, but I'm not sure you'll like it," I started. The girls looked over at me, confused, but Whelan just shook his head.

At least he had the decency to lower his voice. "Look, if you're gonna cheat, I don't want any part of it. I like you guys, but I'm not about to be turned into another of Theid's goons just because I cheated on a test I'm pretty sure I'm gonna pass anyway. So, I'm just going to head out right now with my plausible deniability intact." Then he nodded to us, pinching the front of his wizard hat between thumb and forefinger. "Good luck, and may Pholl have mercy on your souls," he quipped on his way out.

"Oh, shut up!" I called after him, but at least it got a laugh out Haether.

"So, what did you have in mind?" Lilly asked, pronouncing every word slowly once Whelan was out of sight.

"First of all, it would definitely be considered cheating, so if that's a no-go for you, here's your chance." I looked both the girls in the eyes, but neither showed any sign of trepidation.

If anything, Haether was looking more determined than ever. "At this point, I'm willing to consider just about anything. There's only so much progress I can make in two weeks."

"Alright," I said and started to reach into my knapsack. "But you can't tell anyone! Not about what I'm going to tell you, or how I found it, nothing!"

"Okay! Jeez. What, do you have a slave fairy in there?" Lilly shot back in a harsh whisper.

"I literally don't even know what that is."

When I pulled out the book, they had the nerve to look unimpressed. Here I'd been worrying that the book held some historical significance, but they didn't even recognize it. I placed it tenderly in front of Haether and watched the two of them mouth out the title. *Iterad Virtutem*.

"It means The Path to Power. In this book lie some secrets that I don't think people are supposed to know about anymore. My," I took a nervous gulp as I prepared the best lie I could come up with, "my old teacher, the one who helped me get that scholarship, he gave this to me. Told me to burn it if anyone ever found out I had one."

They both slowly nodded and listened intently. The story wasn't true, but the importance it placed on that book was true enough. If a woman like The Lady was desperate to get her hands on it, then it had to be powerful.

"Have you read it?" Lilly asked.

I nodded. "Some of it's basic. Just breathing exercises, really. Other parts refer to foreign Gods or artifacts that might help, but that wouldn't work for us, I did find one thing though. A ritual that would allow the people who formed it together to combine their powers. Theoretically, it would make any one of us three times more powerful. More so, if we could get more girls in on it later."

"More girls?" Haether said, catching on a detail I didn't mean to touch upon quite yet.

"Er, right. You see, it all starts with a ritual that would bind us all together. As one. And as we repeated the ritual, the bond would just grow stronger. To the point of being able to speak in each other's minds."

"Hold. On! Mind reading? That's impossible," Lilly shook her head.

"It didn't sound quite like mind reading, no."

"Of course not. There are some things that even magic can't do," she added.

"Sure, but maybe people don't know as much about magic as they thought," I shot back. Lilly crossed her arms and shrugged. "But from the sounds of it, it would be more like the conversation we're having right now. Only, you know, in our heads."

"I can definitely see how that would be useful," Haether said, clutching her chin in thought. "And definitely cheating. Still, better than death. You never did explain the part about girls... Jake." She said, suddenly sharper. "What is this ritual that's supposed to bind us all together?"

I shot her a grin. "Let's just say, it happens in the

bedroom." Their eyes shot wide and Lilly blushed a deep crimson.

Haether glanced over at the younger woman and chuckled. "Well, it would hardly be my first time." Then she shot me a suspicious look, "So that's why you would only want to add girls to our little study group. Are you sure this is a real ritual and not some lame attempt to sleep with us?"

"I'd hardly call it lame, but yes, it's real." I flipped the book open to section regarding the bond and let them read it.

A few minutes of silence passed as they read through the pages and let the words sink in. As they sat there in thought, I tried my hardest to avoid picturing the two of them naked and in my bed. Not that I didn't want to picture it, but there was a time and place for that kind of thing. I didn't want to be walking around the library with a hard-on.

Finally, Haether nodded and then took on a sly smile. She turned to get a good look at me and ran her eyes down the length of my body. "You're not bad-looking, after all, and it's not like I have any other options. I'm in."

My eyebrows practically blasted off. I mean, obviously I'd been hoping they would both agree to it, but I had a hard time believing either girl would. Besides, Haether was utterly perfect. Long blonde hair, piercing teal eyes the like I'd never seen before. And a body that made my mouth water even before my power let me see her nude.

Lilly, however, wasn't having such an easy time with the decision. "I, um," she took a deep breath. "I think I'll need some time to think it over." She hastily packed her things, all the while looking very worried and nervous. Just before she left, she meekly added, "Promise not to start without me?"

"Of course. Take your time. Think about it. You're probably smarter than the two of us combined, so I wouldn't blame you for thinking you could go it alone. That's certainly what Whelan seems to think."

"And thank Pholl for that," Haether grumbled, crossing her arms under her breasts in a way that made it very difficult to look away.

Lilly nodded. Then muttered a, "Thank you," and sped off.

"Do you think we've scared her away?" Haether asked after a few minutes.

I shook my head. "Honestly... I think she's just a virgin "

It was Haether's eyebrows turn to rise then, but she also started nodding almost immediately. "Now that I think about it, that would make sense. Sometimes I forget how young you all are. Just a year or two over eighteen and fresh out of your hometowns, having hardly experienced the world at all. You think you're ready?" She looked at me with a predatory smile, but I shot one back to match it.

I knew what she was referring to, but it still felt like more. Like I was on the precipice of an entire life that would change based on the decisions I made over the next few days and weeks. But as I thought about the world I was leaving behind, which I did less every day, I couldn't imagine living the rest of my life back there. Without magic, or Gods, or all the exotic women that walked this campus every day.

"Hell yeah, I'm ready."

❧ 27 ❧

Just as Haether and I got back to our dorm and were about to separate, I noticed something.

I looked from the large, golden lettering on the front of my building, then at Haether, and back again.

Denavere Building.

She pursed her lips and nodded, catching on to what I just realized. "In case you were wondering how my father was able to get me in so easily," she waved her hand toward the building with her last name on it. "That's how. His side of the family has always been a big donor, so the school jumped at the chance to do him a favor."

"Wow. You're just full of surprises," I chuckled.

Haether blushed a little at that. "Ready for one more? Part of the stipulations, when he donated the money for this building some decades ago, was that they include a private apartment for any Denavere who should attend one day. It's just around the side of the building, has its own entrance and everything!" Then her eyes narrowed, and her voice lowered to a seductive tone. "Wanna check it out?"

I felt a heat rising under my belt and a bit of redirected

blood flow. "I really would. But we promised Lilly we wouldn't start anything until she made her decision, and I don't think I'd be able to trust myself alone with you."

She walked up to me and ran a fingertip down my chest. "That's okay. You can trust me to take good care of you," she added a wink as her fingers brushed right over my crotch. I tilted my head and gave her a pained look. Then she started laughing to herself, "Sorry. Can't help myself. I just love teasing you. Well I *am* *not* taking care of yourself tonight!" She lifted up on her toes so that she could whisper right in my ear, "And think of me while you do it."

Then she spun and gracefully strolled away, jutting her hips out with every step just to torture me a little bit more.

I shook my head and bit my lip. *God damn, I hope Lilly doesn't keep us waiting long.*

As much as I wanted to spend the rest of the night picturing the two of them in my bed, I had a date with another, much scarier woman. The Lady would be in my room around midnight, so I'd need to finish reading her book at least an hour beforehand. Couldn't risk getting caught breaking her rules. Not yet anyway.

So, I practically ran inside and headed straight for my room. When I rounded the stairs and bounded into the hall-way, however, I ran into a brick wall. A green one, oddly enough. Except this brick wall was built out of a single, seven-foot tall, and insanely muscular orc.

Boba growled as I bounced off him. He gritted his teeth and blew out an angry breath. "Watch where you're going, *shit*. If I wasn't sure you'd be dead by the end of the month anyway, I'd pummel you right now." Then he squinted his dark eyes and lowered his head so that it was level with mine. "And I'm going to be right there in the crowd when it happens."

I glared right back at him. "Once I'm an Acolyte, I can

use the arena grounds freely, right? Practice or duel any time I want?" The big green man nodded with a grunt. "Then you better get training, Shrek. Cause if you keep pushing me, we might as well just duel and get it over with."

Boba reared back and barked a laugh. "Good luck with that, little guy. I don't know who the fuck *Shrek* is supposed to be, but you just paid him a compliment. He'd be lucky to be as strong as me. Now, move."

I realized I was standing in the middle of the doorway, so I crossed my arms and leaned against the frame. "Nope. *You move.*"

He rolled his eyes and chuckled but stepped aside. Then he sarcastically swept a hand in front of himself, as if giving me permission to pass. As soon as I did, though, he wrapped a hand in my shirt and forced me up against the wall, hard. My pointed black hat fell to the floor and the asshole stomped on it. His forearm dug into my back while the other hand squeezed the back of my skull like a vice. I grunted and tried to push myself away from the wall, but his strength was overwhelming.

Boba chuckled. "Go on. Use a bit of Pholl's power. Send me flying through the hallway and see if Theid lets you off easy this time."

"Fuck yourself."

He laughed even louder. Then he released me, tossing me aside so roughly that I nearly lost my footing. *And here I though R.A.'s in the real world were assholes.*

As he walked away, he called over his shoulder. "Don't get yourself killed, *shit.* I want that duel."

I brushed off my hat and stepped into my room, rubbing away the soreness Boba's elbow left in my back. He was an asshole, but he knew what he was doing. I probably wasn't the only Initiate he was trying to push around, but I'd bet I was the only one pushing back. Magic being restricted to us at the lowest end of the totem pole, I should have known that someone would take advantage of their position above us.

Whatever. He'd pay for that, just not quite yet. I had more important things to do.

Immediately, I threw my crumpled hat in the wardrobe, dropped my bag on my bed, and got out the book. There wasn't enough time to finish it, so I flipped through until something caught my eye.

I stopped when I saw the word Pillars. The capital P confirmed exactly what I suspected. That the strange, ancient chambers had something to do with the magic and Gods of this world. Something important.

As I read about them, a few things finally started to click. According to the nameless author, there was an unknown number of them in the world, but they assumed around ten. Each one granted a mysterious power that was beyond anything magic would normally allow. It even listed off a few: Omnitongue, Location sense, and Truevision.

So, Brock was right about what this Power was called. If the name wasn't clear enough, the description was spot on. *The holder of this Pillar has the ability to see everything in the physical world. From the biggest to the smallest, at any distance, through any barriers; they are all-seeing.*

From the sounds of it, I'd be able to focus on any layer of anything I looked at. Since I didn't have control over it, however, the power just latched on to whatever was in my line of sight and scanned through all its layers, as if it didn't actually know what I wanted. That could definitely come in handy.

And not just for seeing under Haether or Lilly's clothes.

My mind already jumped to a few possibilities. I could have found Thuvien's office, for example. If I knew exactly where to look. Theoretically, though, I could see through the dirt and into the basement floors, then look around at whatever I wanted. Even into the deeper floors that none but the highest faculty could access. It was an interesting possibility for another time.

The writer also mentioned a boost in power for whoever held a Pillar. Both for them, and for the God they served.

The process of capturing a Pillar, what Jacobus must have done before we traded places, involved taking in as much power as you could, from the God of your choosing, and infusing the Pillar with it all. As a result, both you and your God got an instant boost.

So, not only did I have an extra power that the other students didn't know about, even the connection I had with Vethris was strengthened. As long as I only used his power in small amounts, to add it to Pholl's power, I'd be able to strengthen everything I did without getting caught.

Theoretically, anyway. Jacobus would have been a force to reckon with, if we hadn't switched places. As it was, I outshone most of the other students without even knowing what I was doing.

It was dark by the time I finished reading. There were plenty of pages left, but once I'd read everything I could find regarding Pillars, I didn't want to risk getting caught. I left the book, closed, on my desk, and hid the other one that I'd taken from Thuvien's office. The Lady didn't tell me *not* to steal any other books, but I didn't want her to take the extra one as well, thinking it a bonus.

I laid in bed for hours before she showed up. It wasn't like I could sleep, knowing what was coming for me.

It started with the sounds of fighting. Metal clashing against metal, grunt meeting grunt. The dark portal appeared in the very same place as before and The Lady stepped out.

As soon as I turned my head to look at her, my eyes burned with pain. It subsided as I clenched them shut.

"Good boy," she drawled in smooth, low voice. She had a patronizing tone that seemed to come naturally to her. "I'll allow you stay in bed this time, considering your success." I heard, rather than saw, her step up to my desk and pick the book up. She hummed to herself proudly as she flipped through it. "Perfect. It's a shame that fool couldn't get his hands on a complete copy, but this will have to do. As for you," she leaned down to whisper in my ear. "I have a gift from our Lord."

She planted a kiss on my forehead, just above the bridge of my nose, and I felt a chill rush through me. I inhaled a sharp gasp as she pulled away and continued to breathe heavily afterwards.

"What... was that?"

"Now, now. I didn't give you permission to speak, did I? We'll let that one go, but don't do it again. *That* was our Lord's blessing. You're a second-rank Shadow, now. As if even a taste of our Lord's power wasn't already enough to set you apart from your classmates, you'll find that your connection to him is even stronger than before. Use it well and at the very least, try to stay alive. We'll have another task for you soon enough."

And with that, she disappeared.

I didn't feel any different. Even reaching out for Vethris' power felt the same, but I didn't dare siphon from it. She was gone, but I still felt The Lady's presence, as if merely touching Vethris' power would bring her back like a moth to a flame, and I didn't want to deal with her any more than I had to. Still, I slept easy knowing that at least one of my problems was solved.

For now, anyway. She'd be back, and now that I'd shown that I was capable, she'd probably give me something even more difficult next time.

Oh, well. At least she didn't torture me that time.

❧ 28 ❧

WE PASSED THE WEEKEND'S TIME IN JUST THE SAME WAY AS any other day. At the library, either working or studying. The first floor was starting to look normal again, with most of the char stains removed and a new bookshelf replacing the old one.

Thuvien was still in a bad mood and avoided me, though he seemed to be avoiding everyone else as well. Ruthie, however, was not around. It was only on Sunday that I actually found out what happened, when I spent a few hours working with Filo.

"She got fired," the fiery haired girl told me. "Thuvien didn't want to, she's been here for decades after all, and some of the faculty think that they even hook up from time to time," though from her tone, I could tell she wasn't sure whether to believe that gossip. "She may have had a near perfect memory, but it made her sloppy. She didn't need to organize things because she always remembered where they were! On the rare occasion that she misplaced something, it was as good as gone forever. Kinda made working under her difficult, and it resulted in more than a few mistakes over the years. Nothing as big as this one, though. And Thuvien hasn't even told anyone exactly what happened. The official story is that Ruthie lost her orb for the final time. It's a huge security risk to the library, so," Filo shrugged, "they couldn't just keep letting her off the hook."

My jaw hung open and my chest felt hollow as I listened to Filo's explanation. The blood ran out of my face and I felt cold. "So, what you're telling me is... I ruined that woman's life?" Filo cringed as if she didn't want to say the words directly, but it was still true. I threw my head back and let out a deep groan. "Fuck. I didn't want that to happen! But what was I supposed to do, let The Lady kill me, instead?"

Filo shook her head in a slow, morose manner. "That's your life now, Jake. And mine, too. Vethris doesn't need simple, painless favors out of us. Everything we do for him will hurt the people around us and we can only go along with it or die. Whoever turned you should have made that clear, but I guess we don't recruit the most well-meaning members. I know it sucks, Jake, but it is what it is."

Of course, that didn't make me feel any better. I ruined a kind woman's life and turned a book with powerful secrets over to the evilest person I know. I had a deadly exam in a couple weeks that could kill me or any of my friends, and I still had no idea what was going on back in my home world.

But I may have convinced the girls to form the bond with me soon, so I had that going for me, which was nice.

MONDAY MORNING BROUGHT WITH IT A NEW UNIT, magical offense this time, as well as another guest speaker.

The head of the Regeneration school elicited a bit of confusion as a man so muscular that he would make The Rock feel insecure walked down the stairs and stepped up to the podium.

The bald man was easily a few inches taller than me, and clad in light leather armor with a sword on his hip. He was clearly a soldier, so how did he come to lead the Regeneration school?

Lilly was the most excited for the lecture, until she saw who would be giving it. Then she grew ambivalent. "Is he the Head Healer's bodyguard, or something?" she whispered to the rest of us.

Andrith sat next to Whelan one row ahead of Haether, Lilly, and I. I took my usual place between the girls. We all just shrugged and shook our heads, indicating that we were just as confused as she was.

Then he started talking. He had the kind of booming voice that filled a room easily and his dark eyes never stopped scanning the amphitheater. "My name is Basset Fowly, but you can call me High Healer." He broke into a smile that looked out of place. Like a rock cracked open to reveal rows of teeth. "I can imagine that I'm not quite what you were expecting, but to be honest, this wasn't at all the path I expected myself to follow, either.

"I was raised as a soldier, just as the men in my family have been for generations. Even those with the gift of magic. But it didn't take long for the horrors of war to reveal themselves. At my first battle, I watched hundreds get slaughtered. Even killed a few, myself. All around me were the dead and dying. And there I stood, healthy and uninjured, yet still unable to do a single thing to help any of them.

"So, I sought out the best healers I could find and learned all that I could from them. Eventually that led me here, and I've been able to not only become one of the most accomplished healers in the world, I've helped hundreds of students begin that very same journey. Through them, I'd like to think that I've saved countless lives."

Lilly glanced over at me, clearly impressed, and I nodded

the same. The High Healer wasn't outwardly what I would have expected but listening to him for the rest of the day made it clear that he was as selfless as a person could be. The body of a soldier, but the mind of a missionary. He was a good man.

So, I decided to keep my distance from him. Partially with the hopes that I wouldn't be tasked with anything that might hurt him, the way I was with Ruthie, but also because that kind of man would always be on the lookout for Shadows. Throughout his entire speech, it felt like he was on high alert. As if an attack could emerge from the crowd of students at any time.

When we left class for the day, Lilly was more excited about her future than ever. "Just think of the possibilities!" She gushed while we headed for our usual spot on the library's fourth floor. "If we ever get into a fight, I could be standing back and healing the rest of you and we'd be a veritable army! Even lethal wounds would be inconsequential. We'd be unstoppable if," then she trailed off and glanced at Haether, then me.

I knew exactly what she was about to say. If we formed the bond, she'd have three times the power to pull from. If I ever got injured and was unable to fight, she could use the strength that I couldn't, and heal me with my own power! Maybe unstoppable was right.

"If....?" Andrith asked after Lilly failed to pick up the end of her sentence.

So, I jumped in. "If we pass the exams, that is. None of us will be particularly powerful without enough time to train and study." Lilly shot me a relieved look and Andrith nodded, accepting my answer.

It wasn't until another couple hours later that Whelan and Andrith took off, leaving me alone once again with Lilly and Haether. The younger woman grew noticeably more nervous those days whenever she was alone with us.

Haether was the one who finally broke the ice. "So, Lilly. Based on what you *almost* said earlier, am I right in assuming that you've made your decision? Not that I'm trying to speed you up or anything, but we do have limited time."

"No, it's alright," Lilly responded in a soft voice. Then she gritted her teeth and nodded. "I'm in. And it's not just about the exams, we'll be able to face any challenge that comes our way once we've bonded. It's... nerve-wracking, to be sure, but I do think it's the right decision. No. I know it is. Just... give me another day or two to prepare myself." She let out an awkward laugh, "This is never how I imagined losing my virginity, but at least I'll get laid before I die."

Haether and I both snorted laughing at that unexpected addition. "That's a good way to put it," Haether added once she collected herself. Then she bumped Lilly with a friendly elbow, "It's not the kind of thing you want to die without experiencing. A threesome, I mean," then she shot me a wink that sent blood rushing into my face. And a grin, of course.

I wouldn't be losing my virginity, but it was certainly going to be my first threesome and I was already getting hard just thinking about it. But, I could wait a few days, considering what I had to look forward to. These two gorgeous girls would be well worth the wait.

My excitement only grew over the rest of the week. Doriah's lectures were almost mirror images of the previous week. She went through things like which element is best used against shields of each kind.

Earth could puncture shields of air best. Fire easily broke through ice, but was dissipated by water. And of course, water would cut through fire easily. Air was good for punching holes through fire or water, but not so good against solid shields, like Earth or ice.

Shields of Earth were the only ones that were best fought with their own element. Breaking through walls of dirt and stone required brute force, and nothing did brute force better than launching a boulder at your enemy.

Friday's class was another practical one. But instead of taking turns attacking each other, Doriah lead the class out to an arena that was set about a half-mile off school grounds. It was shaped like a soccer field, though filled with hard-packed dirt instead of grass. On either side of the arena, and set back about a hundred feet, were the stands.

"This will be the very same arena in which every one of you will be facing your final challenge as Initiates," she started once the class gathered around her at the edge of the arena.

"It is my pleasure to finally inform you as to the actual format of your oncoming exams. They will begin next Saturday morning, so use the following week wisely. First, you will take a written test that will cover every unit and guest speaker that we've had so far. It will likely take you several hours, so it will be the only portion of that day.

"We will grade those tests that very night and use the results to determine your trials on Sunday." She smirked and scanned the crowd as we all anxiously awaited those final, crucial details. "You will each be facing what could only be referred to as a monster. Your task will be to defeat it before it defeats you. Simple as that. It may be a minotaur, a manticore, a young griffon, the possibilities are endless. But take heart, we have made sure that all your adversaries are of similar strengths. Next week, we will be covering a bevy of these magical creatures so that you may know what you are up against." Her smirk widened before she added, "We do have another surprise in order, but that will have to wait until Sunday morning.

"As for today," she reached a hand toward the arena and

then flung it upwards. All across the dirt floor, what looked like training dummies made of clay popped out of the ground. "I want you all to familiarize yourselves with the arena. Practice your attacks not on each other, but on these placeholders, these dummies." And for some reason she glanced at me for that last word. She started walking toward the stands and called back to us, "Do keep in mind that your real targets will be fighting back. I know some of you may be tempted to duel, but that is strictly not allowed. You must make do with the training opportunities we give you. If you've chosen to squander your time here, then you will only be hurting yourselves."

"I don't like her," Lilly whispered, despite our professor being much too far away to hear. "She should be taking more responsibility for her students! We're all at risk of *death* and she treats it just like any other test."

Whelan was the only one who disagreed. "Well, we did all choose to be here. And the school turns away a lot of people; it isn't easy to get in. Those that do make it should know what they're getting themselves into," he shrugged. Lilly glared at him, so I tried to diffuse them a bit.

"Plus, think about it from her perspective. Elves live, like, forever right?" I directed that at Haether, who nodded. "And this one is like a thousand years old. She's probably seen a hundred years' worth of Initiates come and go. After losing students to the exams year after year, I guess it starts to sting a little less."

"Still, you'd think she'd care a bit more."

"She probably did, back when she started," Andrith offered, and I nodded along with him as we found an empty area in the arena.

We let the conversation die there and spread out to face off against our clay enemies. They were surprisingly formidable. I tested mine out first, trying to kick it over, but it felt like kicking a wall. Air and water did nothing to the clay man, and fire just seemed to dry it out.

The only way I could damage them at all was with stone projectiles. Andrith, of course, was the best at that, so he was destroying target after target. I decided to follow his lead and succeeded at peppering my dummy with holes, but nothing close to the clay carnage Andrith created.

It did give me an idea though. I focused within the dummy, on what I imagined would be its center of mass. I fed all the power I could into that small area the size of a baseball and released it in all directions. My proud smile, as the clay dummy disappeared in a satisfying explosion, was only ruined by the bits of dirt that landed in my mouth.

Still, it was progress.

Whelan, however, apparently didn't want me to be too proud of myself. "You won't be able to do that in the real fight, you know!" He called over from his position and trotted closer when I asked him what he meant. "I was watching what you did. Try it on me."

I shot him a look, "What? I'm not going to kill you Whelan."

He grinned. "I know you're not. That's what I'm trying to tell you. Try it."

I shrugged and gave in. It wasn't *really* a duel, so we weren't *really* breaking the rules. Besides, he seemed to know something I didn't. So, a tad reluctantly, I pulled in only a small amount of power and tried to force it into Whelan's core in the same way I did with the dummy. They were both dummies, so I couldn't see why it wouldn't work.

And yet, it didn't. As I tried to press the power into him, I met a barrier.

"Exactly. You can't influence a living thing like that. Against sparring targets, that was a good move, but it won't help you otherwise."

"Good to know," I nodded. "Thanks." He gave me a 'you're welcome' nod just as Doriah was calling an end to the class.

It was a very melancholy group of students that left the arena, then. Some spoke loudly of the creatures they would conquer in just a week, but most were somber and silent.

It was almost here. The day that some of us wouldn't live through.

And it was clear that some students didn't like their chances.

WHELAN AND ANDRITH BROKE OFF FROM THE GROUP AS WE reached campus. On the main pathway that would lead us to the library, Lilly fell behind and it took a few seconds for Haether and I to notice. When we did, we turned to face her.

Lilly was wringing her hands and her eyes were fixed on the ground. "Um," she started and paused to take a nervous gulp. "A-after everything our professor told us today, I realized that I just can't stall any longer." She looked between my eyes and Haether's. We both knew exactly what she was talking about and a nervous, but excited, heat started to grow in my belly. "I'm ready," she said, finally. "I don't know what we'll be facing next Sunday, but I know that our best chance at living through it will be together. Even if we can't fight the same battles, we can lend each other strength."

Haether nodded slowly and stepped up beside the shorter girl, wrapping an arm around her shoulder. "Don't worry, Lil. We'll be gentle. Right, Jake?"

"Right. And afterwards, we're all going to make it through the exams. I know we only met a few weeks ago, but I feel closer to you two than any of my old friends. I can't lose you.

Besides, who knows what'll be waiting for us once we're Acolytes! We're going to need to be strong and have each other's backs." I shrugged in what I hoped was an encouraging way. "We might as well start now."

Lilly nodded and held a tremulous smile. Then she chuckled. "Alright, alright. Let's get on with it before I change my mind."

The walk to our dorm felt like one of my longest ever. I followed behind Lilly and Haether, who walked arm-in-arm, and admired the two of them the entire way. How did I get so lucky? These two girls were flawless beauties, the likes of which I had barely even spoken with back in my world. And yet, here, we were not only best friends, but we were about to add *benefits* to that relationship.

I could hardly believe it was real.

But as soon as we made it inside Haether's personal apartments, which were far more lavish than any dorm I'd ever seen, the reality of the situation slammed into me.

Or, I should say, Haether did. Almost before the door even latched, Haether threw her pointed blue hat on a chair and pushed me up against the wall, then planted her lips on mine. They were soft and plump. She smelled like berries and her tongue was even sweeter as she pushed her way into my mouth. I was fully hard then and grabbed Haether by the waist so that I could spin us, pinning her against the wall instead. Then I pressed my waist into her and started laying kisses down her neck.

A soft, satisfied sound purred in her throat, and I heard her say a very warm, "Come here."

Lilly stepped over to us slowly and Haether pushed me away with a firm hand on my chest. Then she lightly lifted the orange witch's hat from Lilly's head and smiled down at her. She cupped Lilly's face and slowly lowered until their lips met. Lilly's eyes widened at first, but she quickly gave in to the more experienced woman's lips.

For a minute I just stood back and watched as two of the most beautiful girls I'd ever seen made out with each other. Their tongues flicked out and danced, their hands slowly explored each other.

Then, suddenly, Haether pulled away and glanced over at me, her eyes lidded and heavy with the lust that ran through all of us. She looked at Lilly and jerked her head toward me.

The shorter girl took one step toward me and I covered the rest. Restraining myself wasn't easy. I wanted to rip the clothes off each of them and get right to it, but I knew that taking it slow would pay off later.

Still, I wrapped my arms around Lilly and crushed her against me with a little too much enthusiasm. She let out a soft whimper, but then looked up at me and parted her perfect lips. They were thinner than Haether's, but no less satisfying. Her taste reminded me of cinnamon, her scent floral. As I got more excited, I let one of my hands drift down and take Lilly's firm ass into a tight grip.

Her lips were still occupied by my own, but I felt her jolt with shock at first. It only lasted a moment, then she was arching her back, pushing herself into my hand while she wrapped her arms around my chest and pulled me in just as hard as I pulled at her.

"Come on, now, let me have some fun too!" Haether whined as she stepped between us and ran her lithe fingers along the bulge in my trousers. "Mmmm, not bad, Jake." I couldn't help but grin at that. And it grew wider as I saw Lilly's wide eyes staring at the same spot Haether caressed. When the half-elf girl noticed Lilly's expression, she leaned in close to her ear and whispered, "Do you want to see it?"

Lilly's face filled with a deep red, but she let out a quick nod.

Haether released her and one hand reached behind herself. She worked quickly, and soon her long gown fell away. Underneath, she wore something akin to a corset, but it was wound around her chest for some reason. I stepped forward to unlace her while she tucked a few fingers underneath my waistband and pulled.

Lilly gasped as my dick sprung free and I swelled with pride as the two girls feasted their eyes upon me. Moments later, I finished with Haether's corset and let it fall to the ground as I let out a similar gasp myself.

God fucking damn. Elf-girl's hiding some cannons!

She blushed and looked down at my hands as I cupped her perfect tits. So smooth and soft, I could have played with them all day. Especially once Haether started jerking me off. We played with each other for a minute before turning our attentions on Lilly.

She looked nervous and was taking very deep breaths as Haether and I undressed her. She didn't move or even flinch when her dress fell to the floor, with nothing underneath. *I guess that's why it clung to her ass so well.*

Lilly's body was tanned and fit. She wasn't as well-endowed as Haether, but she was just as sexy in her own way. Tan lines showed that, back home, she must have worn some sort of shorts and a top that didn't even reach her belly button. She'd grown up on a farm and had strong, thin arms, but thick legs and a tight ass that equaled Haether's. All that walking around her small town really paid off. Her tits were a nice handful, pale except where the sun would hit her cleavage, with little pink nipples.

Haether and I each took one in hand and tried to ease Lilly into it. Her eyes were clenched shut at first, her face a deep crimson, but she was slowly lightening up. The tension left her body as Haether and I massaged her chest. Then the half-elf shot me a wink and bent down to take one nipple into her mouth.

Lilly's eyes sprung open at that and she let out a soft "Oh!" But she seemed to enjoy it, so I did the same. And gladly. I'd devour every inch of these two perfect women if they'd let me.

Lilly started breathing heavily and jutting her hips out, so I slid my hand down to the small patch of stubble just above her pussy. I placed my hand over her entrance to let her get used to being touched. Her eyes latched onto mine and she bit her lip. At the same time, I leaned down and started kissing her, while rubbing her pussy.

It wasn't long before she was whimpering beneath me, her mouth breathing heavily against mine while Haether and I played with her body.

After a few minutes, she wrapped her hands around my neck as if to stop herself from collapsing. Lilly's face contorted and froze in perfect agony as she let out strangled gasps. Slowly, she returned to her senses and chuckled as we let her recover.

"Dear Pholl! If I knew that *that* was what I was missing out on, I would have jumped you two weeks ago!"

"Girl, we're just getting started," Haether purred. Then she took both me and Lilly by a hand and led us to her bedroom.

Her large bed took up most of the room, it had to be at least a queen, with plenty of space for the three of us, luckily. The twin mattress in my dorm would have made things difficult. Oh, I'd have made it work, just not easily.

Haether led Lilly over to the bed and pushed her onto it, before climbing next to her and waving a hand for me to join them. For a moment, I just stood and admired the view. My shirt hit the floor and just like that, we were all completely nude.

The two girls were intertwined in Haether's bed, their smooth legs rubbing against each other as Haether laid soft kisses on Lilly's throat. All signs of her previous apprehension were gone. Only lust remained.

But there was something I needed to mention before we actually got started. With a grin that I couldn't suppress even if I wanted to, I explained the ritual as I'd read it. "Before we start, we each need to siphon as much power as we can comfortably hold. Then keep it within you the entire time. As you *finish*, you need to force the magic out of yourself and into the other two. That's how the bond is formed."

The girls both nodded and I saw them shine with a very faint blue as they held in their power. It was only the second time that I'd seen an aura like that, and I figured that if we were clothed, the dim light wouldn't be able to shine through. I pulled at Pholl's power too until I felt the power running through my veins and slowly walked around the bed until I stood just at the edge.

Haether purred and separated from Lilly as she crawled over to the edge and took me in hand. She flashed a playful smile up at me and then took my hard length into her mouth.

A satisfying groan immediately came out of me. Her mouth was warm and wet and everything perfect. I was mesmerized by the bobbing motion of her head, the way her long blonde hair fell this way and that as her head jerked back and forth. Lilly craned her head around Haether to watch, a hungry smile playing at her lips.

When Haether pulled away, she grabbed the base of my dick and pointed it at Lilly like it was a loaded gun. "You ready? He certainly is," she added wryly.

Lilly nodded, excited but also nervous as she shuffled toward the edge of the bed and spread her legs to me. Her slit was slick with wetness and looked good enough to eat, but I'd decided that we had all waited long enough. She was ready and willing. I could taste her another time.

Haether climbed up on the bed and started lightly playing with Lilly's boobs and speaking softly to her. "It'll hurt a bit at first, but he'll take it slow." Then she leaned down and placed a heavy kiss on Lilly's lips and when she pulled away, she nodded to me.

Lilly looked up at me and bit her lip. Her cheeks were a deep red and her eyes were practically glazed over with lust. I stepped up between her legs and slowly pressed the head of my cock into her.

The sensation was overwhelming. It wasn't my first time, but this was entirely different from any other girl I'd experienced. Maybe it was the fact that there were three of us, maybe it was due to the magical power we all held within ourselves, I didn't know. But it was fucking amazing.

She was tight and so wet. Her heat pulled me in, but I took it slow. Easing in inch by inch and whenever Lilly gasped sharply, I pulled back and started again. It was a slow, teasing process, but Lilly eventually got used to the feeling. She bled a little bit but wouldn't let me stop. In fact, she ended up asking me to speed up.

And who was I to turn down a pair of busty witch girls in need?

I gradually increased my pace until Lilly was moaning with pleasure. Haether kept playing with Lilly's body as I fucked her, alternating between her breasts and her clit. Another orgasm crept up on Lilly after a few minutes and her hands latched onto the red blanket while a shriek of pure delight escaped her lips.

And I felt something different, something *new* rush into me as Lilly's pleasure ran through her. I immediately assumed it was the bond settling in. It felt like an awareness not unlike that of the Gods and their sources of power, but not quite the same either. Still, I didn't let it distract me. The book mentioned that the ritual wouldn't be complete until all three of us *finished*.

"Ooh, I think I feel it starting," Haether said and both Lilly and I nodded agreement.

While Lilly recovered her breath, Haether took her place. "Come on now, big boy. Show me what you've got," she said with a wink and a challenging grin.

I quirked an eyebrow and grabbed onto her soft thighs, then wrenched her toward me. Haether let out a squeal and wrapped her ankles around my hips, pulling me toward her with an urgency that I felt just as deeply. Then I pressed myself into her.

Again, the feeling was more incredible than anything before. A little more so, even, than it was with Lilly and I attributed that to the bond that was starting to form between us.

I wrapped my hands around Haether's petite waist and held her still while I pumped myself into her harder and faster than I dared with Lilly. The elf girl let out a heavy breath that told of pleasure long awaited. She was the last one to get any real attention after all, I could only imagine how badly she felt teased by Lilly and I going at it.

As Lilly's breathing slowed and returned to normal, Haether looked over at her with a devious grin. "Come here," she said, tapping a hand to her chest just beneath her throat, but Lilly just looked confused. Haether rang out with a short, pure laugh, and added, "I want you to ride my face while he fucks me, Lilly."

The small-town girl's eyes went wide at that, but she nodded and slowly climbed over Haether. I had a perfect view of Haether's body, her perfect tits and toned stomach, as well as Lilly's ass as she hovered just over Haether's mouth.

Haether's hand laid delicately over Lilly's thighs and

pulled her downward. I would imagine it was a little difficult for her, given that my thrusting kept pushing her backward as much as my hands pulled her back into me. But based on the sounds coming out of Lilly, it wasn't an issue.

The three of us played with each other's bodies like that for how long, I had no idea. I just let myself enjoy it and tried to focus on holding back the pressure that kept building in my waist. I wasn't going to let it happen until Haether had hers. And luckily I didn't have to wait terribly long.

"Oh!" The sound rang out from Haether as she pulled herself away from Lilly's slit. "Don't stop. Just like that. I'm so close!"

As her last words rang out, Lilly's hand flashed down and took Haether by the back of the head, pushing it back into place. "Mmmm, me too. Whatever you're doing with your tongue, don't you dare stop!"

Watching those two girls enjoying themselves was too much. Their collective pleasure brought out my own and I pumped a few final, harder thrusts into Haether as I spilled my seed within her.

I felt Pholl's power leak out of me at the very same time, as well as what I finally recognized as both Lilly and Haether's power filling the void. An awareness of them both settled in at the back of my mind and I felt different as I reached out mentally for Pholl's power afterwards.

It wasn't just Vethris and Pholl anymore, it was like the two gods were on one side and I was on the other. Except I wasn't alone anymore. Lilly and Haether were as much as part of me as my own consciousness. Incorporeal, but a part of me all the same.

Lilly collapsed into the bed beside Haether, both smiling and giggling randomly.

As I stood over them, I decided to test my new capabilities. I siphoned at Pholl's power and found that, where I usually would have been tapped out, I could keep going. With a grin, I pushed as far as I could, and power exploded into me. My body felt alive with energy and I clenched my fists as if it would help keep it contained.

The girls looked at me in awe.

"How's my aura?" I asked, with a cocky grin.

A tear came to Haether's eye as she whispered. "I see it." Then she chuckled and repeated herself. "I see it! You look positively radiant, like you're containing the sun itself."

I looked down at myself, a little disappointed I couldn't see my own aura. But it didn't matter. We would all be far stronger than ever before, even more than what I was expecting.

"Ladies. I think our lives just got a lot easier."

$\mathcal{R}$ 30 $\mathcal{R}$

ALL OUR MOODS TOOK A DRASTIC TURN FOR THE BETTER after that night. I mean, how could they not?

After waking up in Haether's bed with the two naked women wrapped around me, I couldn't stop smiling for hours! We even had another round at each other before finally heading to bed, and all woke up a little sore.

But at least it was the weekend. No long walk to the amphitheater at the edge of campus, which was great because my thighs ached from the, uh, exertion last night. We took the steps up to the fourth floor of the library a bit slower than usual but settled into our same spot.

Lilly and Haether got straight to work going through their notes from the previous week on magical offense, trying to figure out what might be on the test and what might be useful for the combat portion. I mostly listened, only speaking up occasionally, and didn't even bother getting my own notes out. They were far less thorough, especially when compared to Lilly's, who tended to go above-and-beyond when it came to schoolwork.

That made her basically the opposite of Whelan, but I

got the sense that Andrith put in at least as much work as any of us, just on his own.

The morning ended up feeling more like a tutoring session than a study group, given that I hardly contributed, but the girls didn't seem to mind.

Afterwards, I pulled out one of Jacobus's books, *The Practical Argument for Eradication*, as I had been neglecting them. The third book, *Pillars: An Examination*, I had already returned without reading. I figured that what I'd read in the *Iterad Virtutem* was enough, so I was better off reading something new.

Given that this book was written by a Brother Hulien, apparently of the Westcroft Monastery, I figured it was a religious text and would be less interesting than the others.

And boy, was I wrong.

These Knights of Eradication were some real assholes. It wasn't like they wanted to eradicate hunger or poverty. Nope. They want to rid the world of all magic. People, objects, literally everything. It was a perversion of God's creation, they said, and therefore a grave sin.

I kept shaking my head and grimacing at the bullshit the author kept pushing. They believed that by ridding the world of magic, their God would finally be able to return to its physical form and he would grant them all immortality or some shit.

Some of it was a little less ridiculous, but not much better. The Knights knew how magic worked; I mean, it wasn't exactly a secret. But one of their tenets was the belief that Pholl did not willingly give up his power. That ancient mages must have overthrown him somehow and dispersed his being throughout the continent, to allow themselves to take hold of his power and use it for themselves.

At least there were some nuggets of truth in there, but they really took it too far. From what I could tell, the more generally accepted story was that Pholl was a benevolent God. That he *chose* to make his power available to humans.

Now if only he could just show up for a minute and clear up all that confusion. All it would take was a few minutes of his time, but no! Just like the Gods in any story I'd ever read, Pholl refused to intervene.

But the lingering question was: What did Jacobus want with these Knights? Why would he even be reading a book about some obscure religion that wanted all mages on the continent, including himself, killed? As much as I wracked my mind for possibilities, I couldn't find any that made sense.

At least *Lost Artifacts of Old Tris* held mentions of ruins that remained to be excavated and the powerful artifacts therein. It even alluded to a Pillar somewhere in the old country, even if the author didn't know where it could be. Still, it was clear why Jacobus picked that book.

Then there was *Pillars: An Examination*. Jacobus wasn't beating around the bush with that one, he must have received his original orders from The Lady, the ones that led him to the ancient chamber where the Pillar made us switch bodies, and immediately went to the library.

But I couldn't think of any reason for his personal interest in the violent sect of knights.

Eventually, Lilly looked up from one of her books on the Regeneration school's recommended reading list and noticed my expression.

"Not much of a fan of that book, are you Jake?"

I looked up and gave my eyes a second to adjust. I'd been looking at words on a page for such a long time that my vision had the anti-image still burned in. "It's just crazy. You two ever heard of the Knights of–"

"Eradication?" Haether finished my sentence and I nodded. "Fuck those guys and their new world order. They're nothing but ignorant murderers."

Meanwhile, Lilly shook her head and interjected, "Never heard of them," in between Haether's angry declarations.

"They had a temple in my city and never stopped trying to convert literally anyone they could get their hands on. They'd cling to stories about mages taking advantage of non-magic folk, then preyed on people's fears and tried to rile them up. And for some reason, my father never took them as a serious threat."

"Yeah, that sounds about right, based on what I've been reading."

"Speaking of which. Why *are* you reading that? Not getting any ideas, are you?" Lilly joked, smirking.

My heart rate picked up as I realized I couldn't just come out with the truth, but I found a convenient lie easily enough. I didn't want to keep lying to them, but it seemed necessary.

At least they weren't able to read my mind. Yet. Although, the *Iterad Virtutem* was pretty vague on how that all worked, all we were able to manage so far was an awareness of each other's feelings and a general location.

"Not at all. We're all finally able to *enjoy each other's company*," the girls smirked at that and Lilly blushed, "and I want that to last as long as possible. We're going to have to leave Aether at some point, and I've no doubt we'll run into these assholes once we do." I shrugged, "So, I wanted to know a little more about them."

They nodded in understanding. I suddenly felt something running up the inseam of my leg and when I gave a jolt, Haether giggled. "Well, if it's stressing you out, I think I know a way to help."

I smirked. "You know, it really is bothering me. I'm not sure how I'll focus on anything else," I said, heavy with sarcasm. "Might even need some help getting it off my mind."

Haether's smile grew but Lilly interrupted our flirting by picking up her heavy book and letting fall back on the table with a loud thump. Our eyes darted over to her. "Now that your minds are out of the gutter, I think we should get back to studying. We can reward ourselves later," she added, sounding like a mother promising her kids a piece of candy so long as they behaved.

"Alright, alright," I grumbled.

But the rest of the book didn't make me feel any better. It was difficult to even read an entire chapter at a time. I kept skipping past passages that felt too stupid or ridiculous to take seriously, only to realize that I ended up hopping straight through the entire book.

Whatever. I got the gist of it, anyway.

I returned the book on the way out and noticed Thuvien looking less angry than he had been lately. Considering that it was my fault, and that I couldn't help but like the guy, I wanted to do something to make up for it. There was also the matter of the woman he had to fire, Ruthie. I felt like I owed them each something but didn't yet know what to do about it.

So, I let Lilly and Haether know that I'd catch up with them later, and not to have too much fun without me. The way the smiled at each other after that made no promises.

I didn't have a lot of experience with this world, but the various races seemed far more open-minded, sexually. Neither girl balked at the idea of playing around with each other. If anything, they seemed into each other at least as much as they liked me! Which was perfect because I'd be lying if I said I didn't worry about the future dynamics of our polyamorous relationship. It could have been enough to make my head spin, dealing with two girlfriends at once, but for the time being it was all play and no work. I only hoped it could stay that way for as long as possible.

The Head Librarian was standing with his arms crossed over his chest, one hand up lingering over his mouth as he mumbled to himself. He perked up as he saw me. "Jake! How's the Initiate life treating you? Should be getting a bit more interesting, these days."

Oh, it just got way more interesting than he could imagine. Unless he had also had a threesome at some point with a pair busty witch girls, in which case he'd probably never stop imagining it in all its glorious detail. I know I wouldn't.

But I knew what he was referring to. "Yeah, we're finally getting to practice what we've learned. We've only covered pretty basic magics so far and used them against training targets when we weren't taking it easy against each other. But still, it's exciting. Much better than several-hour-long lectures. Not that yours was boring, of course," I added.

He smiled widely at me. "Ah, no need to flatter me so! But I do appreciate your *dishonesty*." He jabbed me with an elbow to emphasize his joke, then gave a lazy shrug, "The truth is, that's a lot of what goes on at this academy of ours. Lectures. It might seem boring, but it is important to lay down a solid foundation before we begin to build upon it. Understanding exactly how magic works, and what it's doing, will make your use of it far more efficient. Now, don't give me that look! It might sound trite, but it's true."

I nodded, unable to disagree. Then got to my point of approaching him. "What happened here, anyway? I saw the mess last week and figured I'd let you cool down before asking about it."

"I appreciate that," he said in a more serious tone. "I can't say much, you are still an Initiate after all, and we are keeping the information tight while we investigate. I'll just say that someone broke into the library, due to some of our staff's negligence."

I glanced over at the information desk and Thuvien sighed. "And yes, I suppose that's not a detail I can keep hidden. Ruthie was involved and we had to let her go. With her years of experience, however, I've no doubt she'll find another renowned library that will hire her in a heartbeat.

"But for now, Jake, as much as you might like to help, and I do appreciate your interest, there are some matters regarding our library that can only be dealt with by the most senior faculty."

He clapped an arm on my shoulder and his mood lightened a bit. "Train, study, and pass your exams. That's all you need concern yourself with. Oh, and don't forget to do some of the grunt work around here from time to time." He winked, then patted me on the arm again and took off as I told him to take care of himself.

Whoever shot that fireball at me and destroyed the bookshelf was still out there, after all, and Thuvien may be a senior member of the faculty but I had no idea how well he could protect himself. The man didn't seem worried about it though, so I didn't let it bother me.

Besides, I had more important things on my mind. Like a pair of horny witches who were waiting for me back at Haether's apartment.

And come to find out, they had already started without me. Haether answered her door wrapped in the complex crimson blanket from her bed.

Then she pulled me in and kept my mind occupied for the rest of the weekend.

❧ 31 ❧

THE FINAL WEEK OF CLASSES WAS STARTING, AND THE ROWS of students were as tense as ever.

Most of them were, anyway. Haether, Lilly, and I were less stressed than we'd ever been. It was too bad the school didn't allow partying or alcohol, never mind any other drugs, because this group could really benefit from a bit of stress-relief.

But then again, maybe that was why they didn't allow it. They knew that the students would use them to cope with their potentially impending dooms, which would just take time away from studying, and therefore make the aforementioned doom more likely because they'd be under-prepared.

Or maybe I was just overthinking it.

The lectures on magical creatures, which I was looking forward to more than any other, would have to wait, as we had *two* days of guest lecturers this week. I added my groan to the disappointed chorus as our professor mentioned that little detail.

The High Psymage Phoster Telement was, to put it simply, a creepy-looking old dude. He was bald and frail but moved with a surprising grace. He wore no hat, only long grey robes, but carried a staff of gnarled wood that looked more like a walking stick. His sunken brown eyes scanned the room as if it were a shop whose stock he was interested in.

He was the head of the Mental Magics school and one of the world's foremost forensic scryers, according to Professor Doriah's introduction.

That was an interesting skill, the ability to trace magical signatures back to whoever left them. If I was going to keep working for The Lady, I would need to learn to cover my tracks, if that was possible.

Once he took his place at the podium, he began. "I can sense the tension in this room. Many of you fear for your lives, and I can't say that I blame you. Some of you will not be back next week."

"He's a cheerful one," Lilly quipped softly. Then the speaker's haunting eyes quickly latched onto her and she sunk into her seat.

He didn't call her out though, just kept on as if he heard nothing. "But every one of you that remains will be stronger for it. It is a fact that suffering through such trials builds the will. So, think not of the students who will soon fall and instead look to the future. As a matter of fact, that is exactly one of the disciplines that my school offers. Foretelling. Yes, I can tell that some of you don't believe me. Even today, there are those who think the ability is mere conjecture, or parlor tricks, but nothing could be further from the truth.

"It was a few hundred years ago that the kingdom of Old Tris fell. It is said that one of the last king's advisors told him of the army that was marching on his capital, but he ignored every warning and paid dearly for it. It may not be an exact science. You may not know how large an army is, not without years of practice, but you can know that one is on its way. This, I can teach you.

"As well as many other talents. Mind reading, for example, is a skill thought impossible by many. That it is, indeed, true enough. It is preferable that the laymen believe this, otherwise they would always fear that their thoughts are being tampered with.

"The idea of looking into another person's mind and hearing their thoughts directly or fishing around their memories for information is, however, a complete fallacy. But that does not mean people are indecipherable. You may learn to sense, and even influence, their emotions, and desires. There are even some in this world who claim to have done the impossible by extracting discreet thoughts from a willing participant, but it is a matter of some conjecture.

"Nonetheless, I hope that many of you will commit your efforts toward furthering our study of the Mental Magics. We will continue to push the boundary of what is possible, and the very first true mind reader may very well be sitting in this very room."

I had to admit, the guy made it sound pretty interesting, despite his slow manner of speaking and scratchy voice.

The lecture only went downhill from there, however. The High Psymage went down a meandering tangent as he spoke about some of the past teachers and employers who doubted his abilities and soon met untimely ends that could have been avoided. I was half expecting the guy to start calling out which ones of us were about to die soon! He seemed like the type of guy to think about that sort of thing, even if he kept it to himself.

When we were finally let out, I could not have been happier. Whelan, oddly, seemed a bit offended by that.

"Look, I know he sounded like he was just patting himself on the back and talking about all the people who were wrong about him, but he wasn't exaggerating," Whelan explained after I told him that I almost fell asleep a few times. "My Dad chose the school of Mental Magics and had nothing but good things to say about the High Psymage. Every story he told up there was true, believe it or not."

"Oh, I believe it," I replied. "If only because it prevents him from telling me those stories again."

Whelan rolled his eyes, "I don't think you realize the kind of stuff he was talking about. *Emotional manipulation*, Jake. That doesn't interest you? All it could take is a little nudge on the right emotion and you could get whatever you want! A job that you're not quite qualified for, an item that was a little too expensive." Then he wrapped an arm around my shoulders, leaned in close and lowered his voice, then nodded toward the girls. "A certain attractive lady who isn't giving you the time of day. The possibilities are endless!"

I shrugged him off and shook my head. "Some of us don't need magic to get laid, Whelan."

Haether barked a laugh at that. I realized that, in a way, I did use the bond to get laid, but it was still a far cry from influencing a girl's emotions just to make her give me a chance. I mean, I wasn't *that* pathetic. Whelan though... the jury was still out on that one.

"I'm more excited for tomorrow's lectures," Andrith commented from the sidelines.

We all whipped our heads around to look at him. "How do you know who the guest is tomorrow?" I asked.

Andrith looked at me like I was stupid. Which, given his explanation, maybe I was. Only a little bit, though. He glanced at everyone else with the same expression, so at least I wasn't alone in my confusion. "Well, the academy is broken up into five different schools. Six, I guess, if you count the Natural and Elemental Magics separately. They're the only one left that we haven't heard from," he shrugged, "so it's gotta be them."

"Ah. Well, of course," Lilly muttered, more to herself than any of us.

"Besides, that's the one I've been looking forward to the most," Andrith continued. "I'll be specializing in elemental magics myself. What about you guys?"

I was the first to speak up. "History and Archeology."

"Really? I found Thuvien's lecture a bit boring, to be honest."

"See, in my country, Rhode Island, we have this old legend named Indiana Jones." The girls looked back at me with interest in their eyes, and I had a hard time keeping a straight face. "He was a renowned archeologist who saved the world from men who sought to take it over with the power of the Holy Grail."

"The Holy Grail? Never heard of it," Haether commented, sounding disappointed in herself.

"Oh yeah, it's a big deal. Supposed to be extremely powerful. Anyway, he inspired me as a kid, and I've always wanted to delve ancient tombs and ruins to see what kind of artifacts might be lying around. Plus, ancient peoples always interested me, so it was an easy pick."

"That sounds fun and all, but I think I'll stick with something safer. I'm going into mental magics, myself," Whelan added, jabbing a thumb into his chest. Then he cringed slightly, "Oh yeah. I haven't actually mentioned it yet but, I'm kind of the heir of my house."

"Kind of?" Haether snorted.

"Literally the heir of my house, okay? My Dad's a Count, and I will be one day too. Diplomacy classes are part of the school of mental magics, so," he shrugged and repeated my words, "it was an easy pick."

I nodded. "Simple enough. Ladies?"

"Regeneration," Lilly called back, which she'd mentioned before so it was no surprise.

"I will... also be in the school of mental magics," Haether replied slowly, as if not wanting to admit that she was making the same choice as Whelan.

"Oh really?" he said, much more excited than she was. "That's great, we can compare notes and stuff, since we'll probably be in a lot of the same classes at first."

"Oh. Great," she said in a deadpan voice that made Whelan roll his eyes.

"You can bag on me all you want, but don't think that I haven't noticed how much you two have calmed down over the weekend," Whelan shot back, nodding at both Haether and Lilly. "What changed? It's not like we've learned anything about the creatures we'll be fighting."

From my angle, I could see Lilly's face redden. Haether, however, played it off masterfully. She shrugged and replied in a lazy voice. "Well, it's not like worrying over it will help anything. We spend a lot of time studying, Whelan, more than anyone else in class, as far as we can tell. So, we concluded that we must be doing pretty well. All we can do is work hard and hope for the best. Anything else is a distraction."

Whelan pursed his lips and nodded, clearly satisfied with her answer.

Then she flipped it around on him. "Not that I care, exactly, but since we're talking about it, what have *you* been doing with your free time, Whelan?"

He laughed awkwardly. "Ah, you know. Stuff. Uh," he paused and seemed like he was having trouble coming up with an actual answer. "well, I guess I've just been hanging out with my other friends, mostly. Some other noble's kids who I used to hang out with from time to time. They're able to get their hands on some liquor and are usually willing to share."

Haether snorted. "Typical. You get your first taste of freedom and waste it on drinking with your friends. Well, I hope you enjoyed your last few weeks alive." She left it at that, and I watched her words sink into Whelan.

His brow furrowed and he grew serious. He nudged me and spoke a little quieter, not that it stopped the rest of our group from hearing. "You don't think I actually have a chance at dying, do you?"

Well, shit. Really wished I didn't get dragged into it, but I didn't want to lie to my friend. I shrugged. "Hard to say. We don't really know anything about the monsters yet. And you don't really take many notes in class. And you don't really study. So..." I shrugged again, at a loss for words, "I don't know."

Whelan's gaze dug into me as he nodded, a thoughtful expression on his face. "In that case, maybe I'll join you three. Just for this last week."

"That's probably for the best," Lilly called back.

"Yeah, even I've been spending most of my time in the books," Andrith added, chuckling.

"Oh, lay off!"

❧ 32 ❧

"TODAY, YOU ARE IN FOR A SPECIAL TREAT," PROFESSOR Doriah began, but I got a distinct sense of sarcasm from her. "Not just one guest lecturer, but *two*. The school of Natural and Elemental Magics has grown in recent years and taken on two heads. The High Botanist oversees the Natural Magics side, and the High Wizard does so for Elemental Magics. Be warned, we may end up running a bit late today, as a result. Ah! And here they are now."

Just as she said that two people descended the steps.

The first had to be the High Wizard. He looked to be somewhere in his late thirties, wore long robes of a deep brown and a maroon wizard hat perched on his head. He was pale and had bright orange hair, with a serious face whose deep lines told of years of stress.

The second was a slight woman with pale gray skin, who was rail thin, but topped her colleague by a few inches. She had jet-black hair that reached her waist. She wore a breezy blouse of a light green shade and a golden skirt that billowed around her knees. As serious as the other seemed, this one was lighthearted and friendly. She kept shooting smiles and waves at the students around her as she gracefully flowed down the steps.

The wizard stepped up to the podium first.

He cleared his throat and ran his eyes through the crowd, like he was weighing us up. "Our world can be a dangerous place," he began. "All of our schools have innumerable lessons to teach you that could save your lives one day, but none more so than the school of Elemental Magics. We are the frontline of defense should the school ever be set upon by an army, we are the first line of offense if Vethris should ever gather enough strength for an uprising. The other schools will train you to fight, sure, but as a mere afterthought.

"Even if you don't choose my school, I advise every one of you to pick an element to specialize in and take a few classes in it. We have experts in each of them. I, myself, am an accomplished Fire Mage of some renown. I am High Wizard Bran Lefilio. The youngest head of a school that this academy has ever seen.

"I can teach you to create a flame so hot that it would blind those who look upon it. To create an explosion the likes of which you never dreamed. Or even, should you work hard enough, to create your own familiar. They are companions built of a pure element, not unlike the pure Elementals that some of you descend from." That caught my attention, so I had my Auto-Quill make note of it to look into later.

"Such as this." With a proud smile, he raised his right arm toward the sky. Out of his loose sleeve shot a flaming bird that erupted in size as it left him. Smoke rose from behind it as it careened through the sky and then looped back around. Suddenly, it shrunk to the size of a parrot and alighted on the High Wizard's shoulder. "Blazewing here is a phoenix. Like all familiars, if he should fall in battle, I can bring him back at any time by simply giving up a bit of my capacity for power. You will find yourself weakened by how powerful you make your familiar, but I assure you that they more than make up for it."

Then he glanced up at his friend and Blazewing shot a ball of flame into the air that grew into the size of a car. It flew higher and higher before it ultimately exploded in a violent burst of orange light. Despite being far away from the blast, it felt as if I was sitting in front of a campfire.

The High Wizard watched the ball of flame with adoring eyes. Then he lifted his right hand again and the familiar dove back in. The man proceeded to sell his school to us better than any of the other lecturers.

If I hadn't already made my choice, I might have chosen Elemental Magics instead! Having a familiar like that was tempting, but I already had fighting companions in Lilly and Haether. Still, he succeeded in hyping me up for my time after the exam, when I'd finally be able to choose some of my classes and learn more advanced magics. His school would be the most useful in learning to fight, it seemed. I just had to choose an element.

The sun reached its peak by the time the High Wizard gave up his place at the podium and the High Botanist replaced him. She was a cheery woman, at least part elf based on her grey skin, and had kind, emerald eyes.

She held her arms out at her sides, palms facing up, and began. "The world around us is a magnificent place. Taste the crisp air, observe the beauty of the forest behind me, all the forms of life that inhabit it. Think of the farmers who produce your food, the environment that enables them to grow their crops. These are the domain of the Natural Magics. You might even think of it as just another element. Related to Earth, but not the same. Or almost like a branch of the Regeneration school, but again, quite different.

"We seek to nurture and enhance the world around us. From growing incredible plant life of entirely new species, to healing or boosting the strength of those that already exist. We cure diseases in crops and prevent others. We can make them immune to pests and are even working toward sentience in certain species. The High Wizard is not the only one capable of teaching you to create familiars," she grinned and pointed toward the field just outside of our amphitheater. Just where her hand indicated, a tree began to sprout from the Earth. It grew until it was about a foot tall, then pulled its roots out and trotted over to the High Botanist's side.

"My little Twig here is just the beginning of what is possible with the school of Natural Magics. Look at the tallest trees in the forest at my back. It is far from easy, but this little guy," she indicated the sproutling that clung to her leg, "could gave grown as large as any one of them. Imagine a hundred-foot-tall oak pulling its roots out of the ground and besieging a city. There may be some among you that one day put even my greatest feats to shame."

Lilly was plainly slack jawed at some of the High Botanist's words. Being from a small farming village, I could see why this type of magic appealed to her, even if it didn't particularly interest me. I had to admit, though, it would have been cool to see her summon the largest tree she could manage. My mind immediately went to Treebeard from the Lord of the Rings and it had me seriously tempted to take a few Natural Magics classes.

I knew that I wanted to have a familiar of some kind, even if I didn't always use it, but of what element, I was not sure. Could an air familiar help its owner fly? Or maybe a water familiar could serve almost like a boat. Was lightning even an option? I'd need to find a book about it later.

After classes that day, I took on another shift at the library to fill my night. After a quick bite to eat, I left Lilly, Haether, and Whelan on the fourth floor to go look for Filo.

She was putting books away on the first floor, though in

the minute I spent watching her, I could tell she was distracted. Her eyes kept drifting off and looking toward the information desk, where Thuvien was having a conversation with Ruthie's replacement, a woman I didn't recognize.

Filo reacted with a jolt as I unintentionally snuck up on her. She was so enthralled in the conversation, but from this distance, she couldn't hear a word of it. Unless that was possible with magic, somehow, but I wasn't able to sense her use of either Pholl or Vethuis's power.

"What's up with you?" I asked, as Filo brought herself back to reality and put a book away as if she had never been distracted.

She glanced at me and tightened her expression. "Got some stuff on my mind, is all."

I grabbed a couple books and started to look for their homes, then decided to try making a joke. "You seem as somber as most of my classmates. It could be worse, right? It's not like *you* might get killed by some magical monster this Sunday."

She just sighed, with not so much as a twitch at the corners of her mouth.

"It's about the task The Lady gave you, isn't it?"

Filo froze and blinked a few times, then nodded. Her face was drawn into a resigned expression.

I stepped over to her and took the books out of her hands. When she looked up at me, her beautiful purple eyes were rimmed with tears. "Filo, I know you hate me," I chuckled, "but you still helped me out. That means something to me, and I want to help you in return. You just need to let me know what I can do."

She snorted and shook her head, then wiped a tear as it fell. "Ugh. I don't hate you, Jake. I hate the situation I'm in," she sighed and put one of her hands on my forearm. I tried to hide my shock as it was the first time she'd *touched* me without *hitting* me. Then she held my arm steady while she ripped the books out of my hand. "I know you want to help but I can take care of myself. I always have and always will. There's no way around it, I just have to... to do it. I'm sorry Jake."

I shook my head. "You have nothing to be sorry for, Filo."

"Not yet, I don't," she grumbled.

I wished I knew what was troubling her, but she just wouldn't open up to me. Whatever The Lady expected out of her, it was serious. Probably more so than stealing some book. But what could it be? There were certainly other things worth stealing in this place, but I had no idea what.

But I did have an idea as for how I could find out. One I'd thought of before but not yet tried because I didn't have much control of my Power.

I grabbed a couple books that I suspected were in another aisle and left Filo behind for a minute. Then, when no one was looking, I directed my vision at the floor and flexed the strange new muscle in my eyes that vibrated whenever my power activated.

I pushed through the floor and saw darkness. The basement floors were deeper than I expected, but with magic, normal architectural standards didn't apply.

My vision emerged into a corridor dimly lit by white strips of light at waist height, that I assumed was the first floor, so I just kept going. After passing two more of the same, I expected something more interesting, but the fourth and fifth floors were no different, except that the lights in each hallway changed according to the color orbs that were required for admittance.

Out of curiosity, I kept going.

My breath caught as I found a sixth floor. Initiates like myself weren't even supposed know any of these existed, and Filo only knew about the first five. How far down did it actually go? As much as I wanted to know, I was given pause upon realizing what this floor was used for.

It was a prison.

With tremendous difficulty, I pulled back on my vision as it was zooming in. I was able to stop it where it was, but it was about as easy as balancing a broomstick on one finger. It required constant vigilance. Faltering even slightly resulted in the zooming function starting up again, in either direction.

I fell to one knee as my head swam. It was like vertigo pushed to the extreme. Or like falling off a cliff in virtual reality goggles. My vision didn't match what my hands and feet could feel around me, and my mind was clearly having a hard time reconciling the difference. I steadied myself with one hand on the books that I'd placed on the floor, and the other gripping the bookshelf next to me. *Hard.*

Very carefully, I looked around. These hallways were well-lit and bare of any furnishings. Periodically there were doors set into the walls with slots that I figured were for meals. There wasn't anything special about the inmates, not at a glance anyway, which I found oddly funny. They were a mix of all races; an orc, a few humans, elves, and elementals. All races that I had never even heard of until a few weeks ago and yet, now they seemed like nothing special. A perfectly ordinary rainbow of people.

The inmates seemed off, however, the longer I watched. Some were simply sitting on their beds, others stood staring at the wall or the door. Almost every single one of them looked dazed. *Drugged.*

Except one.

He sat on his bed, leaning forward on elbows planted on his knees, with his fingers steepled together and resting against his lips. Like he was waiting. Suddenly, he perked up. His face twisted in confusion before his head whipped around.

And looked directly at me, then smiled. He was oddly handsome, with thick black curls that fell passed his ears, dark brown skin, and a salt-and-pepper beard of stubble. He started speaking, but my power didn't include noise, so it didn't register. But that didn't matter.

He saw me watching him through who knows how many feet of Earth. He knew I was looking at him and tried to talk to me.

My vision snapped back through layers of darkness and differently lit hallways, until it was back to normal.

But my heart was racing. Fear spiked through me, despite reassuring myself that I was safe.

Whoever that man was, he couldn't do anything, and likely couldn't even see me at all. The Pillars were supposed to give people powers that were impossible with normal magic, so how could he have sensed anything?

After everything I'd learned, my constant reading for the past few weeks, I thought I was starting to get a handle on this world.

But this didn't make sense. Not even close.

33

I WAS SILENT FOR THE REST OF THE NIGHT, TO THE POINT that I was pretty certain Filo thought I was annoyed with her. But I couldn't think about anything else. My hands may have known to pick up books and put them away, with as little input from my brain as possible, but I was barely paying attention.

This place is just full of secrets.

Did Filo know about the lower floors too and just decide against telling me? I knew I couldn't just assume that her task involved that prison, but given her attitude toward the job she refused to tell me about, I couldn't imagine anything else that made sense. Maybe the Shadows wanted her to break someone out.

But I also kept wondering why they would keep a prison beneath the library, anyway? It would make far more sense to be beneath the Natural and Elemental Magics school. At least the faculty in that building specialized in combat.

If any of those inmates were particularly powerful, which I had no doubt they all were, what chance would a bunch of librarians have at stopping them?

Great. With just a few days left before the exams, I ended up with a whole list of questions to distract me and no way to find out the answers.

Even some of the most interesting lectures so far couldn't keep my attention. As important as I knew they were, I didn't care to learn about griffins or minotaurs, nor any other creature that, to me, was mythical until just a few weeks ago.

Besides, I knew that two of the best students in class had my back. Lilly and Haether took extremely detailed notes that, when put together, were probably more thorough than the class itself. As long as I had them nearby when I went up against whatever creature Doriah pitted me against, I'd be safe.

So far, we'd only managed to communicate vague meanings and images, but we kept getting better, and we were determined to reach the point where we could actually talk to each other mentally, even if it meant performing our little ritual every night.

Which was a sacrifice I was *very* willing to make.

Especially since it just kept getting better. We were starting to learn each other's bodies, knowing just the right places to kiss or caress to drive each other wild.

In my case, it was pretty simple. Lilly and Haether were so hot that they could slap me with mashed potatoes, and I'd still find a way to get turned on. Just watching those two walk around campus, knowing what I got to do to them behind closed doors every night, was enough to get me hard.

With each of us there to have each other's backs, the girls didn't have anything to fear anymore. Whereas the rest of our class was growing more panicky by the hour, Lilly and Haether weren't even concerned. I was a bit of a mess, considering the several layers of secrets that I was still trying to hide, but at least I had two gorgeous women to keep me distracted.

And then Doriah decided to cap off her last lecture by scaring the shit out of everyone.

Her last creature she decided to tell us about? Dragons, obviously.

When she brought them up, the class grew abnormally quiet, and she smiled as if that was just the reaction she'd been hoping for. "That's right. Dragons," she continued. "One of the most formidable foes this world has to offer. Just about everything you've heard about them is true. They have greater control over their given element than even the strongest mages in history. There are dragons that spit venom, lightning, ice, fire of course, and even more."

An elemental that I'd never met stuck up her hand shyly. When Doriah nodded to the pink-skinned girl, she asked, "Um. We're not going to have to actually fight a dragon on Sunday, though. Are we?"

Professor Doriah started chuckling and some of the tension seemed to drain out of the rows of students. That is, until she said, "Oh, you didn't think I'd actually answer that question, did you? These creatures you've been learning about over the past few days, you never know when one of them will catch you off guard. As Acolytes, some of you will leave the academy to run errands or even simple missions, and you need to know how to protect yourselves. From *everything*. Not because they might be on the test, but because they are *real*."

Both Lilly and Haether fidgeted uncomfortably at that. Even Whelan and Andrith shared a nervous glance.

I reached both hands out to my sides and grabbed onto Haether and Lilly. Then I gave them each a solemn nod in turn that I hoped would reassure them. With it, I whispered, "We've got this. We've been working hard. We have an *edge*. We've got this." I nodded again to try to drive the point home, and while it seemed to help, they both still seemed on edge.

When we left class that day, they rushed me straight to Haether's apartment.

Lilly dropped her skirt to the floor and threw her breezy blouse over a chair before jumping me. Her orange hat fell off her head as she latched onto me. Behind me, I heard Haether close and lock the door, then start undressing herself, too. Which was a shame, I liked doing that for them.

"We have only one night left," Lilly said between heavy kisses, "and we still can't read each other's minds. Not the way we want to. So, you know what that means." She shot me a wink and then lowered to her knees. Her hands shook as they started to unlace my trousers.

I took her hands in mine and pulled her up to me. As much as I loved feeling her mouth wrapped around me, I hated seeing the two of them this way. Worried and anxious. They hadn't been so jittery ever since we formed the bond.

I pulled Lilly up to meet my eyes and looked between her and Haether as I spoke. "I know. One last night, and one last chance to pour as much power into our bond as possible. In other words, we're in for a busy night," I chuckled. "But first, I want to help you two unwind. So, for now anyway, I'm in charge. Got it?"

They both looked a little confused and shot each other glance as if to ask if the other knew about this. They shrugged and looked back at me.

"I don't want you two to worry about anything tonight. So just relax and let me take care of you."

Haether blushed, "Ooh. I like this new bossy Jake." As she waltzed by me, I slapped her ass and she let out a playful yelp that made Lilly giggle.

"Alright, onto the bed. Both of you."

They both grew redder by the second but obeyed loyally. Haether plopped herself onto bed as if she were about to go to sleep, but Lilly crawled over to her seductively.

I couldn't tear my eyes away from her ass, nor the way she arched her back to emphasize it. So, I kneeled by the edge of the bed and barked a quick order. "Lilly. Right here," I pointed to the edge of the bed and the brunette flipped onto her back, then edged herself toward me.

Then she spread her legs and inched her mound toward my mouth. When she was close enough, I wrapped my hands around her soft thighs and started kissing my way closer to her center.

"Mmm," Haether purred, "What about me?" She matched Lilly's position and shimmied up to the edge right next to her.

"For now," I said between light kisses around Lilly's slit that made her shudder, "you just watch."

Haether's pout looked insanely sexy. "I don't like being teased," she said in a heavy whisper, "but for you, I guess I'll allow it."

As I finally ran my tongue along Lilly's hot entrance, I held eye contact with Haether. The elf girl's smile grew hungry, and she bit her lip. Without looking away, I started focusing on Lilly's clit and moved one of my hands up to grab one of her firm tits.

One of Haether's hands inched up to her own chest to mirror what I was doing to Lilly. She barely even seemed to realize she was doing it.

As Lilly's breathing grew heavy, I pulled back. Her head had been lolled back against the red comforter, but she shot up and glared at me like I'd just betrayed her. "Oh, you can't stop now! I was getting close!"

"I know. But Haether's been nice and patient so far. I need to reward her." The busty half-elf nodded incessantly at that and edged herself closer to me just as Lilly did the same.

"But it's not fair! You started with me, you should at least finish," Lilly whined.

I chuckled as I switched over to Haether and started warming her up. "We're a team, here Lilly. We need to take care of each other. I'll make it up to you after, alright?"

As I placed my mouth over Haether's slit and started running my tongue over her, Lilly responded, sounding out of breath. "O-okay."

Then, as she watched me eating Haether out, I noticed one of Lilly's hands drifting southward. I caught it before she could touch herself, though. "Nope. No pleasuring yourself. You're in my hands tonight, remember?"

"No fair!" she called out, and I finally felt a bit of guilt for teasing her.

"Alright, alright. I was going to wait for this, but I can't risk leaving either of you unsatisfied."

Haether, for one, barely seemed to notice what we were saying, her head merely laid back as she let me do as I wished to her. She perked up as I got to my feet and undressed. Then I climbed onto the bed next to them.

"First," I grinned, "Put your hats back on, and nothing else." They both made wry expressions but giggled as they went along with my request. "Now, Haether," I got her attention and pointed at my mouth. "And Lilly," then I pointed to my waist.

They both nodded and jumped to action. Haether planted her knees beside my head and lowered herself down to me. She braced herself against the headboard and looked down at me with lidded, teal eyes. Her dark blue hat flopped against the wall and laid crooked on her head.

Lilly caught me by surprise as she took me into her mouth. I groaned into Haether's pussy as Lilly covered me in her spit, but it wasn't long before she climbed on top of me and started grinding away. Her center was warm and tight, but I tried to focus on taking care of Haether, as hard as that was.

Lilly's hands were planted on my stomach as she ground into me with a circular motion. Haether kept bucking her hips harder against my face as she grew closer and closer to completion.

It was Lilly that finished first, but she kept right on going. I felt the bond strengthen a little as she shuddered with the pleasure of her orgasm.

I was next. I pulled away from Haether's slit just long enough to warn Lilly. To my surprise, Lilly hopped off and took me into her mouth as she sucked the seed right out of me.

Haether looked back to watch and started grinding herself against my face with a renewed frenzy. "That's so fucking hot," she let out in a breathy whisper.

Her body was twisted so that she could look at Lilly with my cock in her mouth, my seed dripping out, while her orgasm hit her. A deep, pleasurable sound erupted in her throat and her hand tightened its grip on my head so hard that it felt close to ripping out hair. Her head flung backwards, and the witch's hat slipped off.

When she was finished convulsing, she was out of breath. Haether pushed off the headboard and crawled over to join Lilly as they took turns cleaning me off.

Yeah, at this point, I think I could die happy.

🎇 34 🎇

As much as we tried, Lilly, Haether, and I weren't able to reach the point in the bond where we could speak in each other's minds. We could, however, send clear images such that we could basically see through each other's eyes freely.

We could also pass along simple ideas. Not sentences or words, but meanings. Things like, "Come here," or "Help." It wasn't so much that we could hear the word in our minds, instead we just knew what each other wanted.

It would need to be good enough.

Whelan and Andrith joined us on our walk to the exams. We were all nervous. It was one of the most important days of our lives, after all, but most of the other students who were headed in the same direction looked far worse.

There were a lot of grim faces heading toward the arena. It was much larger than the amphitheater and made it possible to spread hundreds of desks over the hard-packed dirt.

A crowd of students was gathered near Doriah, who was busy speaking with some people I hadn't seen before. They weren't much older than the class, so I assumed they were there to help Doriah keep an eye on the students so that they couldn't cheat.

Not that they'd be able to stop us.

Normally, I wouldn't be in favor of cheating, but when the school put us in the position where we could lose our lives, they should have expected people to do whatever it took to pass. So, I didn't have a single regret or second thought.

As we approached the crowd, the test organizers started letting people into the arena to find seats. We wished each other well and took up a block of five desks in a corner.

I felt the positivity that Lilly was sending Haether and I and tried to return the same. Not able to resist, I pictured a few of the positions we'd tried out last night and was rewarded with Lilly's deep blush and wide eyes. Haether, however, just chuckled and sent back her own point of view of the same positions.

I tucked my hardening friend under my waistband just as Doriah began her introduction. "Welcome, class, to your exam. You will have all day, so do not rush yourselves. How well you do on this written portion will help decide your place tomorrow. So do your best. Do *not* cheat. And make me proud." She nodded her head and a small stack of papers rose out of the desk, along with an Auto-Quill.

I shot my friends an encouraging look and got started.

"Eyes on your own paper," I heard from a sharp voice nearby and just nodded my head, while rolling my eyes. Haether sent an image of her own papers and a wry feeling to go along with it. I snorted a laugh and cleared my throat to hide it.

Then we got started. The questions were a mix of multiple choice, short answer, and open-ended. I was a bit disappointed, to be honest. It felt almost exactly like a test back in my world, which was a bit anti-climactic for a fantastical magic academy, but there was also tomorrow's battle to worry about.

We started off a bit slow as we established our method of communicating. One of us would pick an answer and send an image of the question to the other two, who would then respond with an image of the same answer if they agreed. There were a few disagreements, which amounted to sending back a different image along with a few notes written next to the question that explained why. They were short, simple notes that no one could know were written for anyone but the test taker.

The longer-form questions were a little harder to discuss, but it was easy enough to just write out an answer and send it to each other.

The two girls were guiding the group along far more than I was. By the time I finished reading the next question, they had already answered it, most of the time.

The sun reached its peak and still we were jotting down answers. The sounds of test-evaluators' soft footsteps were joined by the scratching of hundreds of Auto-Quills and shuffling papers.

Eventually, students started trickling out. They raised their hands and when an evaluator came by to confirm that they were finished, the test materials sunk back into the desks. Andrith was one of the earlier finishers. The first was a small orc girl I hadn't met yet.

By the time we were done, my butt was sore, and my brain felt fried. We didn't all raise our hands at the same time, though, that would have been suspicious. We even made a point of changing some of our answers, particularly on the questions that we couldn't reach a consensus on. Having all the same answers was a sure-fire way to get caught, even if they would have trouble figuring out our method.

So, Lilly was the first to raise her hand and leave.

Followed by Haether a few minutes later and myself about fifteen minutes after that. Whelan, along with about half of the rest of the class, was still working as we left the arena behind in near silence.

It wasn't until we were walking along the dirt path that led through the forest and back to the school that we spoke up again. It had to be no more than a few hours past noon. Birds flitted between branches and sung to each other as rays of sunshine peeked through the canopy of leaves.

I walked between the two girls and was the first to say something. "Well, I think that went pretty well. They didn't catch on to us at all!"

Lilly shushed me and glanced behind us, despite there being no one close enough to see, never mind hear us. She lowered her voice, "We should keep that kind of talk inside our heads as soon as we can. Or at least in our dorm rooms while we can't."

Haether nodded wisely and I did so reluctantly. There was no one around, but better safe than sorry, after all.

"Still," I said a moment later, "I think that I did pretty well. On my own of course, with not even a single person's help!"

Lilly rolled her eyes and Haether snorted a laugh.

"How was Whelan looking when you left?" Haether asked, clearly amused that our confident friend wasn't done yet.

I sent them an image of the last time I saw him and Haether smirked widely. Whelan had been hunched over his desk with a hand tangled up in his long black curls, looking frustrated.

"Oh, I don't wish him any harm, I really don't. But... after teasing us for working so hard the past few weeks, it's nice to see that he's finally realizing his mistake."

"I just hope his Dad taught him more about fighting than

test-taking," I added, only half-joking. I really was worried about the guy and kind of wished that I'd pressured him to join us more often. But he'd made his own choices and would need to deal with their consequences.

We stopped by Haether's apartment for a quick *celebration*, and had her Alchemical Chef whip us up some food before heading to the library.

There wasn't much left to study, but we agreed with Whelan and Andrith to meet afterwards and discuss the exam.

As we stepped out of the stairway, Whelan held out his arms and called to us, "What took you guys so long? You all finished well before I did, and yet me and Andy have been waiting here for like twenty minutes!"

"So, you're calling him Andy, now?" Haether quipped.

"Well, I'm sure as hell not calling any of *you* Andy," Whelan shot back. "But yeah, I think he likes it." Andrith just shrugged. "Well, he doesn't hate it, so I'm sticking to it."

I shook my head, grinning, as I sat down across from the two guys. Haether and Lilly took their places by my sides. "So? How'd you two do?" I asked.

"Not as well as I would have liked," Whelan replied, cringing, "But I wasn't the last person to finish, so it could have been worse."

"Er, yeah. I guess that's one way of looking at it," Lilly muttered.

"Andrith?" I nodded to our newest member.

He glanced at Whelan with a shy smile. "Well…" he hesitated, "it really wasn't as bad as I was expecting. It was long, sure, but most of the questions were pretty basic."

"For you, maybe," Whelan cut in. "Did you three realize we befriended a genius? This guy's only *seventeen*, which makes him one of the youngest to ever attend Aether. The school normally doesn't let people in that young, but he aced the mock exam they gave him months ago and even came to campus a month early so that he could get involved with some research team in the school of Elemental Magics."

Andrith blushed and seemed like he was trying to hide in his chair. "It's not that big a deal," he mumbled.

But from the feelings I was getting from the two girls, I could tell they were at least as surprised as I was. "Jeez. I mean, I knew you were pretty good with Earth magic but didn't realize you were *that far ahead* of the rest of us. Though, now that I think about it, you do look a little younger." I had just assumed he was scrawny.

"You'll have to study with us more often," Lilly added, "Especially once we start Elemental magics classes."

Andrith brightened at that. "Once we're able to practice magic on school grounds, I'm sure we'll all have a few tricks to teach each other. I'm part Earth elemental, so it comes more naturally to me, but I'm sure you've all got your own specialties."

The rest of us glanced around at each other uncertainly. I was the first one to speak, "I can't speak for anyone else, but no. I really don't. Not yet anyway." Then I thought better of it and added, "That is, unless you wanna learn about some obscure ruins I've been reading about," I chuckled, but Andrith responded with an enthusiastic nod.

"That counts!" He assured me. "Either way, we can't be experts in everything this school has to teach us. Over the years we spend here we'll just keep getting better at whatever niche magic we decide to study. If we keep working together like this, we can at least have a passing knowledge in each other's disciplines."

"True enough," Whelan said, then addressed my side of the table. "By the way, how do you guys think you did?"

"Really well," I replied, and the two girls nodded agreement. "All our work definitely paid off," I added with a sly grin. Haether and Lilly both sent images of our extracurricular activities in Haether's apartment, nursing grins of their own.

"And it was *so* worth it," Haether added.

"Nice, nice. In that case, I think an intermediate celebration is in order," Whelan announced as he pulled a bottle of dark brown liquid with light blue, glowing specks collected at the bottom that suffused the liquid as he shook the bottle. "Who here has never tried Aetherian whisky?"

Lilly, Andrith, and I raised our hands. Whelan shot an impressed look at Haether.

She rolled her eyes and shrugged. "I'm eighty-two, remember? I've tried things that would put hair on even *your* chest."

"Oh, well then. I didn't realize I was dealing with such a renowned expert! In that case, I suppose you wouldn't mind starting us off?" His reply was laden with sarcasm as he held the bottle across the table.

Haether snatched it out of his hands and shook it a bit. The blue specks lazily floating around reminded me of a snow-globe. Without another word, she uncorked the bottle and took a swig. With a grimace, she set it back down on the table, wiped the back of her hand over her mouth and then wiped it on my sleeve.

"See?" She said in a strained voice. "Nothing to it."

"Right. Well, no use stalling," Whelan took a sip as well and his face tightened as he set it down. "The after taste really isn't all that bad." Haether shrugged a non-committal answer.

"So, what's with all the blue specks, anyway?" I asked, grabbed the bottle, but wanting to know more before I drank it.

"Ahh, well, to me, they're a dark green. It's just concentrated magic. They brew it in areas of high magical potency, with enchanted barrels and all that. Granted, I'm not expert, but the result are these little globules of power. Try it, you'll feel pretty great afterwards. In more ways than one."

Curious, I tilted the bottle back and took a big swig. The liquid burned as much as anything I'd ever tried, and I once had a sip of Everclear on a dare with a friend. But the taste wasn't terrible, and it left a slightly nutty aftertaste.

When it hit my stomach, however, I felt like I had just pulled in a bit of Pholl's power. I made a confused face and Whelan burst out laughing.

"Yup, you're feeling it! The concentrated magic isn't just there for show, you could use something like this as a source of power instead of Pholl, if you really wanted to. You'd need to get pretty damn drunk to do anything useful," he shrugged, "but it would work. You should check out the flasks they sell at the alchemist's shop near the square. They're full of the stuff. Expensive shit, though."

"Hold on, how am I only hearing about this now?" I asked.

Whelan shrugged. "Mate, if I tried to fill you in on all the shit I thought you'd never heard of, I'd never stop talking."

"Fair enough," I noted, handing the bottle to Lilly.

She looked at the bottle inquisitively and tilted it back. Her eyes widened and eyebrows shot up. As the bottle clinked roughly against the table, one tan hand rose and covered her mouth. "Ugh. That is disgusting!"

Whelan grinned. "Yeah. Andrith? Andy, I mean," he corrected himself and handed the drink over.

Andrith took a deep breath and shrugged before leaning back and taking an impressive drink. "Oooh. Yeah. I don't like that, but it is certainly interesting."

"Just wait til you've had a few more, mate, it just keeps tasting better."

I noticed Haether nod at that, seemingly reluctant to

agree with Whelan. He took another drink and passed it back to Haether, who replaced the cork on the top instead of drinking. "That's all for now," she said, much to Whelan's disappointment. "Tomorrow's going to be even worse than today. There's no way I'm fighting some unknown beast hungover."

"Right," Lilly added. "Tonight, we need to get rested up and ready to fight. Tomorrow, though," she trailed off and let her eyes linger on the bottle.

"Alright, alright," Whelan gave in and put the bottle away. "Tomorrow."

I nodded. "When we're all out there fighting for our lives, this is what we'll need to keep in mind. We're going to need each other's help over the next few years if we want to be the best mages this school has ever had. So be smart and live long enough to come back here and finish that bottle! Then the real fun begins."

35

Fog covered the campus grounds on the morning of the battles. Every face in the crowd of students had the signs of nerves. Many were fidgety, others just stared aimlessly toward the arena.

They were all clearly garbed for battle. Some wore armor and weapons, but most dressed light and held their staffs or wands in tight grips.

Most of the men, like myself, wore close-fitting robes that wouldn't slow us down or cause unnecessary risks with all that extra fabric. Almost no one wore their wizard or witch's hats. They would just fall off as soon as the battles began, anyway.

My robes were black with accents of gold running down each limb and bright yellow buttons running down the front.

Haether wore a dress that was only a slight deviation from her usual gowns; this one's skirt parted mid-thigh, showing just a bit of skin before black stockings ran down the rest of her leg, ending in frilled, dark brown moccasins.

Lilly wore a light brown skirt that reached her knees but was loose enough to not restrict movement. Her tight black top clung to her skin, and its long sleeves ended in little loops that her thumbs slid through.

They both grasped my hands at either side, and we stayed close to each other for comfort as we waited for it to begin. In Lilly's other hand was her branch-like staff. Mine was strapped across my back; I was excited to finally use it.

Andrith didn't notice, but when Whelan saw the three of us, it was like he finally made the connection. His jaw dropped, and he gave me an impressed look and a nod. I noticed an ornate sheath holding a sword at his side and gave him a similarly impressed nod.

Before either of us could say anything, though, our professor's voice boomed over the hundreds of anxious students.

"Welcome to your final day as Initiates. You've all come a long way and I'm looking forward to seeing you put all that you've learned to the test. I can only hope that you've put in as much work outside the classroom as in. If not," she shrugged and let her sentence trail off.

Then she changed the subject. "You may notice that we have a crowd this time," her hand swept over a balcony that floated high above the arena, on the opposite end from where we were gathered. "Our department heads regularly attend these final exams, eager to see what their new students have to offer.

"There is also a collection of nobility from the surrounding areas and neighboring kingdoms," she added with an excited tone. "Some are here just to watch, but others regularly hire our more senior students for jobs of all sorts. Impress them and you just may find yourself employed before you even graduate!

"Now, as for the structure of today's events. The order will be determined by how well each student performed in yesterday's test. The lowest scores will go first, leading to the top score at the end. Observing your fellow students and learning from their mistakes is the reward some of you receive for doing so well. Those of you who failed to take your studies seriously will fight before having a chance to learn by example." I saw Whelan shift his weight from foot to foot as that detail sunk in.

Doriah went on, "We have procured a number of creatures, all of which were covered in class, and we have taken care to be sure that they should all provide a roughly equivalent challenge. There will be no easy fights, nor impossible ones. There is, however, the surprise that I've previously mentioned," she took on a devious grin. "Recall that I said the top scoring student will fight last. I've not yet mentioned *what* they will be fighting. So, if our esteemed Andrith would just join me up front," she started scanning the crowd for my friend as her sentence trailed off.

But he was frozen. I released the girls' hands and stepped up beside him, clapping a hand on his shoulder. Andrith's jaw was clenched, and he was blinking rapidly. "It's gonna be alright," I tried to assure him, but his worried glance told me that I wasn't very convincing. Slowly, I watched him wade through the crowd until he emerged near Doriah.

"Ah! There you are. Took your time getting up here, didn't you? Nonetheless, congratulations. Andrith here has gained some hype among the faculty by receiving one of the highest scores we have ever given out! And for your reward," she stepped back so that she could see Andrith's reaction, "here is your adversary." She waved a hand over the arena and a terrifying image came into view.

It was a dragon.

Golden scales covered its body, which was about the size of a mini-van. Long wings stretched out at least fifteen feet and a tail that was just as long had several long spikes sticking out of its end. Its head could have bit me in two. Smoke emerged from its nostrils with every breath and its large, sharp teeth were covered in brown stains.

Andrith seemed about to have a panic attack. His eyes looked like they were about to pop out of their sockets and his chest heaved. His jaw dropped and his hands shot up to tangle within his hair.

Professor Doriah didn't seem fazed by his terror, though, she went on just as excited as before. "That's right! I imagine many of you have never seen a dragon before. They certainly aren't as common as they used to be. This one is young, but still a far greater challenge than any of the other creatures you might face this day. And for that very same reason, we will be allowing Andrith to be joined by three companions! So, if any of you would rather take your chances facing a stronger foe with a few allies by your side, speak up now!"

And, just like all of my college classes at home, as Doriah asked for a volunteer, not one hand rose.

Well, none except mine.

Haether and Lilly shot me horrified glances. I lowered my voice to address them. "You see how terrified he is, I can't let him do this on his own. We need to help," I added and saw the 'we' sink in as they both looked appalled at first, then gave resolute nods. Their hands shot up next to mine.

"Ah, yes. Come forward, please, whoever that is."

When we stood next to Andrith, I gave him a pat on the back, and he seemed slightly less likely to piss his pants than a minute ago.

"So. Jake, Haether, and Lilly, is that right?" We all nodded, and she continued, "Brave of you to volunteer. I must admit, I'm looking forward to this." Then her voice boomed across the arena and I knew that she was addressing the audience as well as the students. "And there we have it! Our final match is squared away," she waved another hand over the arena and the dragon vanished. "Let us begin!"

Doriah called out the name of the first student and a very embarrassed, and muscular, orc with a large hammer in his hands, joined her while her assistants gathered the crowd at the bleachers nearby. They sat us in the same order as our fights, so Whelan was separated from the rest of us. Each row easily fit fifty students. The four of us were placed at the very top, a few empty rows separating us from the rest.

While the students got organized on the bleachers, Doriah kept going "I will be choosing all fighting for the rest of you at random. Like so," as she spoke a small, circular rift open in the air. She stuck her arm through it and returned with a tile in her hand. "First up, a pair of hobgoblins!"

Two brown, gnarled creatures appeared in the middle of the arena. They looked frightened and clung tightly to the spears they each held.

The orc man who had stood by Doriah looked satisfied as he walked out to join them. By the time Doriah told them to begin, he was already rushing the pair, who almost looked like miniature orcs, but brown. They couldn't have been taller than four feet and reached only as high as the orc's chest.

The pair separated as the orc approached, hammer reared back as he roared. He took on a faint blue light that suffused his hammer as he brought it down on the first hobgoblin, who jumped out of the way just in time.

The hammer slammed into the ground and sent dirt flying away from the small crater his magic-enriched attack created. I took note of his technique for later but doubted that even a super-powerful blow from my staff would faze a dragon.

As he spun to face the dodging hobgoblin, the other dove in behind and raked his spear along the man's green ribs. Blood spurted out and one of his hands shot to his side. He growled and did a spinning flourish with his weapon to gain himself some space.

They took it a bit slower then, testing each other's

defenses as the orc struggled to keep his two enemies in sight. One would dive in to draw his attention and when he struck back, the other would attack his opening.

They were relentless. The hobgoblins used their superior reach, their spears being as tall as they were, to their advantage and wore the orc down slowly.

Until finally, he was able to grab on to one of their spears and swing his hammer down one-handed on the suddenly defenseless creature. He crushed his enemy's skull just as a spearhead emerged from his chest cavity.

The hobgoblin behind him hopped back as the orc collapsed next to his fallen foe. The large green man struggled to rise to his feet and even sent a crescent of fire at the weaponless hobgoblin, but it was pointless. The orc's strength faded, and he was gone within seconds.

All three combatants, living and dead, slowly faded from the grounds as I assumed the still-alive hobgoblin was sent back to his prison, and the dead were sent to their graves.

It continued much like that for a while. The earlier students were clearly less prepared and sadly, they died off with alarming, not to mention disgusting, frequency. They were maimed, dismembered, even partially eaten while their former classmates watched in horror.

More than a few times, Lilly buried her face in my shoulder to avoid watching the grisly scenes. Haether took it with more grit, but still looked away from time to time.

Meanwhile Andrith had sweat stains on his brown tunic, his hands gripping the fabric of his pants so tight that I thought they might rip.

While a pale elemental girl fought off a small griffin, I tried to get through to Andrith. I reached over Haether, who was sitting between us, and tapped one of his tight fists. His head whirled over to look at me, fear plain on his face.

"Look, I know it isn't getting any easier, but we need to

stay as calm as we possibly can. Panicking won't help and shaky hands will make for inaccurate attacks. We'll spread out and attack the dragon from all sides. As it chooses one of us, the other three will strike hard. We can do this," I assured him but all I got back was a weak smile.

I turned my attention back to the arena just as the griffin's claws raked through the girl's left thigh and as she collapsed, it pounced and finished the job. By my counting, about a third of the students who had gone up had fallen.

And Whelan was next.

Since the griffin was unharmed, it didn't fade away with its enemy. Whelan looked back at us as he rose from his seat and I shouted, "You've got this Whelan! Pick that thing apart feather by feather!" He broke into a weak grin and nodded, then grew tense as he took his place in the arena.

As soon as he stepped on the dirt, the half-eagle half-lion charged for him. Its front legs had talons, while the back sported claws and a flicking, bushy tail.

The beak opened and let out a squawking challenge as Whelan pulled out an ornate, glowing blue sword with a gemstone set into its hilt.

Whelan shot a fireball in its direction, but the creature met it head-on and burst through. A few feathers were singed, but it didn't falter. As the griffin dove in to strike at my friend, he swept one arm to the side and a powerful gust of wind pushed the creature aside as Whelan swiped at it and bounced away.

The tip of his sword dripped red with blood, but the animal didn't slow. It beat its wings, but was luckily too young to fly, even if Whelan hadn't sliced it.

He gripped his sword tight and kept the same strategy as the griffin charged in with an animalistic focus. Time and again he dove away and struck in with his sword, whittling away at his opponent, but it wasn't enough. The creature was able to sink its talons into Whelan's side and he barely managed to duck away just as its beak closed over where his head used to be.

But the griffin knew it had the advantage now and kept pressing its human enemy. Whelan beat away beak and talon with his sword as the animal struck over and over again. Suddenly, it feigned an attack with its talon and bowled right into Whelan, butting its head into his chest so hard that it sent him tumbling, the sword flying from his grip.

He raced along the ground, but the griffin was coming after him. Whelan swung a hand upwards as the Earth beneath the griffin erupted. The animal might not have been able to fly, but it beat its wings and was able to right itself in the air to continue its assault. The winged beast landed and in a single leap engulfed my friend in a mass of feathers.

The two fighters lay still for the briefest moment and when the griffin's head started to twitch, my heart dropped.

That is, until its head tumbled free of its body and Whelan shuffled out from underneath it. Blood and dirt covered him from head-to-toe. His sword slid from his grip as he let out a triumphant roar and started kicking the dead griffin in its side over and over, cursing the entire time, until it faded away.

Whelan collapsed to his knees and took the sword into his hands, carefully returning it to the sheath at his side as one of Doriah's assistants helped him off the arena and over to the area where they were healing the injured students.

He looked up at us and thrust a fist into the air, before he let it fall, clearly exhausted.

Finally, I could breathe easy again.

For a little bit longer, anyway.

36

AT LAST, THE FINAL BATTLE ENDED AS A MALE STUDENT pierced the chest of his opponent, a young ogre about his size, with a jet of flame that looked like a blowtorch. He pulled away and smoke rose from the wound.

When the battlefield was cleared, Doriah called for us.

I put my hand on Andrith's shoulder as we all rose to climb down the steps. "You ready?" He shook his head slowly. "Yeah, me neither."

"You're a fool," Andrith whispered, and I reared back, surprised. "You barely know me. And now you're going to die by the side of someone you've been friends with for, what, a week?"

I shook him by the shoulder I gripped. "Come on, man! Don't talk like that. I know this won't be a walk in the park, but we still have a chance. I can't even tell you how many times in the past few hours I've thought someone was about to die, but they ended up pulling through. Hell, Whelan was one of those! And you've got three friends by your side. They were all alone! We can do this," I repeated my words from earlier. "Giving up before the fight has even begun is the only way to be sure we'll lose."

Andrith's jaw clenched, but he nodded and lead the way down the stairs. Doriah nodded to us and wished us luck as we walked by. Then she waved a hand toward the center of the arena.

The golden dragon reappeared and roared its anger. The monster whirled around, whipping its tail behind it, until its black eyes found us. Then heavy footsteps that sent dust into the air in their wake headed straight for us.

"Alright, remember what I said. We'll spread out and strike from afar. Do whatever you can to stay out of range!"

They all nodded, and I felt the girls sending feelings of affection both to me and each other. I returned the feeling and chose to put myself in front of the dragon. My heart raced, my legs and arms trembled until I got them under control and gripped my long, thin, black staff.

Haether snapped her fingers and the silver wand from her necklace disappeared, materializing in her hand. Lilly held her branch-like staff out in front of her. Andrith slapped a hand against the Earth and pulled out a long stone rod a little thicker than my staff. It looked heavy, but he spun it with ease.

The girls took the dragon's sides, while Andrith rounded to its back. Its head kept swiveling between us, its tail constantly flicking back and forth in case one tried to sneak up behind.

But I wanted its attention on me. As it glanced over at Lilly, I pulled some rocks out of the ground and sent them at the dragon's head as fast as I could manage, filling the stone with magical energy. One missed, but two crashed right into the side of the dragon's huge head, then burst into pieces.

I'd never seen something as terrifying as an angry dragon. It whirled on me and charged in my direction. Gesturing with my staff, I swung it upward and burst the ground beneath my enemy just as spears of ice and fire struck at its sides, one of stone coming from behind.

But none seemed to even register as they crashed into the dragon. It shrugged off all attacks as easily as mosquito bites and I felt fear spike in both Haether and Lilly. They must have been able to feel mine as well, despite my efforts to push it down.

I switched between elements and tried to backpedal, but none were any better. Even shields didn't slow the thing down, it just crashed straight through. When it finally reached me, it swung a heavy claw that barely missed as I dropped to the ground and rolled away. By the time I rose to my feet, though, the dragon drew its hand back and sent me flying, the air forced out of my chest.

I crashed to the ground hard against my right shoulder and cringed as I pushed myself to my feet. But the dragon was already there. Thinking fast, I sent a ball of fire into its face. Not to hurt it, as if fire could even harm a dragon, but to block its vision as I dove out of the way of another clawed hand. I picked up my staff and ran to join Haether.

"Got any ideas?" I said through heavy breaths.

She nodded. "If we can immobilize it long enough, I think one of Andrith's spears should be able to pierce it's hide. You distract it, Lilly and I will try to freeze a couple of its feet in place, and Andrith will need to put all the strength he has into one throw."

Lilly sent us a feeling of understanding, so I told Haether to share the plan with Andrith while the dragon approached. I held its attention as the bastard approached slowly, confidently. None of our attacks had so much as scratched it so far, but it had been able to toss me with ease.

Thinking of one of the earlier fights, I siphoned Pholl's power and forced all the heat I could into a spearpoint at the end of my staff. A jet of white flame jutted out a foot long and gave the golden beast some pause.

Or maybe it was just gathering strength. As soon as the dragon reared back and started opening its mouth, I knew what was coming. I brought up a wall of Earth between us and started condensing water in front of me to put out the flames I knew were coming. Lilly and Haether's strengths poured into me and bolstered the defenses.

But the dragon's spout of flames crashed right through the rock wall and turned the water into a mass of hot steam that crashed into me. The searing heat bit at every inch of my exposed skin and it came with a gust of smoke from the doused flames. I couldn't see anything while I was in the middle of it until a sudden gust of wind, from one of the girls, blew it away just as the dragon swiped at me again.

A large rock rose out of the ground and shoved me back just in time. Not bothering to wonder who sent it, I tried to put some more space between myself and the monster.

I kept an eye on the dragon to make sure it kept chasing me until Haether sent a feeling that I identified as 'ready.' Then I spun and held my ground against the speeding mass of scale and muscle. When it swiped at me, I ducked forward under its arm and thrust the flaming tip of my staff upwards.

It bounced right off the dragon's hide just as I saw ice start collecting around two of its feet. The dragon's long neck suddenly wound down to bite at me, so I ran forward and came out behind it.

Right next to the tail. It tossed me aside like a rag doll.

My staff flew out of my hands again and I came to a rolling stop near Haether. She ran to help me up, but by that time the dragon had turned to face us. Lilly was trying to freeze its feet with so much power that Haether and I were left dry.

And still, it didn't work. Powerless, we clung to each other as flames erupted from its throat and hurtled toward us.

Suddenly, Andrith bowled into the two us and we crashed into the ground. He planted his hands in the dirt and pulled out what looked like a blanket made of stone. His arms swept over us just in time as the blast of fire crashed into our dome of protection.

Andrith's hands were planted against it and he was breathing heavily, sweating profusely. The three of us were lit in light blue, despite being entirely closed off from the world by Andrith's improvised defense.

When the wall stopped shaking, he let it fall and the first thing I saw was the dragon's back as it went after Lilly.

I flexed the muscle in my eyes and activated my power, scanning through the dragon's anatomy, hoping to find a weakness. There wasn't a weak point on its hide, but I did manage to find its heart.

"Fuck," I grumbled, eyes darting around desperately. They landed on Andrith's spear, which lay nearby. I thrust it into his hands with the command to harden its tip as much as possible as I laid out my plan.

Seconds later, I took the hardened spear and gripped it so tight that my fingers hurt. My shoulder screamed pain at me, but I ignored it as much as possible as I charged up a ramp of Earth that Andrith brought up for me just behind the dragon. I leaped with a gust of Haether's wind behind me, now that Lilly had let go of some of our power.

Then I did something people kept telling me not to do.

I reached out for Vethris and took in every morsel of power that I could until it felt like my very veins were on fire, desperate to release some of the energy I'd collected. I focused it all into the point of Andrith's spear, to suffuse my blow with the strength of a dark God and drove the spear in between the dragon's spiny shoulder blades, where I'd located its heart.

The monster reared its head back and let out an ear-shattering scream accompanied by flames roaring twenty feet into the sky, but I held firm to the spear, driving it even further in as the dragon flailed around desperately.

But it was weak. Haether and Lilly came from either side and gathered ice around its limbs, too weak to break through now. Andrith summoned a blanket of Earth and crashed it over the dragon, forcing it to collapse onto its stomach.

With another, final thrust, I pushed the stone spear deeper again and held it there until the beast stopped moving.

Vethris power leaked out of me as I fell to my knees on the dragon's back. I felt something scrape against me and my body crashed to the dirt floor of the arena as I passed out.

Totally exhausted, but victorious.

❧ 37 ❧

I came to in a small white tent. I was lying in a cot and there were some bandages and other medical supplies nearby.

As I looked down at my battered body, I noticed several burns that hadn't even registered during the fight, as well as numerous cuts and bruises.

My right shoulder was killing me, but I was okay. I opened my mouth to call out for one of my friends, but only coughed. That did the job, though, as the girls rushed in and the guys were stopped by one of Doriah's assistants, who insisted on giving me space.

They were covered in dirt and streaked with sweat, but beautiful anyway. Haether sobbed into my shoulder while Lilly held my hand and inspected my wounds.

"I don't know how you managed to move by the end of it," she murmured. "You look like that thing ate you up and spat you out." She tilted her head and shot me a bright smile, but a few fresh tears ran down her face.

Haether pulled back from my shoulder. "You did it! I can't believe it worked. When nothing we tried even seemed to faze that thing, I thought we were dead! I cursed my father for sending me here and myself for being so useless!"

She buried her head in my shoulder again, the one that wasn't injured. Her voice was muffled. "I never want to feel that way again. You'll see, next time we fight something like that, I won't freeze up. I'll be leaping onto it's back right beside you."

She looked up at me with tears in her eyes and I leaned forward, ignoring the pain that flared up in my side, and kissed her soft lips. I held her there a moment and just enjoyed the feeling. I wasn't sure I'd get to do that again.

Then I waved Lilly closer and wrapped my hand around the back of her head, pulling her in as well. She tasted of sweat, they both did, but I didn't care. We were alive, and that was all that mattered.

"There are some healers from the Regeneration school here to take care of everyone, but with all the students that went before us, they're pretty busy," Lilly explained. "But don't worry, we'll be right here until they come, okay?"

I nodded and let my head fall back against my pillow. Sleep took me over before I even realized it.

Some hours later, I could tell because it was suddenly dark out, I woke up to a heat that engulfed my body. My mind shot back to the cone of flames the dragon shot at me more than once and I lashed out, trying to get away.

"Jake!" I heard several voices ring out and my eyes focused on the world around me. Haether and Lilly stood in one corner of the tent, huddled together, and a pair of white-garbed healers stood at my bed side, struggling to hold me down. A man and a woman.

The man forced me back into a lying position, easily I might add, while the woman said, "You'll need to rest for a few days, and you'll certainly be sore, but you're all set. Now, you two," she turned toward the girls and they refused her help at first, but the woman was unrelenting. They shuddered as I assumed a similar heat washed over them, then the pair of healers left us alone.

The girls were sweating lightly from their recent healing, whereas I felt like I'd been drenched in water. I reached for Pholl's source to take the sweat away but fumbled as I grasped it. Too tired from my recent exertion, I guessed. Lilly, apparently knowing what I was trying to do, took care of it for me and I thanked her.

Whelan bowled through the tent flaps with Andrith just behind him. "That was fucking amazing, mate! You should have seen yourself soaring through the air with that spear and planting it right through that bastard's hide. And it wasn't even glowing green, how'd you know it had a weak spot?"

My mind swam for a minute as I put together those details. I poured more power into that spear than I'd ever tried to hold before, so why wasn't it glowing?

It all came back to me. Whelan wouldn't have been able to see it because it was Vethris's power that I used. It had worked, so I didn't exactly regret it, but with a crowd that large, I was sure someone noticed. It was just a question of who.

Luckily, Haether spoke up before I had to come up with an answer. She pushed Whelan away and berated him, "Give the guy some space! He just saved our lives and almost died in the process; he can answer your dumb questions later." Whelan looked offended, but gave in.

Andrith stood by the entrance with his arms crossed, smirking. "She's right, you know. You saved all of us."

"Not me," Whelan added, "I saved myself, thanks for noticing."

"Shut up," Haether and Lilly said at the same time, then nodded at each other.

"Don't forget, Andy, you saved me too. Haether and I

would have been burned to ash if you didn't come in with that dome thing of yours."

He blushed and ran a hand along the back of his neck. "It was nothing. To be honest, I wasn't even sure it would work. I thought you'd be mad at me for shoving you two to the ground!" He laughed.

"After that, you can shove me to the ground any time," I quipped. "Say, Whelan. I don't suppose you have that bottle with you, do you? I don't think I'll make it to the library today."

He grinned as widely as I'd ever seen. "You know me too well." He reached into his robes, which he'd changed while I was asleep, and pulled out a brown bottle with blue specks in it. He popped the cork off and took a long swig. Then cleared his throat as some threatened to come back up. While wiping his mouth with the back of his sleeve, he handed it over. "Small tip. Pace yourself," he added in a croaking voice.

I chuckled and raised the glass bottle to my lips, then took a mouthful. It burned and tasted terrible. But I loved it.

We'd made it through the exams, and nothing could soil that.

THE NEXT DAY, AROUND NOON, THOSE OF US THAT LIVED were once again gathered at the arena. Somehow, they had already cleared away all the bloodstains and broken ground. Our Headmaster, and Heads of each school department were gathered behind our ruby-eyed professor.

The surviving students sat in the same order as the day before while Professor Doriah called us down one-by-one to receive our mark of advancement.

She handed the badge to me with a proud smile. "I knew you'd be one of the ones to make it through. There's something special about you, Jake. I don't know what it is yet, but you didn't kill that dragon by the strength of your arm alone. Still, congratulations."

Even though she seemed suspicious, there was more curiosity in her voice than anything else. *She mustn't suspect that it has anything to do with Vethris, then.*

As I left her behind, Head Librarian Thuvien gave me a thumbs up and a big smile. Headmaster Theid merely nodded his head reverently, while the rest of the department Heads added their congratulations.

I inspected my new badge. It was a small globe with two ravens flying within a red background. The back of it held no pin, nor was it sticky, but I mimicked what I saw other students doing and stuck it to my chest over my heart. It stayed there, just as I'd seen from similar badges on countless other students over the past few weeks.

First Haether, and then Lilly squealed in excitement as they ambushed me with hugs and high-fives and gushed over their memory of our fight with the dragon. It was only a day ago, but they spoke of it like some old adventure that we could all laugh about already. We wore our badges with pride and joined Whelan and Andrith to have another celebratory drink.

And afterwards, I brought Haether and Lilly back to my dorm to celebrate in our own way.

EPILOGUE

Jacobus gritted his teeth against the cold and wrapped the tattered cloth around him tighter yet again. He had no idea how many nights he'd spent outside in the last month, but it sure as hell wasn't getting any easier. He hid behind a dumpster, in a dry alleyway, alone.

He didn't make it in time that night. The shelter closed, all its beds filled, and turned him away. He spent his days scrounging for food, begging for work, or at least for directions back to Aether Academy. After the first few tries, and the strange reactions he got from these oddly dressed humans, he knew he had to change his strategy, just not how.

There were things in his pockets.

A small leather pouch that held what he assumed was money, as well as some cards made of a strange bendable material, one of which had his face on it. Most of them had a variation of his name as well. 'Jacob Pratt.' Not quite his name, but not entirely different either.

Then there was the case of his body. It had been distinctly larger ever since he woke up in the Pillar chamber, alone for some reason. His clothes were different, there were strange supplies by the entrance.

Worst of all was when he tried to use Vethris's power. The source of magic that he had sacrificed so much for was gone. Not even Pholl's presence was there.

It was a strange place and he hated it. It had been years since he had been so helpless, and he hated that too. These people spoke the same language as him, and yet he couldn't get them to understand what he was asking for. Arthur Bond City! Magic? They all thought he was crazy!

And he was starting to believe it too. When a dark portal appeared in the brick wall in front of him, he thought it a hallucination.

The woman who stepped out was the last person he would ever wish to see.

The Lady looked around and for once her face wasn't shrouded in black fog. Nor was he in any pain as he laid eyes on her.

She was an older woman, to his surprise since she had sounded younger. Dark grey hair was pulled into a tight bun and her wrinkled face looked down at him with disappointment and disgust. She wore a long black dress that was elaborately decorated with red accents.

"Hm. So this is where you got to. Found yourself a little lost there, Jacobus?" She said, as if she were speaking to a lost puppy. He just grunted in reply and she chuckled. "Yes, that's the boy I know. You did seem oddly... friendly when last we spoke. I'm almost glad to see your usually grim countenance has returned."

He perked up and rose to his feet. The Lady always exerted her power over him whenever she had the chance. The fact that he wasn't in pain meant that she couldn't siphon any power in this place either. "What the fuck are you talking about?"

The Lady chuckled, "Oh yes, I missed that directness of yours, too." She held her hands out to either side to emphasize the alleyway she found herself in. "This place? It's an alternate version of our world, without any magic. They exist in the same location, in a way, just occupying different dimensions. It's quite fascinating really, and you have no idea the lengths I've gone to retrieve you." She let her last words sink in for a moment.

Retrieve me? he thought. *Great. Now she'll think I owe her even more than I already did. She'll pay for all the pain she's caused me. Somehow this last month was her fault, I know it. But first, I need to get home. Need to feel that power seeping through my veins again.*

The Lady snapped her fingers in front of his face and Jacobus gritted his teeth before glaring at her. "There's a good boy, if a bit poorly trained after all," she pouted. "If I'm to take you back with me I want your word. You'll do as I say, when I say it. No questions, no trouble. You work for me now, or you stay in this shithole for the rest of your life. How's that sound?"

He hated her as much as the father he barely knew. She moved up a few spots in his list for that, but he needed her. As much as he didn't want to admit it. As much as he hated to need her, it didn't change anything.

Jacobus let out a sigh that he thought sounded regretful. "Fine."

She broke into a wicked grin and clapped her hands together. "Fantastic! Come along then," and she turned around, stepping through the portal in the wall on the opposite side of the alleyway.

Jacobus bit back a growl and tried to smile. He was going home, after all, he should have been happy.

But he barely felt anything anymore.

Anything but hate.

THANK YOU FOR READING!

I hope you liked the story and would consider leaving a review! It's a big part of how people decide to take the risk on newer authors like myself. You can also find me on Facebook or send feedback to me directly here:
MiloStormBooks@gmail.com
You should also check out these Facebook groups for some more great book recommendations!
https://www.facebook.com/groups/haremlit
https://www.facebook.com/groups/HaremGamelit
https://www.facebook.com/groups/MonsterGirlFiction/
I'm off to work on your next book!
Milo Storm

Made in the USA
Monee, IL
27 September 2023